Richard Laymon was born in Chicago in 1947. He grew up in California and has a BA in English Literature from Willamette University, Oregon, and an MA from Loyola University, Los Angeles. He has worked as a schoolteacher, a librarian, a mystery magazine editor and a report writer for a law firm. He now works full-time as a writer. His novel FLESH   named Best Horror Novel of 1988 by *Science Fiction Chronicle* and also shortlisted for the prestigious Bram Stoker Award, as were FUNLAND and his short story collection, A GOOD, SECRET PLACE. Richard Laymon is the author of many acclaimed works of horror and suspense, including THE STAKE, SAVAGE, AFTER MIDNIGHT and the three novels in the Beast House Chronicles: THE CELLAR, THE BEAST HOUSE and THE MIDNIGHT TOUR. He died in February 2001.

'In Laymon's books, blood doesn't so much drip drip as explode, splatter and coagulate' *Independent*

'Stephen King without a conscience' Dan Marlowe

'A gut-crunching writer' *Time Out*

'An uncanny grasp of just what makes characters work . . . readers turn the pages so fast they leave burn marks on the paper' *Horrorstruck*

'Incapable of writing a disappointing book' *New York Review of Science Fiction*

'One of the best and most reliable writers working today' *AFRAID*

'Laymon's biggest strength is that he is able to provide lighthearted fun and disturb at the same time' *Fear*

'He's got a knack for creating characters you care about' *Cemetery Dance*

Among The Missing

Richard Laymon

headline

First published in 1999
by HEADLINE BOOK PUBLISHING

First published in paperback in 1999
by HEADLINE BOOK PUBLISHING

11

ISBN 978 0 7472 6072 1

Printed and bound in Great Britain by
CPI Antony Rowe, Chippenham and Eastbourne

Typeset by CBS, Martlesham Heath, Ipswich, Suffolk

HEADLINE BOOK PUBLISHING
A division of the Hodder Headline Group
338 Euston Road
London NW1 3BH
www.headline.co.uk
www.hodderheadline.com

This book is dedicated to
The Deadline Boys
Peter Enfantino, Robert Morrish, John Scoleri

Thanks for the books and the fun.
May there be plenty more of both.

Chapter One

THE RENDEZVOUS

When he heard the car, the man stood up. He brushed pine needles off the seat of his jeans, then hurried out of the forest and trotted down to the roadside. As he neared the moonlit pavement, headlights swept around a corner to the south. They were very low and close together.

Could be a Jaguar.

Has to be, he thought.

He glanced at his wristwatch. 2:32.

It's gotta be her. An hour late.

With a grin, he showed his thumb.

The car sped closer, its engine tearing the silence, its headlights growing.

A Jag, all right. So how come she's not slowing down?

He took his eyes away as the car blasted by. Then he looked again. The Jaguar's tail-lights vanished around a wooded curve.

'Bitch,' he muttered.

But the engine noise didn't fade with distance. Instead, it decelerated from a roar to a choppy grumble. A few seconds later, the tail-lights reappeared. This time, they were accompanied by a pair of white back-up lights. With jerking bursts of speed, the Jaguar made its way toward him.

It stopped in front of him.

'How about a lift, stranger?' a familiar voice called through the open window.

'I could go for that.'

When he opened the door, a map-light came on above the glove compartment. He bent low to climb into the car and looked at the woman behind the wheel. 'Nice outfit,' he said.

'It's the latest thing in tryst-wear.'

It was a see-through white nightgown that hung by cords from her shoulders, clung to her breasts, and covered very little of her lap.

'The door?'

'Almost forgot, the view's so nice.' He shut it and the light died.

'Thank you,' she said.

'You're very welcome.'

'And where would you like to go?'

'Well . . . Anywhere's fine.'

'Somewhere not too far away?' she asked, and started to drive. 'I shouldn't be out too long under the circumstances.'

'How long have you got?'

'Well, I really should be home before dawn. I wouldn't exactly like to be *seen* in this outfit. Not by just anyone.' Turning her head, she smiled at him. 'Only by someone extra special, like you.'

'You're pretty special yourself.'

'Are you surprised I actually showed up?' she asked.

'I was starting to wonder.'

'Well, I made it, didn't I?'

'A little late.'

'A smidgen.'

'I guess they can call you "the late Mrs Parkington."'

'That's not terribly funny.'

'Sorry.'

'That's the sort of quip I might expect from Grant, the pretentious asshole. Always with the quips. *Nasty* quips. I can't imagine why I stay married to him.'

'It's not his good looks?'

She laughed. 'Now, *that's* funny! *Very* good.' Reaching over, she patted his thigh. 'Anyway, where shall we go?'

'Well, how about Harrah's at South Tahoe?'

'I'm not dressed for *that* sort of gambling, buster.'

'I hear they've got great guest rooms.'

'Well, isn't Tahoe a trifle far?'

'Less than an hour.'

'That's too far for me. I don't want to spend the whole night driving. Can't you think of a nice, romantic place that's perhaps five minutes from here?'

'Well . . .'

'Help me out here, fellow. *I* haven't a clue. For all I know, we could be in the Black Fucking Forest of Bavaria.'

'Guess you could say *every* forest is a fucking forest, if you're in the mood.'

'Oh, please. I may *lose* the mood.'

'How about the Woody Pines Motor Lodge?'

'Where's that?'

'I don't know. I made it up.'

She reached over, slapped his thigh, and said, 'Stop that.'

3

'I know a place,' he said.

'A *real* place?'

'A beautiful, romantic place with a view of the river.'

'That sounds promising.'

'We'll have the stars overhead, treetops whispering in the breeze, and moonlight rippling on the water.'

'Fabulous! Where is it?'

'The Bend.'

'The Bend?'

'You don't know the Bend?'

'We've only been here two months, dear. I can hardly be expected to know every detail of your backwoods, albeit quaint geography. So if you'd like to fill me in . . .?'

'It's a bend, or turn, in the Silver River.'

She nodded. 'Runs into Silver Lake, I presume.'

'That's right. The river widens and slows down at the Bend, and there's a nice, sandy beach.'

'I'm not so sure about sand . . .'

'You'll have to make up your mind pretty soon. The turn-off's coming up.'

'Well, I do have a blanket. I suppose the sand shouldn't present *too* much of a problem.'

'You'd better slow down.'

Taking her foot off the gas pedal, she said, 'It does get everywhere.'

'What?'

'Sand. The nasty little grains like to go where they've got no business.'

'The turn-off's right after this curve.'

'Ah.' She pressed down gently on the brake pedal. 'I suppose we might as well give it a try.'

'Sure. Get ready to turn.'

'Right?'

'Left.' He closely watched the roadside. 'There!'

She jammed on the brake and swung the Jaguar in a hard left that took it onto a road both unmarked and unpaved. Trees crowded in close, blocking out the moon. 'This is a bit spooky,' she announced.

'I'll protect you.'

'You're such a gentleman.'

'So was Count Dracula,' he said.

Her head turned. 'Now, stop that.'

'Vampires are *real* gentlemen, right up to the moment they sink their fangs into your neck.'

She slapped his thigh again. 'Cut that out! You're frightening me.'

'Sorry.'

'How far does this road go, anyway?'

'Not much farther,' he told her.

'I hope not.'

Moments later, the trees moved back from the sides of the road, letting moonlight in. The road continued into a broad clearing – a parking area, deserted except for a garbage barrel and a single, dark car.

'Oh, dear,' she said. 'Company.'

'Don't worry about it.'

She parked beside the garbage barrel. 'So where is this Bend of yours?'

'We'll have to walk down to it.'

'Oh, charming. Far?'

'Not very.'

She twisted the ignition key and silence replaced the

5

engine's roar. She killed the headlights. Darkness clamped down on the clearing ahead of them.

'All set?' she asked.

'All set,' he said, and tried to open his door.

'Push down.'

He pushed the lever down and the door unlatched. 'Complicated contraption,' he said, climbing out.

'It only responds if you handle it properly. Like a woman.' Standing by the driver's door, she said, 'Just a sec while I grab the blanket.' She lifted a lever. The back of the front seat tipped forward.

'You sure came prepared.'

'Why not? One can't always count on a bed. And as much as I adore the great out of doors, I do like to have a little something between me and the ground. Most *especially* between me and the beach.' Bending down, she reached behind the front seat.

The man shut his door. He stepped to the other side of the car and saw her still bent over. Her slim legs were pale in the moonlight. Her nightgown, no longer than a shirt, left her buttocks bare.

She ducked out of the low car and stood up straight, holding a knitted blanket.

'*Voilà!*' she said.

'I'll carry it.'

'See? I knew you were a gentleman. But I believe I'll keep it, thank you. A trifle nippy out here.' She spread the blanket open and wrapped it around her body. 'You're the native, so tell me. It's the middle of August. It rarely fails to be as hot as blazes during the daytime, but after dark we seem on the verge of the next Ice Age. Why is that?'

'Just how it is,' he said. 'It's the mountains. We're about a mile high, for one thing.'

'Are *you* freezing?'

'I'm fine,' he said, and held out his hand.

Holding the blanket shut with one hand, she reached out through the front with her other and took hold of his hand. She gave it a squeeze.

'Nervous?' he asked.

'A trifle.'

'Me too.'

'You're not nervous. You're only saying that.'

'Think so?' Lifting her hand, he placed it against the front of his shirt. 'Feel that?'

'Oh, my Lord! Is that your *heart*?'

'Sure is.'

'You *are* nervous.' She patted his chest. 'Or are you just excited?'

'I'll never tell.'

'I bet I could find out.'

'Wouldn't you rather wait until we get down to the river?'

'Not necessarily. At least there's no sand up here.'

'But there's no wonderful view of the moonlit river, either.'

'Ah. True.'

He led her forward, away from the parking area and over a narrow, grassy rise. From there, he could see the start of a trail that curved down the wooded slope. Far below, visible through breaks in the trees, was a pale stretch of beach, a curving lane of dark water, and woods on the other side.

'It does look lovely down there,' she said.

'Nice and private.'

'I hope so. Who do you suppose might belong to the car?' She glanced over her shoulder at it.

'Campers, maybe. Backpackers leave their cars here, sometimes, when they're going off on a long trek. They could be miles away.'

'If anyone is around,' she said, 'we'll have to go someplace else. I'm not a great believer in public displays.'

'Nobody'll be around. It's nearly three o'clock.'

She squeezed his hand. 'Have you ever been here with *her*?'

'Hey. Never mind about her, the bitch.'

'Just asking.'

'Don't.'

'So sorry.'

At the bottom of the slope, the trail vanished as it led into pale, moonlit sand.

'Wait just a second.' Letting go of his hand, she put her hand inside the blanket and bent down.

'What're you doing?'

'Taking off my slippers. I don't want to get them all full of sand.' Moments later, she said, 'Oooo, cold! A *very* good thing I brought the blanket, or we'd freeze our tushes the minute we lie down. Brrr.' She stood up straight, keeping both hands inside the blanket. 'All set,' she said.

Side by side, they walked on toward the river.

'Now how can it be that the sand feels so much colder than the air?' she asked. 'Does that make any sense?'

'Mountain sense.'

'Oh, my God, I've fallen in league with Daniel Boone.' He laughed.

'I *do* love this, though. Just smell the air!' Hurrying ahead of him, she whirled around and pranced backward. 'This is so delicious. So *invigorating*!' Suddenly, one of her hands darted out from inside the blanket and tossed both her slippers at him. 'Catch!'

He caught one, but fumbled the other. As he crouched to pick it up, she whipped the blanket from around her shoulders and flung it toward him. 'Catch!'

It fluttered to the ground in front of him.

Laughing, she lifted the nightgown over her head. She threw it. The wind spread it open and lifted it, carrying it high. The wispy white gown twirled and swooped like an exuberant ghost.

'Don't let it get away!' she called. Then she ran through the moonlight and shadows, her arms waving in the air.

At the water's edge, she stopped. She looked back. 'Coming?' she called.

'Might take me a minute,' he said, standing up with her slippers and blanket. 'I've got to chase down your nightgown.'

'Oh, leave it.'

'No, I'll get it.' Moments before, a low pine limb had snagged the cavorting nightie.

'I'm going in the water!'

'I'll be along in a minute.' He hurried over to the gown, carefully freed it from the pine snare, then turned around and headed for the beach with it in his hands, blanket and slippers clutched to his chest.

Standing naked at the river's edge, she looked over her shoulder at him.

'Don't take all night!' she called.

'I'm coming.'

'I do hope that's not intended to be some sort of lame, Grant-like orgasm pun.'

'Huh?'

'Never mind.' Turning her head forward, she dipped a foot into the water.

'How is it?'

'Bearable, but only just.'

Against the dark surface of the water, her body looked stark white. She had no tan lines. She might have been molded out of fresh snow or sculptured from ivory – pure white from neck to foot except for the shadowed gray crescent between her buttocks.

As she waded slowly into the river, her white feet seemed to disappear into blackness. Then the black void climbed her white calves. As she moved forward, her arms out for balance, the black consumed the backs of her thighs, then her buttocks.

She turned around.

Her pure white front was dabbed with dark areas: her eyes, her mouth, her nipples. Below each breast was a crescent of shadow that reminded him of the crevice behind her. But these were horizontal, not vertical, and much smaller.

'Coming in?' she called.

'You bet!'

He dropped the blanket, gown and slippers into the sand in front of him, then took off his shirt.

'Nice chest, babe! Now let's see the rest!'

He let his shirt fall onto the pile. As fast as he could, he pulled off his boots and socks. Then he pulled down his jeans.

'Wow!'

'Wow yourself!' he called.

'I'm impressed!'

'You're not so bad either.'

'Don't just stand there. Come on out and show me what you can do with that baby.'

'Here I come, ready or not!' He stepped around the pile of clothing and headed for the water.

'Come and get me!' she cried out. Laughing, she dived toward him. The water shut over her and for moments the river looked deserted – as if she had never been there at all. Then her face appeared, a pale laughing oval. 'Ever do it in the water?' she asked, gliding closer.

'A couple of times.'

'How was it?'

'Dry.' He dived and swam toward her underwater. When he surfaced, she was close enough to reach. Standing shoulder-deep in the river, he found her hand and pulled her toward him.

'You got your hair all wet,' he said.

'It'll dry.' She rubbed herself against him.

'Not in an hour or so.'

'"So" can be a long time.'

'It can be forever,' he said. Below the surface, his fist shot toward her. Water resistance slowed the punch, robbed it of power, but his fist connected well anyway.

With the first shock of the blow, her eyes bulged. Her mouth sprang wide. She gagged, trying to suck in air but getting none.

He struck her again in the same place, dead center, just below the sternum.

Then he grabbed her behind the neck and pushed her down. Climbing onto her back, he rode her, hands around her neck, knees squeezing her sides. She twisted beneath him. She tried to roll. She tried to throw him off. Once, she managed to force the top of her head to the surface. Before her mouth could make it to air, he leaned forward, shifting his weight, and her head went down again.

After that, she seemed to give up.

He stayed on her, keeping her down while he counted slowly to three hundred.

Then he climbed off. Gripping her hair, he dragged her slowly toward the shore. When the water was waist-high, he ducked beneath her and lifted her onto his shoulder. He carried her up the beach, then dropped her onto the blanket.

He looked down at her. The breeze on his wet skin made him shiver.

She'd brought along that blanket. The bitch should've brought along a couple of towels, too.

He tried to dry himself using her nightgown. It was so small and so wispy that he had to wring it out a few times. But he finally managed to wipe most of the water off his body. He tossed the nightgown aside.

Then he walked to the foot of the trail. He faced the river, turned to the right, counted off ten paces, then dropped to his knees.

With both hands, he dug into the sand. The cold grains hurt his fingertips, but he continued to work. After a few seconds, he wondered if he had the location wrong.

Then he found what he wanted.

He pulled it out of the sand and stood up.

As he walked toward the woman's corpse, moonlight

gleamed on the polished steel surface of the hacksaw swinging in his hand.

Chapter Two

THE RIVER TRIP

Bass Paxton left a trail through the dew as he crossed the front yard to the house. He climbed the porch stairs and stopped in front of the door. His knuckles rapped it, shaking it in its frame. Through the screen, he saw Faye walking toward him across the shadowy foyer.

She pushed open the door, stepped into his arms, and kissed him.

Bass gave her a good squeeze. He patted her rump through the seat of her bikini pants. Easing her away, he said, 'Good morning, doll.'

'Good morning, stranger.'

He laughed. 'Stranger, huh? It hasn't been *that* long, has it?'

'Two days is long. Very long. The way I miss you.'

'Well, business before pleasure.'

'My ass,' she said, and smiled up at him. 'Anyhow, it's nice to have you back.'

'The pleasure's all mine.'

Turning away from him, she stepped back into the house. 'I'm almost done making the picnic lunch. Would you rather have mustard or mayonnaise on your turkey sandwich?'

'Tough call.'

'Or both?'

'Mustard. That'd be fine.'

'Mustard it is.'

He followed her toward the kitchen, watching her. The sleeves had been cut off her white T-shirt. So had its lower half. The shirt ended just below her ribcage, leaving her bare all the way down to her bikini pants. She wore the skimpy pants low around her hips. They clinged to her tight, firm buttocks, and moved with every step she took. Her legs were slim and tanned. Her feet were bare.

'You're sure looking good this morning,' Bass said.

She grinned over her shoulder at him. 'Thank you, thank you.'

In the kitchen, she stepped up to the refrigerator. 'Wine or beer?'

'Beer.'

'Natch.' She opened the refrigerator and lifted out a six-pack of Budweiser. She handed it to Bass. 'I believe I'll stick with wine,' she said, and pulled out a bottle of Chablis. Then she took out mustard and shut the refrigerator door.

'Can I give you a hand with anything?' Bass asked.

'No, that's fine. Just keep me company. I'll be done in a jiff.'

So he stepped back and leaned against a counter and watched Faye prepare the sandwiches.

She was awfully good to watch.

Probably the best-looking woman he knew, if you didn't count Pac. And he tried *not* to count Pac, since she was married to his best friend.

15

He wondered how Pac might look in an outfit like this. *I'll never find out*, he thought.

But she couldn't look *much* better than Faye. Nobody could.

Soon, she finished preparing the lunches. 'Ready when you are,' she said.

'The river's waiting,' Bass said. He picked up the picnic basket and cooler, and headed for the front door. Faye walked behind him. Before leaving the house, she grabbed a couple of beach towels and her big, cloth purse.

After following him onto the porch, she shut the main door and locked it. As she eased the screen door shut, she asked, 'How far are we planning to go?'

'All the way down to the lake,' Bass said. He trotted down the stairs.

'From where?' Faye asked.

'The Bend.'

'We're going all the way from the Bend to the lake?'

'It's only about twenty miles. I've got a borrowed car waiting down at the marina so we can drive back.'

'But twenty *miles*?' Isn't that an awfully long way to paddle a canoe?'

'It's not so far. Besides, it's all downstream. The current'll do most of the work for us.'

'Even still . . .'

'You'll love it. You'll want to do it *every* Saturday.'

'All I can say is, it's a good thing I brought my sun block.'

'Yeah,' Bass said. Approaching the trunk of his ancient Pontiac Grand Prix, he ducked to keep his head from bumping the stern of the canoe lashed to the roof. He set down the basket and cooler.

His trunk hadn't worked right since he'd come back from a canoe trip a few weeks earlier and found it broken open. He didn't know what sort of valuables the thief had expected to find in there. But it was a mighty large trunk, so the jerk probably figured it was sure to contain a wealth of goodies.

He'd stolen nothing except the spare tire – a treadless old thing of no use to anyone.

But he'd done lasting damage to the trunk's latch and lock.

The key no longer did the trick, so Bass didn't bother to try it. Instead, he pounded the trunk's lid with his fist. The latch released. Stepping back, he watched the lid rise.

Then he stowed away the basket and cooler. 'Anything else you want in here?' he asked Faye.

She shook her head. 'When're you going to get that thing fixed, anyway?'

'Maybe never. I sort of like it this way.'

He needed two attempts at shutting it before the latch caught and held the trunk closed.

The rough, dirt parking area above the river was deserted except for a single car, a blue Jaguar parked near the garbage barrel.

'Bet they didn't haul a canoe over here on top of *that*,' Bass said.

'Doesn't seem likely.'

He and Faye climbed out of his car.

Faye stood back and watched.

Bass untied the bow and stern lines anchoring his

aluminum canoe to the front and rear bumpers of his Pontiac, then unbuckled the cloth straps that latched it to the roof rack.

'Could you give me a hand lifting it down?'

'I don't know, Bass.'

'It's not very heavy.'

'Not for you, maybe.'

'All those work-outs you do, you shouldn't have any trouble at all holding up one end of this little thing.'

'Well, I'll give it a try.'

Bass took the bow and Faye took the stern. 'Okay,' he said. 'Ready?'

'Oh, I guess so.'

'Now!'

They both lifted the canoe off its rack. Holding it high, they sidestepped away from the car.

'This isn't so bad,' Faye said. 'I thought it'd be a lot heavier.'

'You're stronger than you think.'

'Maybe so.'

With her arms raised, the bottom slopes of her breasts showed beneath the ragged edge of her T-shirt.

'Ready to carry it down to the river?' Bass asked, enjoying the view.

'How far *is* the river?'

'At the bottom of the hill behind you.'

She gave him a thin smile. 'Pardon me if I don't turn around and look.'

'You wouldn't be able to see it, anyway. Too many trees in the way.'

'I don't know how far I can carry this thing.'

'Just do the best you can.'

'Holy Moses, you didn't tell me this would be an endurance test.'

'You're doing just fine.'

'Why don't we carry the other stuff down first? The light stuff?'

'Do you think that'll make things easier?'

She grinned. 'Sure.'

'We'd have to set down the canoe. Then pick it up again.'

'Oh, I wouldn't mind. Let's, okay?'

It made no sense at all, putting down the canoe at this point. But he didn't want to start an argument. Forcing himself to smile, he said, 'Okay. Let's set her down.'

Slowly, they lowered the canoe to the dirt. Then Faye straightened up. She brushed strands of short blonde hair away from her brow and took a deep breath. 'Whew,' she said. 'Glad to have *that* done with.'

'We'll just have to pick it up again in a few minutes.'

'It'll give me time to rest and recuperate.'

'Ah. Okay.' Bass stepped to the trunk of his car and pounded on the lid. The latch opened and the lid swung up. Reaching in, he grabbed the towels. He tossed them to Faye, throwing them high to make her reach. 'Catch,' he called.

She leaped for them, her cut-off T-shirt rising above her breasts for a moment before she snagged the towels out of the air, laughing.

'Nice catch,' Bass said.

'Nice throw.'

He lifted out the picnic basket, set it on the ground behind his car, then ducked into the trunk and hauled out the cooler chest.

'Do you think I should leave my purse in the car?' Faye asked.

'Might not be a bad idea. In case we capsize.'

'Wonderful. Capsize?'

'It isn't likely.'

'Are you taking your wallet?'

He patted the rear pocket of his cut-off jeans. 'I need mine. I'll have to drive after we get to the lake.'

'Oh. That's right. Okay, I'll leave my purse here. Do you think it'll be safe?'

'Probably. Just hide it under the front seat.'

'What about my cell phone?'

'You'd better leave it, too. You definitely don't want *that* going into the river.'

'I don't want *anything* going into the river.'

'More than likely, nothing will. Just our paddles.'

'I hope so.'

Faye removed a plastic bottle of sun block from her purse, then opened the passenger door, bent down and shoved her purse under the seat.

'All set?' Bass asked.

'Yeah.' She locked and shut the door.

Bass shut the trunk. Its latch caught on the first try. As he picked up the picnic basket and cooler, Faye started on ahead of him with her sun block and the towels.

'That's a long way down,' she said.

'It's not as bad as it looks.'

'I'll just bet.' With a laugh, she started down the trail.

Bass walked behind her. He didn't try to catch up, but

walked steadily with his load, watching her. In spite of her complaining, she seemed eager and happy about being here, doing this.

She hurried down the trail, stopped, turned around to smile at Bass and wait for him to get closer, then chided, 'Slow poke' and hurried on.

'I'm saving my energy for the canoe,' he called.

She turned her head and grimaced at him. 'I know! Let's *forget* about the canoe. Why don't we just leave it up at the car? We can swim in the river, instead. Lie in the sand, soak up the sun, have our picnic right here on the beach.'

'Where's the fun in that?'

'Oh, we might think of something.'

'You stay if you want. *I'm* taking the canoe down to the lake.'

'And leave me here without you?'

'You've done other things without me.'

The fun seemed to drain from her. 'For God's sake, Bass. I know what I did. I told you I'm sorry. What do I have to do?'

'I don't know.'

'God, why did you have to bring *that* up?'

'I'm sorry. Forget it.' He set down the basket and cooler beside the trail and went to her. He took the towels and sun block from her hands and let them fall to the ground.

Faye threw herself against him. She clutched him tightly, pressing her face to his chest. 'I'm sorry.' She was crying, 'I'm so damn sorry.'

'It's okay.' He gently stroked her back.

'I wish to God it'd never happened.'

'It's okay.'

'I love you, Bass.'

'I know. I love you, too.'

'I was so stupid. I only did it . . .'

'Hey, hey. It's all right.'

'If you want your ring back . . .?'

'I don't. Of course I don't. Come on, now. We've been through all this. Everything's fine.'

She nodded, her face wet against his shoulder.

'And we'll still get married,' he said. 'If *you* still want to.'

She sniffed. 'Of course I do. Of course. I want to marry you so badly.'

'Now let's get down to the river while we've still got some Saturday left.'

She turned her face up to him. It was red and wet. Her nose was running. She wiped it dry and Bass kissed her. Then he gave her a gentle swat through the seat of her bikini pants. She flinched a little and laughed.

'Let's go,' he said.

She gave him a hard squeeze, then let go. While Bass hurried up the trail, she picked up her things. Then she waited for him. As he walked quickly toward her, the basket and cooler swinging by his sides, she used one of the towels to wipe the tears from her face.

'Go,' he said, bearing down on her.

With a laugh, she whirled around and scampered on ahead of him.

And suddenly stopped at the foot of the trail.

Bass, about to run her down, dodged to the right and halted beside her. 'Look,' she said, and ducked her head slightly.

Bass turned his eyes toward the river.

With trees no longer in the way, he saw two people lying in the sand near the water's edge.

'What are they doing?' Faye whispered.

'Sleeping.'

'She's *naked*.'

'Sure looks that way,' Bass whispered.

'What'll we do?'

'Take a closer look?'

Faye's eyes, playful again but still red from the recent tears, gave him a mocking scold.

'Pretend they're not here?' Bass suggested.

'They're bound to wake up. I mean, we still have to bring the *canoe* down, and everything.'

'So?' Bass said.

'She's *naked*. I don't want them to wake up and *find* us here. Anyway, we don't even know what kind of people they might be.'

'Well, I know one thing. We're not going to let them mess up our canoe trip. We'll just go on with our plans as if they aren't even here.'

'But they *are* here.'

'We've got as much right to be on this beach as they do.'

'But she's *naked*.'

'Probably just working on an even tan.'

'Let's go back, honey. Please?'

'No. Look, don't worry about it. If we disturb them, too bad. Let them call the cops.'

Faye made a nervous laugh and quickly pressed a towel to her lips. Lowering the towel, she whispered, 'We do have friends on the force, don't we?'

'Sure do.'

'Man, would *these* two be in for a surprise.'

'Anyway, nobody's going to call the cops. We'll just mind our own business and let them mind theirs.'

Lips pressed together, Faye nodded briskly.

'Come on,' Bass said.

He started walking forward, Faye close to his side. The motionless couple was still a fair distance away. The man wore blue jeans, but no shirt. He looked slender and fit. His feet were bare. Curled on his side, his body blocked some of the woman from their view. Her legs were visible. Her nest of pubic hair glistened in the sun. One breast showed, but the closer one was hidden behind the man's upthrust shoulder.

'I've got an idea,' Faye whispered. 'Maybe if we sing . . .'

'What on earth for?'

'To warn them, let them know we're coming. It'll give the woman a chance to throw something on before we're right on top of her.'

'I wasn't planning to get on top of her.'

'I'm serious.'

'I thought we wanted to *not* wake them up.'

'It'd be better this way,' Faye whispered.

'Okay. What'll we sing?'

'How about, "We're off to See the Wizard"?'

'I don't know the words.'

'What *do* you know?'

'"Things to Do in Denver When You're Dead."'

'I don't know that. How about "Deck the Halls"? You've *got* to know that one.'

'Sure.'

'Ready? Get set. Go.'

They began to sing.

The man's arm moved. He flopped onto his back, exposing the rest of the woman. She had no head.

Screaming, Faye stumbled sideways against Bass. He pulled her tightly against him and held her as the man sat up.

'Stay back!' the man yelled. He looked at Bass and Faye, then at the woman beside him. Scurrying to his feet, he ran for the river.

'My God!' Bass blurted. 'He's got her head!'

Faye pushed her face hard against Bass's chest.

The man reached the river running full speed, splashing water high as his bare feet hit it, pulled out, and hit it again.

'I'm going after him.' Bass started to let go of Faye.

'No! Stay with me!' She clutched him hard, mashing herself against him.

The man dived into the river and started to swim.

'He's getting away. I've gotta go after him.'

'No! Don't! He might *kill* you!'

'I can't just stand here and let him . . .'

'Stay! Please!' She hugged Bass even more tightly than before. 'Stay. Just let him go. It doesn't matter.'

'But . . .'

'No! *You can't leave me here!*'

'All right. All right.'

He made no more efforts to get free. They stood together on the sand, embracing, as the man swam to the other side of the river, climbed the far shore and, after a quick glance backward, disappeared into the thick forest of pine.

Chapter Three

THE SHERIFF

Rusty Hodges, the sheriff of Sierra County, squeezed the trigger of his Smith & Wesson .44 magnum. The shot crashed through the silence and his revolver leaped like a strong, startled dog. Thirty feet in front of him, the hollow-point struck a water-filled beer can. The can jumped off the ground, tumbling and blasting out water. The water glistened like silver in the sunlight. The can fell to the forest floor and rolled.

That's about enough for today, Rusty thought. *Might as well quit on a winning note.*

Besides, he'd managed to destroy the two dozen beer cans he'd brought with him to the clearing.

At the rear of the patrol car, he tossed his ear protectors into the trunk. Then he ejected his brass. The six shiny shells felt warm in his palm. He poured them into the left front pocket of his uniform trousers and patted them. They made a nice jangle.

Leaning into the trunk, he plucked six fresh cartridges out of their box. He held them in his left hand and stepped away from the trunk so he could look at them in the sunlight.

Beauties, he thought.

They were sleek and heavy. Their blunt tips gleamed like silver; their shells shone like gold.

He remembered a bit of a poem from high school. It went, *A thing of beauty is a joy forever.*

These were things of beauty, all right.

He wondered if women felt this way about their best jewelry.

Smiling, he shook his head and started sliding the rounds, one at a time, into the snug holes of the cylinder.

He supposed it was terrible to be so fond of his weapons and ammo. A lot of people, if they knew about it, would take him for a nut. You weren't supposed to like guns. Not in this day and age. So he pretty much kept quiet on the subject.

When his hand was empty, he snapped the cylinder into place with his thumb. Then he brought his left hand close to his face. It was big and grimy. He inhaled, sucking in the aromas of oil and brass and blasted powder.

He closed his eyes.

Somebody oughta bottle this smell, he thought, *and sell it as a men's cologne.*

He holstered his weapon.

Call it Gunfire, he thought, and grinned.

'Shit,' he muttered. 'It'd sell like hotcakes.'

Leaning into the trunk, he grabbed a plastic garbage bag.

'Especially on Father's Day,' he added, and laughed quietly.

Swinging the bag by his side, he started ambling away from the car. Just as he passed the open door, however, the radio crackled. 'Headquarters to Car One.' He ducked inside, let go of the garbage bag, and grabbed the mike.

'Car One,' he said. 'Go ahead, Madge.'

'We've got a homicide, Rusty.' Her voice sounded excited. 'We've finally got another homicide. Over.'

'Don't sound so overjoyed, darling. It isn't lady-like. What's the location?'

'It's at the Bend. They found it at the Bend. And there was a suspect seen fleeing the scene, but that was back at about oh-nine-hundred. Over.'

Rusty glanced at his wristwatch. 9:35. 'Let's bring in the Pac,' he said. 'She'll be at home. Where's Jack?'

'He's Code Seven at Wilma's Grill.'

'Send him over to the Bend as soon as he checks in. And get in touch with George Birkus, have him send over his meat wagon. I'm on my way. Who should I see?'

'Bass Paxton. He found the body. He called from a car phone there at the roadhead.'

'Which roadhead?'

'The one this side of the Bend. You know. Where everybody parks? Not that other one, whatever they call it.'

'Sweet Meadow.'

'Right. It's *not* the Sweet Meadow roadhead, it's the closer one.'

'The *Bend* roadhead?'

'Well, isn't that what I said?'

'More than likely.'

'Don't be a so-and-so, Sheriff.'

'Sorry.'

'He'll be waiting for you. Bass Paxton. At *the Bend* roadhead.'

'Got it. I'll be there in about twenty minutes.'

Just over fifteen minutes later, Rusty reached the turn-off to the Bend. He knew the dirt road well. As a boy, he'd hiked it with his buddies, wrestled in the sand, gone swimming in the Silver River's cold currents, camped on its shores and in the surrounding woods. Later, he'd driven the road with girls, walked them down to the Bend, wrestled in the sand, gone in swimming. The first time with Millie, it was on the sand of the Bend. God, what a night! Over the years, they'd returned to the Bend each anniversary. It was a very special place for both of them.

And now some creep had committed a murder there.

Should've done it someplace else.

The pines thinned out, and Rusty drove across the bare dirt of the parking area. A Jaguar was parked beside the garbage can. He rolled past it, and drove closer to Bass Paxton's old red Grand Prix.

The Pontiac's windows were rolled down. Bass was sitting in the driver's seat. In the passenger seat was a woman. Rusty couldn't see her face clearly, but he supposed she must be Faye Everett. The two had been going together, off and on, for a couple of years.

Bass waved and opened his door.

Rusty steered around a canoe on the ground near the Pontiac, then stopped his patrol car. As he climbed out, Bass came walking over.

'Morning, Bass.'

'Rusty.'

'They tell me you found a body.'

Bass shook his head, wrinkling his nose as if he smelled

29

a foul odor. 'Sure did. Faye and I were gonna take my canoe down the river and we walked right up to it.'

'Where abouts?' Rusty asked.

'Down by the shore.'

'It's down there now?'

Bass nodded.

'What is it? Male, female?'

'A female.'

'You're absolutely sure she's dead? We should call in an ambulance . . .'

'She's dead, all right. She's been decapitated.'

Rusty gaped at him. 'De-*what*?'

'Decapitated. Her head was cut off.'

'You're shitting me.'

'I wish.'

Shaking his head, Rusty stepped over to the Jaguar. He took a close look at the orange decal on a corner of its windshield. 'Do you know anything about this car?' he asked.

'It was here when we came.'

He opened the door, bent down and peered inside. Looking for the registration, he tried to open the glove compartment. It was locked.

A brown leather strap curved across the floor under the driver's seat. He slipped a finger beneath the strap and pulled out a purse. Setting it on the seat, he opened it. The billfold inside was a rough twill fabric. He lifted it out, opened it, and removed the driver's license from its plastic holder. After studying the license for a few moments, he slipped it into his shirt pocket.

He nodded to Bass. 'Let's go down and have a look.'

'Do I have to? I mean, I hate to leave Faye alone.'

'We can have her come with us.'

'I don't think she'd want to do that. She's pretty shaken up. She was sick to her stomach a while ago. She's still scared half to death.'

'Well, go and ask her to come along with us. She shouldn't stay up here by herself, and I need to go down there and have a look at things.'

'I'll talk to her.'

He watched Bass walk over to the Pontiac's window and bend down. Inside, Faye nodded. Then Bass opened the door and she climbed out.

She looked good in her bikini shorts and cut-off T-shirt. She was dressed for a good time, dressed for sun and splashing and laughter and probably sex. But the fun had been wiped out before it even began. Her head hung low. Her shoulders drooped. She walked unsteadily, holding Bass's arm as if she might fall without it.

'I'm sorry this had to happen,' Rusty told her.

Faye looked up. 'He cut her head off, Sheriff.'

'Bass was telling me.'

'He did.' She nodded, frowning. 'He cut it off.'

'Why don't we go on down, now?'

'But *she's* down there.'

'Come on, Faye.' Bass started leading her.

She jerked her arm free, lurched away and fell. She landed hard on her back. The impact made her grunt. Her T-shirt slid up a few inches, baring the undersides of her breasts, showing one of her nipples entirely and draping the other like a ragged white hood.

Instead of giving the shirt a pull, she rolled onto her

31

stomach. 'Not me,' she said. 'Not me. You go down, not me. Oh, no. Not me.'

'Okay,' Rusty said. 'That's okay. You don't have to come with us.'

After helping her into the Pontiac, Rusty and Bass stepped far enough away to prevent her from hearing them. 'I've got a couple of deputies on the way,' Rusty explained. 'We can stay with Faye till one of them gets here.'

Bass nodded.

'Let's go over the whole story, okay?' Rusty took a small notebook and a pen out of his shirt pocket. 'Give me as much detail as you can recall.'

'Well, I went over to Faye's place at about eight to pick her up for our canoe trip. It's not Faye's place, really. She rooms there with Ina Jones. It's Ina's house.'

'Do you know the address off hand?'

Nodding, Bass gave him Ina's address and he wrote it down.

'We were planning to take the canoe down river to the lake. We were going to have a picnic . . .'

Bass went on telling his story until a car engine interrupted. Then he and Rusty watched the shaded area where the dirt road emerged from the woods. In moments, a brown patrol car appeared, its tires raising dust. It pulled alongside Rusty's car and stopped. The door flew open. Deputy Jack Staffer stepped out. He walked quickly with the stiffness of a soldier approaching a general.

'Sorry I took so long, sir.'

'We all have to eat,' Rusty told him.

'Yes, sir.'

'Jack, do you know Bass Paxton?'

'We've met.' He nodded smartly toward Bass.

'We found a body,' Bass told him. 'Me and Faye Everett. Down by the river.'

'Faye's in the car,' Rusty said. 'I want you to stay with her while we have a look down below. And talk to her. Find out what she has to say about all this.'

Jack nodded briskly.

'The Pac'll be here pretty soon. Send her down when she arrives. And send down Birkus. He won't be able to get his Good Humor truck down to the shore, so he'll need to carry her up.'

'Right.'

'Faye's in bad shape, so be nice.'

'Right, sir. Nice.'

Rusty turned to Bass. 'Let's go down and have a look.'

They walked quickly down the trail. When they reached the bottom, trees no longer blocked the way and Rusty noticed a shape on the sand near the shore.

Even from this distance, he could tell that it was a naked woman. He could tell that she was dead, too. She looked all wrong. Her skin color was off. The positioning of her body looked awkward and unnatural. Even her *shape* looked strange and off kilter, though he couldn't really see from here that her head was gone.

'Where were you standing when you first saw the two of them?' Rusty asked.

'Just about here, I guess.'

He glanced at his notes. 'You said the man was a Caucasian, about thirty, five-eleven, a hundred and sixty pounds, and bald. Did he wear glasses?'

'No.'

'Any physical irregularities? Did he limp? Have a scar? Any tattoos?'

'No, I don't think so. Not that I noticed.'

They walked closer to the body.

'What about his voice? Did he speak with an accent?'

'Nothing foreign or anything. I mean, he sounded like he could be from around here. But all he said was "Stay back."'

Rusty could now make out details of the woman's body.

It looked as if it had been a very fine body.

By the blue tint of her skin, he figured that she must've died by suffocation. Either she'd drowned or had been strangled. By her proximity to the river, death by drowning seemed likely.

Rusty looked at Bass.

The young man was gazing at her, a sickish look on his face.

'So after the man ran into the river with her head, did you come over and take a closer look at her?'

He nodded slightly.

'Did you touch her?'

'*Touch* her? No. Are you kidding? Why would I . . .? No, I sure didn't.'

'So she was in exactly this position when you found her?'

'Yeah.'

'You didn't touch *anything*?'

'No.'

'Okay. Just asking. I need to make sure everything's just the way you found it.'

'Exactly the same. I mean, I know you're not supposed to fool with a crime scene.'

'What about Faye?'

Turning slightly, Bass pointed. 'She was over there barfing her guts out.'

'So she didn't touch anything either?'

'No. Huh-uh.'

'Good. Now, why don't you wait here?'

Rusty walked alone toward the body, moving his eyes carefully over the area near it. Slowly, he circled it. Then he approached, knelt down, and studied the neck stump. Flies were already on it. Though he started feeling nauseous, he stayed on his knees and refused to look away.

The spinal column looked as if it had been neatly severed with a fine-toothed saw.

Feeling more woosy than ever, Rusty realized he was holding his breath.

He scurried backward, got to his feet, and breathed again. Turning to Bass, he asked, 'Where did the man enter the river?'

Bass pointed. 'About there.'

Unwrapping a cigar, Rusty walked over to the shore. 'He was running?'

'Yeah.'

Rusty stuffed the cellophane wrapper into his pocket. Then he bit off the end of his cigar and spat it out. 'He entered about here?'

'That's right.'

'What kind of stroke did he use?'

'Stroke?'

Rusty struck a match. Cupping it against the breeze, he sucked the flame into his cigar. He took a few puffs. '*How* did he swim? Breaststroke, sidestroke, crawl?'

'He was carrying her head.'

'How'd he swim?'

'It was a sidestroke, I guess.'

'He carried the head in one hand?'

'Sort of clutched against his chest. You know, like a football.'

'Was the other hand free?'

Bass nodded. 'I guess so.'

'How long did you watch him?'

'Till he got across. I kept thinking I should chase him, but Faye wouldn't let go of me. And I didn't want to leave her alone.'

'Just as well. You might've ended up as dead as that woman.'

'Maybe.'

'Did you see him get out on the other side?'

'Yeah.'

'Was he still carrying her head?'

'Sure was.'

Chapter Four

THE DEPUTY

Deputy Mary Hodges, known from childhood as the Pac or just Pac because of her father's allegiance to his native Green Bay football heros, had never been accused of looking like a fullback. At five foot eleven, she didn't look much like a gymnast, either. Not until you saw her on the uneven parallel bars or vaulting horse. When a knee injury knocked her out of the Olympic finals, she'd joined the Sierra County Sheriff's Department.

Nepotism had nothing to do with her success; she'd been on the force two years before marrying the sheriff's son, Harney Hodges.

She smiled, remembering the way Harney was this morning when the telephone rang at the worst possible moment.

Celebrating the third anniversary of their wedding.

On top of her and madly thrusting.

'No!' he'd gasped.

'Yes.'

'No!'

'Don't stop,' she'd gasped. 'God. No. Don't. Stop!'

37

It had still been ringing by the time they got done and they both rolled, still embracing, Harney still deep inside her. The rolling took them sideways across the bed and closer to the phone. From her position on top of Harney, she was able to reach out and pick up the handset.

'A homicide,' she'd explained after hanging up.

'I'd like to homicide Madge.'

'You're so mean when you're angry.'

He'd laughed.

Pac took her foot off the gas pedal as the car broke through the last of the trees. Jack Staffer was standing between a Jaguar and a big old red Pontiac, talking to a young blonde . . .

Bass Paxton's Grand Prix.

Bass is involved in this?

And that's Faye!

Pac drove past Bass's canoe, parked beside another patrol car and leaped out. 'Faye, are you all right?'

'No, not really.'

Pac turned to Jack. 'What's going on?' she asked.

'She and Bass Paxton had a run-in with a headless corpse,' Jack said. 'Down there.' He pointed toward the wooded slope. 'Rusty wants you to do your stuff.'

Pac nodded. To Faye, she said, 'How do you feel?'

'Not too good.' She made a feeble smile. 'I'm feeling a little better though, I guess.'

'You'll be all right.'

'Sure.'

'You're staying with her?' she asked Jack.

'Right.'

She turned to Faye. 'I have to go down. I'll probably be

gone a while, but Jack'll stay here with you.'

'Okay.'

She hurried back to her patrol car and took a Nikon and a crime-scene kit out of the back seat. With a final glance at Jack and Faye, she started down the trail.

Normally, she would have enjoyed the heavy, sweet odor of pine. She might even have stopped to take photos of the cone-littered trail or of the dust-swirling, golden sunlight slanting down through the trees. But not this morning. Not with a dead body down below.

At the bottom of the trail, the trees ended and she could see Rusty wandering over the sand, head down, a cigar protruding from his mouth. Bass was standing a few yards from the body, not looking at it.

Her shoes dug into the sand as she hurried forward.

Rusty came over to her. 'Sorry we had to drag you out of bed, darling.'

She felt herself blush.

And Rusty noticed it. 'Oh?' he said. 'Hmm. Now I'm twice as sorry. Please tender my apologies to Harney, too.'

'Nothing to apologize for.'

'Bet he doesn't see it that way.'

'Ah, he's all right.'

'And happy anniversary. Sorry we had to interrupt it like this.'

'These things happen.'

'Not too often around here, they don't. You going out to dinner tonight?'

She nodded. 'We've got reservations for the Fireside. Think I'll be able to keep 'em?'

'Sure. I don't see why not. But the sooner we get this

situation wrapped up, the better.'

'Who's our body?' Pac asked.

'If she belongs to the purse I found in the Jag, she's Alison Parkington. Resides in Santa Monica.'

'Long way from home.'

'Hi, Pac,' Bass said, striding toward her.

She turned to him. 'Hey, Bass.'

'How you doing?' he asked.

'Not bad,' she said.

'Wish I could say the same.'

'You can go back up to Faye if you'd like,' Rusty told him. 'We'll want statements, though, so stay with Deputy Staffer.'

Bass nodded. He muttered, 'Guess I'll go on up.' He glanced toward the body, but quickly looked away. To Pac, he said, 'See you later. Say hi to Harney for me.'

'Sure. See you.'

He started walking toward the trail.

Rusty stepped closer to Pac. 'Bass and Faye found the body at about nine o'clock this morning,' he explained. 'They were planning on a canoe trip to the lake. When they got down here, they saw the body. It was where it is right now. But it wasn't alone. An adult male was in the sand beside the body, apparently asleep. About thirty years old, five-eleven, a hundred and sixty pounds, bald.'

'Bald?' Pac asked.

'He sounds a lot like you.'

'I'm not . . . *Rusty!*'

'Sorry,' he said, grinning. 'Couldn't help it.'

Pac glanced around. She saw nobody. So she slugged Rusty in the upper arm.

He grimaced.

'Sorry,' Pac said. 'Couldn't help it. So, what was this guy wearing?'

Rusty rubbed his arm, then glanced at his notebook. 'Blue jeans, no shirt, no shoes.'

'Did Bass and Faye get a look at his face?'

'Just for a moment, apparently. Faye might not've even seen that much. The way Bass tells it, the guy had his back to them most of the time. And Faye freaked out when she saw that the gal was short a head. We'll have to talk to her and get the details, but it sounds like she tried to see as little as possible.'

'She's a pretty squeamish girl,' Pac said.

'Well, I might get squeamish myself if I saw a fellow go running off with somebody's head.'

'He took it?'

'Bass said he ran into the river with it and swam to the other side. Apparently, he wanted to take it home as a souvenir, or something.'

'Maybe he'll have it stuffed and mounted,' Pac said. Then she switched her camera on. 'Guess I'd better get this show on the road.'

Nodding, Rusty said, 'Make sure you get some good close-ups of the neck. And take shots of the tracks that go over to the river, too. They aren't much, but you never know. We'll get Jack down here with a rake. Maybe we can come up with the saw or whatever our bad guy used. And the clothes. Doesn't look like there're clothes around here anywhere. I can't imagine the gal walked all the way down from the parking lot bare-ass naked.'

'Doesn't seem too likely.'

'Of course, she might've had no say in it.'

'Might've already been dead,' Pac suggested.

'Could be, could be.' Rusty nodded, frowning. Then he said, 'When you get finished down here, go on up and take care of the Jaguar. The gal *might've* come out here alone, but I doubt it. If we're going to come up with any latents, they'll probably be on the car.'

'Or the saw.'

'If we find it,' Rusty said. 'Now, I'm going to have myself a look on the other side of the river.' He tossed away his cigar. 'You stay here.'

'How're you going to get over there?'

'Swim, of course.' He grinned. Then he walked to the shore, staying well to the left of the shallow indentations in the sand he'd asked Pac to photograph. Near the water's edge, he took off his shirt.

His back was tanned and freckled. He looked like a heavier, more powerful version of Harney.

He set his folded shirt in the sand, unstrapped his gun belt, and put it down on the shirt.

'You're going unarmed?' Pac asked.

'You're not supposed to be watching me, young lady. The sight of my pulchritude's likely to stir you up and get us both in trouble.'

She laughed.

'Go on and take your pictures.'

She waited until Rusty had stripped down to his boxer shorts, then snapped one.

He spun around, his face redder than usual.

'For the family scrapbook,' she explained.

'You're a terrible woman, Mary.'

'I know, I know.'

'No wonder my kid fell for you.'

Turning away from her, he waded into the river.

Pac watched him trudge out. When the water was nearly waist deep, he dived. Then he swam to the other side and climbed onto the bank, his shorts low and clinging. Standing on dry land, he hitched the shorts up. Then he glanced over his shoulder.

Pac, grinning, showed him a thumbs-up.

He returned the gesture.

After Rusty had disappeared into the trees, Pac began taking photos of the crime scene. The area photos went well. She took more than necessary, postponing the time when she would need to do detail shots of the body.

But that time came. She took the photos slowly, carefully. When the roll of film was used up, she reloaded, set the camera aside, and drew sketches of the scene.

That took care of it. She wanted to start working on the car, but she couldn't leave the body unattended. The sun pressed down on her. With a sleeve, she wiped sweat off her forehead.

A swim would feel great.

She didn't dare.

Instead, she picked up her camera and fingerprint box and walked to the foot of the trail. She found a shaded area, kicked aside some pine cones and sat down. The mat of needles made quiet crushing sounds.

She sat there waiting until she heard the voices. Then she stood up and brushed needles off the seat of her trousers.

Two men came down the trail carrying an empty stretcher.

'Top of the morning,' called Birkus. 'They say you've got a present for us.'

Pac got to her feet.

Chapter Five

WITNESSES

On the other side of the river, Rusty walked carefully down the narrow path through the woods, watching for the killer, for clues, for the missing head, for pine cones.

The pine cones, whenever he stepped on one, hurt like hell.

Except for an empty mashed pack of Camels, a Hershey wrapper and a couple of crushed beer cans, the path was clean. None of the debris looked fresh.

Half a dozen overgrown footpaths led into the path he was following. The suspect could have taken any of them, but Rusty doubted it. This was the main path, the one leading most directly to the Sweet Meadow roadhead.

When the ground began to rise, he knew he was close to the roadhead. He left the path and approached cautiously. Pine needles scratched his arms. Lines of spider webs stuck to his face and shoulders.

At last, he could see the parking area.

It was deserted except for a battered old Chevy pick-up truck.

Though he could see no one, he heard a man's quiet laughter.

It came from the truck.

The pick-up was about twenty feet away. Through its windshield, Rusty saw an empty rifle rack. Nobody was visible inside the cab.

He looked to the left and right. He saw no one.

Before stepping into the open, he memorized the license plate number.

He walked quietly toward the truck. His hand moved to his hip. Though he sought the comfort of his Smith & Wesson, he found only the damp fabric of his underwear. He almost muttered a curse, but stopped himself.

At the truck, he glanced through an open window. The cab was empty. A faded purse made of blue jeans, complete with pockets but without any legs, lay on the passenger seat. There were sandals on the floor. Stepping toward the back, he looked down into the truck bed.

He grinned.

Then he slammed his hand against the side panel, making the metal ring out.

'Hey!' the girl blurted. 'Shit! What the fuck?' Rolling over, she scowled up at Rusty. A teenager. She had frizzy blonde hair and a pierced eyebrow with a ring in it that made Rusty hurt, just looking. She had one through her left nostril, too. And one in her upper lip. And about six running down the rim of each ear.

Hell on metal detectors, Rusty thought.

She wore a pink T-shirt, and was covered almost to the shoulders by an old brown blanket. 'Hey,' she said, 'what's happening?'

'Saturday morning,' Rusty told her.

'Yer a riot.'

Beside her, a boy pulled down a blanket that had been hiding his face. He frowned at Rusty. Like the girl, he had a ring through one eyebrow. None in his nose or lips, though, and only one ear was pierced. Its lobe was decorated with a small, silver skull.

Rusty guessed his age at seventeen, maybe eighteen.

Not thirty and certainly not bald.

Though his hair was cut so short it resembled a three-day growth of whiskers, it was jet black. Nobody would be likely to describe him as bald.

Not our guy, Rusty thought. Not unless the Bass's description had been *way* off.

The boy said nothing. Underneath the blanket, his arms were moving. Rusty figured he was probably fastening his pants.

'So, what're ya doin' here?' the girl asked.

'Taking a look around.'

'Well, now that y'seen us, how about gettin' the fuck outa here?'

'You got any clothes on?' the boy asked him. Sitting up, he looked over the side panel. 'Not much. What are you, some kind of degenerate?'

'What's he got on?' the girl asked.

'Just his undies.'

'No shit?'

'I'd like to ask you some questions,' Rusty said.

'I'd like to ask *you* something,' the girl said. 'Briefs or boxers?'

'Maybe we can be serious here for a minute,' Rusty said.

'*I'm* serious,' the girl said. 'I'm *always* serious, right Bill?'

'That's right,' her boyfriend said. To Rusty, he said, 'Trink's *always* serious.'

'I haven't got a funny bone in my body,' she said, and giggled.

'If you're looking for your clothes,' Bill said, 'I haven't seen them. Have you seen his clothes, Trink?'

'Nope.' She sat up, crawled over Bill, and looked down at Rusty's shorts. 'Boxers. Hmm.' She looked him up and down, then said, 'Hey, mister, you wanta climb in and join us?'

'Thanks for the invitation, but no thanks. I'd like you both to climb out.'

Bill frowned again. 'What for?'

'I want to talk.'

'We don't have your clothes.'

'Maybe he thinks you're layin' on 'em, Bill.'

'Well, I'm not.'

'*I* know that, tell *him*.'

'Why? It's none of his business.'

'It's his business if you're on top of his clothes.'

'But I'm not,' Bill said.

'I'm not looking for my clothes,' Rusty explained. 'I need some information.'

'Why *aren't* you looking for 'em?' Trink asked. 'Seems to me you *oughta* be.'

'Maybe he's a flasher,' Bill told her.

'Are you a flasher, mister? Go on and flash us if you want.'

'Did either of you see a man here this morning?' Rusty asked.

'I did.' The girl glanced at Bill. 'Did you?'

'Not me.'

'You must be blind.'

'What did the man look like?' Rusty asked.

Frowning, she rubbed her chin. 'Oh, he was about forty-five. He was some six feet tall or more, and maybe weighed a couple hundred pounds. Had him a good build, a real nice build. Had red hair and green eyes and freckles. And, let's see . . . yeah . . . he was wearin' boxer shorts.'

'You're a big help,' Rusty said. 'I'm Sheriff Rusty Hodges. This is an official investigation, so I suggest you cooperate unless you want to find yourselves in a jam.'

'He claims he's a sheriff,' Trink told Bill.

'I heard.'

'So where's your badge, Sheriff?'

'He don't *need* no steenking badges!' Bill blurted.

'Think we should talk to him?'

'Hell, no!'

Frowning seriously at Rusty, she said, 'We never talk to cops in undies. Not without our lawyers.'

'You may need a lawyer,' Rusty said, 'if I decide to search this truck.'

'You can't search it,' Bill complained.

'Watch me.'

'You need a warrant.'

'I don't need no *steenking* warrant.' He nodded toward the tweezers that lay in plain sight on their blanket. 'That looks like a roach clip to me, and it's right out in plain sight. That's all . . .'

'That ain't no roach clip,' Trick said. 'That's my eyebrow pluckers.'

'Both of you climb down, please.'

49

Bill shook his head. 'Why should we?'

'Now.'

'Okay, okay. Don't get your shorts in a twist.'

Trink laughed.

'You first, Bill. Trink, you stay there till I tell you to move. Come on down, Bill.'

The boy stood up. He was wearing a rumpled T-shirt with the logo, 'Eat Shit and Die,' a pair of torn and faded blue jeans, and sandals. The waist button of the jeans was fastened, but his zipper was down. He pulled it up. Fastening his belt, he stepped to the rear of the truck bed. Then he climbed over the tailgate and jumped down.

Rusty turned him around. Standing behind the boy, he bent him over. 'Hands on the tailgate,' he said. After Bill complied, Rusty nudged his feet apart and started to frisk him.

'Hey, that tickles.'

Rusty worked his way down to Bill's waist, then stopped. 'Anything sharp in your pockets? Razors, needles?'

'No. No, sir.'

'I put my hand in, nothing's going to poke me?'

'I told you . . .'

'Okay.' Keeping one hand on Bill's back, he searched the jeans pockets with the other.

They were empty.

'Where's your ID?'

'In the cab. You gonna bust us?'

'We'll see.' He backed away from Bill. 'Stand over there,' he said.

Bill stepped aside. 'Here?'

'That's good. Okay, young lady. Please step down.'

Trink swept the blanket away and stood up. Her T-shirt was pink, fairly clean, and had no sayings or decorations. It might've fit her when she was nine years old. It hugged her body, clinging to her breasts. She didn't wear a bra, but she obviously wore nipple rings. The T-shirt didn't quite reach down to her navel. On purpose, Rusty supposed. So everyone would be able to admire the ring in her belly button. Down low on her hips, she wore a flower patterned skirt. Long and billowy, it reminded Rusty of the 'granny dresses' that gals used to wear back in his college days.

If I had a daughter and she looked like this . . .

Straddling the pick-up's tailgate, Trink raised her skirt waist-high. She wore nothing beneath it. Except a few small, gold rings. 'Give me a hand, Sheriff?' She laughed.

'Go on, Sheriff,' Bill added, sounding amused.

Rusty turned to Bill. 'You knock it off.'

Out of the corner of his eye, he saw Trink leap. He didn't have time to get out of the way, so he braced himself for the impact. When she dropped onto him, he staggered sideways but didn't go down. She clung to him with her arms and legs.

He twisted, trying to free himself.

Bill, rushing in, threw a right cross.

Rusty blocked it with one arm. At the same moment, teeth clamped down on his shoulder. He jabbed his elbow sideways into Trink's belly. With a *whuff* of escaping air, she collapsed.

Rusty turned all his attention to Bill. He walked into the boy's punches, catching them on his wrists and forearms, brushing them away until he grabbed the boy's shirt front.

'Hey, okay!'

'Okay what?' Rusty swung him sideways and slammed him against the truck.

'What do you want to know, man? Hey, just ask. Whatever you want, okay? I'll tell you anything. Just ask.'

'Who did you see this morning?'

'Nobody.'

'The truth.'

'We heard a car start. That's what woke us up.'

'When was that?'

'I don't know, maybe an hour ago.'

'What did the car look like?'

'We didn't see it.'

'What about the driver?'

'Didn't see him.'

'You're not being very helpful, Billy.'

'Well, shit . . .'

'Okay. Fine. You have the right to remain silent.'

'Hey!'

'If you choose to give up the right to . . .'

'Hey, man! No! Don't bust me! Please! I saw the guy. Okay? Only not this morning.'

'When?'

'Last night.'

'What time?'

'I don't know. One or two, when we pulled in here.'

'What did you see?'

'Not much. It was so dark. But there was this van parked . . .'

Rusty heard movement behind him.

Before he could turn, a fist swung up between his legs. A grenade seemed to explode, blasting up through his groin

52

and bowels, tearing out his backbone, his lungs, his brain.

Vaguely, he knew he was down. He heard voices. They didn't matter. He heard the truck engine start. He didn't care. He watched the truck drive away and didn't give a damn.

He only cared about the pain.

Chapter Six

MERTON DROPS IN

The man trotted up the porch stairs of the brightly painted house and jabbed his finger into the doorbell button. From inside came the ring of chimes. He wiped his sweaty hands on his jeans. He looked behind him. No cars were approaching on the quiet, sunny street. Two boys on bikes pedaled by, hunched low over their handlebars, racing. Across the street, a young woman was walking her dog.

He hit the button again. Then two more times.

Inside the house, a toilet flushed.

So that's *why he's making me wait*, the man thought. *I suppose I can't blame him for that.*

Somewhere behind him, a house door banged shut. He didn't turn around to look. He stuffed his hands into his jeans pockets and waited.

'Who's there?' asked a voice from inside the house.

'It's me – Merton,' he answered, pulling open the aluminum framed screen door.

A guard chain rattled. A dead bolt clacked. Then the wooden door swung open and Merton stepped into the house.

He found Walter half hidden behind the door, gazing at

him. 'Good heavens!' Walter blurted. 'What on earth happened to you? You look an absolute fright!'

'Is your car in the garage?'

'Certainly.'

'Move it. Fast.'

'My God, what have you done *this* time?'

'If you're not going to let me use your garage . . .'

'I didn't *say* that. Of course you may use my garage.'

'Then let's get your car out of it.'

'Just one minute, please. I'm hardly dressed for an excursion outside.' In his robe, his bare chest showed. And so did his white, scrawny legs. He had the pale and bony look of a hospital patient. 'Just let me throw on some clothes.'

'You look fine, Walter. Grab your keys.'

'Really, now . . .'

'Hurry.'

'All right, all right.' Scampering away to find the keys, he said, 'Don't get snippy with me, thank you very much.' He rushed out of sight.

Merton waited in the foyer.

'Found them!' Walter sang out. A few moments later, he came scurrying along, holding the keys high and jangling them like bells.

Merton opened the front door.

Following him outside, Walter said, 'I do hope you haven't done anything awful.'

'Just move your car.'

Merton crossed the neatly trimmed front yard to the curb where his van was parked. He climbed inside and started the engine. At the end of the block, a Jeep Cherokee turned left and headed toward him. He ducked until he heard it pass. When he sat up again, the garage door was open. White exhaust spurted from the tailpipe of Walter's old Dodge.

As the Dodge backed out of the garage, Merton shifted into first gear. He waited until Walter pulled into the street. Then he drove forward and swung into the driveway. The open garage ahead of him looked cool and shady and safe, like a cave. He drove forward slowly. The shadow covered him. The noise of his engine swelled. He turned the key. The noise died, and he climbed out of his van.

Not waiting for Walter, he shut and locked the garage door. He entered the house, walked directly to the bathroom, stripped off his clothes and stepped under the shower.

He was drying himself when Walter pushed open the bathroom door.

'Haven't you ever heard of knocking?' Merton asked.

'It's my bathroom. I don't *have* to knock. Especially when someone barges in without so much as a "may I please" and helps himself to a hot shower.'

'You're just a dirty old man.'

'Be that as it may . . .'

'Would you like to finish drying me?' Merton asked, holding out the towel.

Walter shook his head. 'No, I would not. You're just trying to change the subject.'

'Sucky-wucky, Wally?'

'I didn't come in here for that, and you know it.'

'Right.'

'Are you ready to explain yourself?'

Merton raised his eyebrows. 'Explain what, for instance?'

'Oh, don't be that way with me. This is Walter. Walter?

Remember me? Of course you do, or you wouldn't have
come running to me this way. So don't treat me like a nobody.
I won't have it.'

'Would you like me to leave?'

'No!'

'I'd be happy to leave.'

'I'm not suggesting that you *leave*. I'm merely saying
that I deserve some consideration and the least you can do
is offer an explanation as to why you simply barged in the
way you did. Don't you think I'm entitled to that?'

'Sure.' Merton wrapped the towel around his waist and
tucked down a corner.

'Are the police after you again?'

'Could be.'

'Are they?'

'I wouldn't be terribly surprised.'

'Don't you be coy with me.'

'My clothes are filthy. How about throwing them in the
washer?'

'What did you *do*, Merton?'

'I had a little trouble, that's all.'

'Oh my dear God, you did it again, didn't you? I knew it.
I knew it the moment I saw your face.'

'Hey, look, I'm a little tired. I'm gonna sack out for a
while. Why don't you make yourself useful and wash my
clothes?'

'You haven't changed, Merton. You haven't changed at
all.'

'I've changed. Just watch them try to nail me this time.
Isn't gonna happen.'

Chapter Seven

RUSTY'S RETURN

Pac watched the tow truck drag the Jaguar, like a carcass, into the trees.

'What happens now?' Bass asked her.

'We'll need formal statements from you and Faye. We'll also want you to look at some mug shots.'

'Just like TV, huh?'

'Sort of. Excuse me.' Turning away, she called to Jack. 'Could you come here a second?' As the deputy walked toward her, she said to him, 'I'll wait here for Rusty. You go ahead and drive Faye back to the station.'

'Why can't she go with me?' Bass asked.

'It's just standard procedure. We like to keep witnesses separated.'

'Afraid we'll try to cook up a story?'

'Well, not particularly in your case, but—'

'We weren't separate before. I mean, it we'd had any intention of making up lies, we could've done it before I phoned you guys. The thing is, Faye's really shook up. I think she'd be better off staying with me.'

Jack stepped in. 'The longer you argue about it,' he said,

'the shorter your Saturday's getting.'

'Good Christ, maybe we should've just *left* the damn body down there. If I'd known we'd get hassled like this . . .'

'Nobody's trying to hassle you, Bass. If you'll just take it easy, everything'll be taken care of and you can probably be on your way in an hour or so.'

'I don't see why I can't drive Faye to the station, that's all.'

'If we let you,' Pac said, 'Rusty'll find out we violated procedure. He'll have our butts.'

'Well, I'm not looking to get anyone in trouble.'

'Okay. I know. Now, why don't you just follow Deputy Staffer's car back to the station? He'll take Faye. It's only a ten or fifteen minute drive.'

'I guess it'll be all right,' Bass muttered. 'But can somebody give me a hand with the canoe? Or do I have to leave it here so somebody can steal it?'

'Oh, I think we can let you have it.' Pac stepped toward the canoe.

'I'll get that for you,' Jack said, hurrying ahead of her.

'Thanks, Jack. You're a gentleman and a scholar.'

'Well, I might be a gentleman, anyhow.'

Together, Bass and Jack hoisted the canoe off the ground and set it onto the roof rack of the Pontiac.

'Thanks,' Bass said. 'I'll take care of it from here.' He started securing it.

While Jack stood nearby and watched, Pac walked over to him. He smiled at her. 'And how's that ol' Harney doing?' he asked.

'Oh, he wasn't real keen on me running off to work on our anniversary.'

'Your anniversary, huh? How many does that make it?'

'It's our third.'

'Well, congratulations. And give my best to Harney, okay?'

'Will do. Thanks. By the way, Rusty said he wants you to bring back a rake and go over the beach down there, see what you can find.'

'Sure thing.'

When they were gone, Pac opened the passenger door of Rusty's patrol car. His uniform and service revolver were there, where she'd put them after coming up from the beach. She picked them up, then locked the car and walked over to her patrol car. With a beach towel from her trunk, she started down the steep trail.

She half expected to meet Rusty on his way up, but there was no sign of him, not even when she reached the sand. She walked to the shore. She looked across the river, past the embankment at the far side and into the shadows of the pine forest.

No Rusty.

I'll give him fifteen minutes, Pac thought.

Sitting in the sand at the edge of the river, she crossed her legs and waited. The minutes passed slowly. The sun felt hot. After thirteen minutes, she got to her feet, walked to the foot of the trail and entered the trees. Between two manzanita trees growing close together, she hid Rusty's uniform and revolver.

Then she stripped down to her brassiere and panties. The breeze felt good on her bare skin as she walked to the shore. Dropping the towel, she entered the water. Its cold clamped her feet. She gritted her teeth and groaned, but didn't turn back. It flowed around her ankles, her calves, her knees. Not so bad anymore, now that the initial shock had passed. But she dreaded how it would feel when she took the plunge.

Let's put that off for a while.

She took shorter, slower steps, the frigid water climbing her thighs.

Across the river, movement caught her eye.

She stopped. As the water swirled around her thighs, she saw a man stagger out of the pines.

'Rusty!'

He raised an arm and waved, then worked his way down to the shore, bent over and hobbling.

'Are you all right?' Pac called.

'Far from it. Feel like nitro went off in my drawers.'

'Can you swim?'

'Time will tell.'

She watched him wade into the river, dive and begin swimming toward her. Though he seemed to have very little kick, his powerful arms pulled him along. As he neared Pac, he said, 'Sure beats walking.'

'What happened?'

'Caught one in the nuts.'

'Ouch.'

'There's an informed opinion.'

Suddenly feeling a rush of embarrassment, Pac bent her knees. The water surged up her body. Fresh from the melting snow pack higher up the mountains, it felt like ice shoving up against her groin and between her buttocks. She half expected steam to rise. She felt as if somebody'd clamped frozen pliers onto her nipples. But at least she was covered, now, to the shoulders.

Turning into his side, Rusty sidestroked past her. 'Were you coming to look for me?'

'Just felt like taking a swim.'

'Sure,' Rusty said.

He swam almost to the shore, then got to his knees and stood in the shallow water. He looked back at Pac. 'Coming?' he asked.

'Would you bring my clothes? They're with yours between those two manzanitas over by the bottom of the trail.'

'Trying to hide them?'

'What else? I couldn't just leave them out in the open when I went to your rescue.'

'Where's everyone else?'

'Birkus got here and took the body. Jack's taking Faye to the station, and Bass is following in his own car.'

When Rusty began walking in his careful, stooped way toward the line of trees, Pac started wading for shore. She stepped onto dry land as Rusty vanished into the trees. While he was out of sight, she used the towel to dry herself.

The sunlight felt wonderful. Its heat spread over her skin like a soothing warm fluid. She wanted to take off her bra and panties, but she didn't know when Rusty – or someone else – might come along. So she kept them on. Though she rubbed them with the towel, they remained damp and clingy and nearly transparent.

Rusty didn't reappear for several minutes. Finally, he stepped out of the trees fully dressed and carrying Pac's uniform.

Pac held the towel against herself.

Rusty handed the uniform to her, then turned away.

'Thanks,' she said. She dropped her towel to the sand, bent over, and stepped into her trousers. 'So what'd you come up with on your excursion beyond the river?'

'Other than a sore pair of *cojones*? Some kids. Teenagers. A creep named Bill and a creep-ette by the name of Trink. A couple of real prizes. They were in the back of a pick-up truck over at the Sweet Meadow roadhead. I got Bill to admit he'd seen a car last night. It was there when they arrived to smoke their weed or compare ring holes or what-ever.'

'Ring holes?' Pac asked, pulling her blouse on.

'These two pieces of work had more perforations than Bonnie and Clyde. Anyway, Bill was just starting to tell me about the car, and that's when disaster struck. Trink nailed me from behind. Next thing I knew, I was coming to and they were long gone.'

'You figure they know more?' Pac finished buttoning her blouse.

'Sure. If nothing else, they oughta be able to tell us something about the car they saw.'

'I'm decent now,' Pac announced.

Rusty turned to her and held out her holstered Colt. 'I must say, you look better out of uniform.'

'Thank you, sir. So do you.' She buckled the gunbelt around her waist. 'By the way, I told Jack to bring back a rake.'

'Good. You stay here till he arrives. Give him a hand. Did you get any good latents off the Jag?'

'Some partials on the driver's side. The passenger side was clean, though. Somebody'd wiped it.'

'Anything else?'

'I'll vacuum the car after we get it to the station. Maybe that'll turn up something.'

They walked toward the slope. 'What do you think happened here, Pac?'

'I'd say the victim drove out last night with a man in her car. Otherwise, why did he wipe the passenger side? He'd planned to kill her, so he had a car of his own planted across the river at Sweet Meadow. Maybe he kept the saw in that car, too. Anyway, they walked down to the river and did some swimming. Looks like she died of suffocation, so he may have drowned her.'

'It's a good possibility,' Rusty said.

'Well, the autopsy'll tell us.'

'So what else happened?'

'After she was out of the river, he raped her.'

'Raped?'

'You testing me, boss?'

'More like testing myself,' he said. 'You're more observant than me and you're not exactly a dummy.'

'Well, thanks.'

'Okay. Why do you say he raped her?'

'She obviously didn't give consent. Being already dead.'

'Sharp as a tack. So how do you know it was *after* she'd drowned.'

'If it'd been before, the river would've washed the semen off her.'

'One more question,' Rusty said.

'Fire away.'

'The rape. Did he do it before or after he cut off her head?'

'Rusty!'

'I'm serious.'

'Before.'

'What makes you think so?'

'Just a gut feeling,' Pac said.

'Go on.'

'Without her head on, I just don't think he'd feel very inclined. You know?'

Rusty smiled grimly and shook his head. 'You don't know guys.'

Chapter Eight

ZELDA

Leaving his daughter-in-law sitting in a shaded area near her patrol car, Rusty drove out to the main road. As he headed north, he radioed Madge and had her put out an APB on the 1994 gray Chevrolet pick-up truck, license plate Bob-William-David 793.

He stopped at the Texaco station. The owner, Herby Swaymen, came out of the office. 'Morning, Sheriff,' he said. 'Beautiful day, don't you think?'

'Lovely,' Rusty said, and climbed out of his car. 'Just want to use the phone,' he explained.

'Public phone. Help yourself.'

Rusty walked over to the telephone booth. He flipped through the directory, running his eyes down the listings for Sierra College. He didn't want the student residence hall, the student book store, or the campus food service. Academic and administrative offices had to be the number. He picked up the phone, fed it a quarter, and tapped the number in. As he listened to the ringing, he clamped the handset against the side of his neck and took out his notepad and pen.

After several rings, a woman's voice spoke to him.

'Sierra College, Betty Morris speaking. May I help you?'

'You sound like a real person, Betty,' Rusty said.

'Why, thank you. I *am*.'

'Not voice mail?'

'No, sir. We like to keep the personal touch.'

'Well, here's one fellow who appreciates it.'

'And who might you be?'

'Name's Russell Hodges. I'm with the county sheriff's office.'

'You *are* the county sheriff.'

'That's right, ma'am.'

'How may I help you, Sheriff?'

'I'd like to speak to someone about the identity of a woman who might be connected to your school.'

'You may speak to me about it, if you'd like.'

'Do you have access to the various records?'

'I'm the only person on campus with such access, Sheriff Hodges. Unless you'd prefer to wait until Monday morning.'

'You'll do just fine, Betty. What I'd like is some information about Alison Parkington. She apparently resides in Santa Monica, but her car windshield has one of your summer parking stickers.'

'Ah. Well, she would be the wife of Dr Grant Parkington. He's a guest lecturer for our summer literature program. From UCLA? The Coleridge man.'

'May I have his address?'

'His Santa Monica address, or . . .?'

'Where I can find him today.'

'Just a moment, please. I'll have to look that up.' After a brief silence, Betty's voice returned. 'His summer residence is sixty-eight Cove Road. He and Mrs Parkington are staying in Professor Dill's condominium. Dr Dill is away on sabbatical leave.'

Rusty jotted the information in his notebook. 'Very good,' he said. 'Thank you so much for your help, Betty.'

'You're very welcome, Sheriff. Let me just say, I vote for you every chance I get.'

'Well, I appreciate that.' He hung up and started back toward his patrol car.

'Hey, Sheriff.' It was Herby Swaymen's way of saying goodbye.

'Hey, Herby,' Rusty called. Then he climbed into his car and headed for Cove Road.

The condominiums at Pyramid Cove were nicely kept, and the sign that proclaimed COUNTRY CLUB LIVING wasn't far wrong. Rusty drove along Cove Road, looking at the tennis courts, at the condos with their well-kept lawns, at the people walking by in swimsuits or tennis whites.

A major change from the days when the Cove had been an overgrown inlet visited by men in puttering motorboats and boys with cane fishing poles. A change not necessarily for the worse. It saddened Rusty to see the old ways go. They were part of him, but also he liked the carefree, well-off atmosphere at the new Pyramid Cove where everyone seemed to be on vacation.

He parked in front of number sixty-eight, crossed the perfectly trimmed yard, and rang the doorbell. The door opened quickly. For a moment, the bearded face of the man inside showed relief. But it quickly turned to disappointment, then alarm.

'Are you Grant Parkington?' Rusty asked.

The man nodded. He appeared to be about fifty years old. Fairly handsome, tanned, in good shape. His light brown hair, shiny with a scattering of gray, was rumpled as if he'd just awakened. He wore glasses with round lenses and wire frames that made him look very academic and old-fashioned. He also sported a bushy mustache.

Quite the professor, Rusty thought.

But like everyone else at the Cove, he looked as if he were vacationing at an upscale resort. His bright, flowered shirt was open to the middle of his chest, and untucked. His knee length white shorts looked clean but wrinkled. He was barefoot.

'I'm Sheriff Hodges.'

'*Sheriff?* What's happened?'

'May I come in?'

'Yes. Of course.' He stepped back. After Rusty was inside, he shut the door. 'What's happened to her?' he asked. 'This is about Alison, isn't it?'

'We're not a hundred percent sure it's your wife, Dr Parkington, but a woman's body was found this morning near the river. Your wife's car was nearby.' He unbuttoned the flap of his shirt pocket and pulled out a driver's license. 'I took this from a purse in the car.'

'That's Alison's,' Grant muttered. 'Oh, God.'

'As I said, we're not sure it's her body.'

Grant reached out with a trembling hand and tapped his forefinger against the license's color photo. 'Her picture. That's her picture. Did you . . .?'

'I'm afraid there are circumstances . . .' Rusty's voice faltered as he tried to figure a tasteful way to describe the situation.

'What circumstances?'

'Maybe you'd like to sit down, Dr Parkington.' Gently, he took the man by the elbow and led him to a sofa that seemed to be upholstered in zebra skin.

'Why couldn't you tell from the photo? She wasn't . . . disfigured? She was always so beautiful . . . a thing of beauty, a joy forever. Oh, God!'

'I'm afraid the killer took . . .' Rusty started over. 'She was decapitated. So far, I'm afraid we haven't been able to locate the head.'

Grant gazed up at him, his eyes red and wide. 'Decapitated? No. You're . . . You're having me on.'

'We'll need you to identify the body. She must've had certain freckles, scars . . .'

'Her head is gone?'

'I'm afraid so.'

'And you can't find it?'

'Apparently, the killer took it with him.'

'Oh, dear God!' Grant shook his head, rubbing his tangled hair. 'She was so beautiful. The most . . . *he* must've thought so, too.'

'Who's that?'

'The killer. The man who did this.'

'Uh-huh.'

'Do you know Byron?' Grant asked, looking into Rusty's eyes.

'Byron who?'

'*Lord* Byron. The poet.'

'Oh. Sure. I've heard of him.'

'He wanted Shelley's head. He wanted it for a drinking mug. After Shelley drowned off Viareggio. Maybe that's why the killer wanted Alison's head. For a mug. Do you suppose?'

'I guess it's possible.'

While Rusty drove, Grant Parkington stared at the dashboard of the patrol car, his head moving slowly from side to side.

'Was your wife with you last night?' Rusty asked.

'Oh, yes.'

'What time did she leave?'

'I don't know. Very late. In the vicinity of one, one-thirty, I should think.'

'That *is* late. Why did she go out?'

'"What makes her in the wood so late, a furlong from the castle gate?" Maybe dreams of knights. I don't know.'

'What?' Rusty asked.

The professor smiled strangely. '"Christabel."'

'That another poet?'

'A poem. By Samuel Taylor Coleridge.'

'Had you and your wife been arguing at the time she left?'

'No. Oh, no, not at all.'

'Did she go by herself?'

'All alone.'

'But you weren't having any sort of fight?'

'No. I already told you that. This was just a thing she enjoyed doing. Taking off for a wild drive through the night.'

'What was she wearing?'

'Her nightgown. A diaphanous white negligee.'

'What else?'

'Slippers? I believe she wore slippers. And naturally she had her purse. She never went anywhere without her purse.'

'Is that all?'

'Nothing more.'

'Why didn't she get dressed before she left?'

'It was simply her way. She liked to think of herself as quite scandalous. Something of a Zelda Fitzgerald, you know. It excited her, made her feel special.'

'Did she tell you where she was going?'

'Out. "I'm going out."' He turned toward Rusty and slowly smoothed one side of his mustache with a forefinger. 'She did go out, too. She went out, and went out. Snuffed like a candle.'

'Do you know anyone she might've gone to meet?'

'No. No.' He shook his head. 'No. Nobody.'

At the morgue, Rusty studied Grant Parkington's reaction to the sight of his wife's body. The man pressed a hand to his open mouth as if to hold in a scream. But he examined her with care, pointing out the mole beneath her left breast, the brown oblong birthmark on her right thigh, how the small toenail of her right foot was missing. Then he broke down crying.

Rusty led him out of the room.

Chapter Nine

THE DIGS

As Pac watched, a tine of her rake snagged a white cord. Jack Staffer dropped to his knees in front of her, slipped a finger beneath the cord, and lifted. Sand fell away as he pulled the nightgown free. 'This belong to you?' he asked Pac.

'Never use the things,' she said.

'Lucky Harn.'

'You betcha.'

'Do you think it's hers?' Jack asked.

'Until I find out otherwise.' She dropped the rake, hurried over to her case and took out a clear plastic bag. She brought it to Jack. He dropped the nightgown inside. 'How would you like to get the shovel?' she asked.

'Sure thing.'

While Jack went for it, Pac looked down at the shallow dip in the sand. She felt a chill and rubbed her arms.

'You want me to do the honors?' Jack asked.

'Go ahead.'

He pushed the broad head of the shovel into the sand and lifted out a load. Fine granules spilled off the shovel like water. He dumped the rest off to the side, turned again to the hole, and jabbed the blade in. It made a harsh, scraping sound.

'Maybe got something here,' Jack said. He lifted out the shovel, and a pink slipper came up with the sand. 'Its twin must be around here someplace.'

Soon, the second slipper came up.

'The guy must've thrown everything into the same hole,' Pac said.

'Nice for us.'

Jack kept digging, pushing the shovel deep into the sand. Soon, its blade clinked against steel. Dropping to his knees, he brushed sand away until he uncovered a black plastic handle.

'Be careful. Prints.'

The hacksaw was all there, its steel back glaring with sunlight, its blade coated with a fine crust of sand.

'Looks like we've got us the murder weapon,' Jack said.

'Not exactly,' Pac told him. 'The murder weapon was probably the river. This is what he used afterward.'

'Nice guy,' Jack muttered.

'A real prince,' said Pac.

Chapter Ten

TWO WOMEN

'Look who's here.'

'I was in the neighborhood,' Rusty said, 'so I thought I'd drop by for lunch.'

Millie unplugged the iron, set it upright, and stepped around the ironing board. She was barefoot. She wore white jeans. The tails of her pale blue blouse hung out.

Rusty wrapped his arms around ten, pulled her tightly against him and kissed her. They kissed for a long time, Rusty enjoying the warm moist smoothness of her lips, the curves of her back, the pressure of her breasts against him, her flat belly and the jut of her hip bones.

When she started to unzip his trousers, he caught her hand.

'A slight injury,' he explained.

'Hernia?' she asked.

'Fist.'

'Oh, you poor thing. How did it happen?'

'Some freaky girl got me from behind while I was questioning her boyfriend.'

'Beware the freaky girls.'

'She had an *eyebrow* ring. And a *lip* ring.' He thought

about the other parts of Trink that had been pierced and adorned with rings, but decided not to mention them. He could just imagine Millie giving him *the look*, and saying, *And how exactly did you happen to get a look there?* The less Millie heard about that, the better.

'It must've really hurt,' she said.

'Getting her eyebrow pierced?'

'Getting hit in the family jewels.'

'It wasn't fun.'

'Let's have a little peek.'

'Suit yourself.'

Rusty helped by removing his gunbelt. Millie unfastened his waist button, lowered the zipper, and let his pants fall around his ankles. Then she pulled down his boxer shorts. If she noticed they were damp, she probably assumed the moisture was from his sweat.

Probably is sweat, Rusty thought. They'd had plenty of time to dry after his swim.

Millie crouched in front of him. 'Everything *looks* okay down here.'

'Doesn't feel so good.'

'You know, maybe it *does* look a little swollen. Maybe we should put some steak on it. Some meat for your meat.'

'Real nice. Anyway, that's for black eyes.'

'Same principle, don't you think?'

'I think we should save the steak for a meal and keep it away from my equipment.'

She laughed. 'Equipment?'

'You know.'

'Maybe I can help the equipment feel a little better.' She lifted his penis and kissed it. 'Does that help?'

'Sure does.'

He decided not to mention that his injury was slightly lower.

She kissed him again.

He felt her open, slippery lips.

When they went away, she said, 'I guess that wasn't such a good idea.' She smiled up at him. 'The swelling got worse.'

'Sure did.'

'Better quit that,' she said, and pulled his shorts up. 'We don't want to do something that'll make the situation worse.'

'I think you helped.'

'Think so? Glad to hear it.' She stood, lifting his trousers. 'Now, how about some lunch?'

'That'd be great.'

'What would you like?'

'That steak you mentioned?' he asked as he fastened his waist button.

'It's frozen. How about an omelet?'

'Great.' He pulled his zipper up.

'It'll take a few minutes.'

'That's fine. I need some rest, anyway.' He sat down gently on a kitchen chair and watched Millie begin to prepare his lunch. 'You remember Bass Paxton?' he asked.

'Harney's friend? Sure I do.'

'He and his girlfriend found a body this morning.'

'Oh, yuck.'

'To say the least.'

'That's one thing I'd sure hate to find. Some stiff. Nasty. Funerals are bad enough, God knows. But if you go to a funeral, at least you can *expect* to meet up with a corpse. To have one pop up when you're not even expecting it – awful.'

'They weren't ecstatic about it.'

'I should think not. Do you want some nice diced ham in this?'

'Sounds good.'

'How'd the person die?'

'We're not sure yet. From the look of her, I'd say she was either strangled or drowned. The autopsy should be going on right now.'

'Right at this moment?'

'Should be.'

'How appetizing.'

'She was a beautiful woman, Millie. Before someone did a job on her.'

'Was she married?'

Rusty nodded. He knew what was coming.

'The husband did it,' Millie said.

'According to you, it's *always* the husband.'

'It *is* always the husband.'

'Not all the time,' Rusty told her.

'Often enough so the rest hardly matters.'

Rusty smiled and shook his head. 'In this case, I don't think the guy did it. He was expecting her back. In fact, he looked like he thought *I'd* be her when he opened his door this morning.'

'Maybe he's a good actor.'

'Could be.'

'I'll bet you he's involved. One way or another, every motive comes down to sex.'

'Even greed?'

'Especially greed. A greedy man is after power. Why does he want power?'

'To improve his sex life?'

'Exactly,' Millie said. 'If you're rich and powerful, all the luscious young things throw themselves at you. It's *always* sex. Or the lack of it. So the husband *has* to be involved one way or another.'

'You have a wonderful way of simplifying matters.'

'Thank you. Most matters *are* simple once you cut through the malarky.'

'But you're wrong about this. The husband didn't do it.'

'Of course he did.'

'Bass and Faye *saw* the killer. And I've met the husband. He doesn't even come close to the guy they described.'

'Well then, maybe I'm wrong.' She smiled over her shoulder at Rusty. 'There's a first time for everything.'

When Rusty left home half an hour later, he radioed Madge. 'Anything on the Chevy pick-up?'

'It hasn't been spotted, but I ran the tag. The vehicle is registered to Blake Elwood White, three four two Muir Road. No wants or warrants.'

'Thanks. Thank you very much.'

The trip to Muir Road took him ten minutes. After driving past the small, weathered wooden house, he circled the block. No sign of the pick-up truck.

When he reached the house again, he pulled into its rough dirt driveway. He climbed out of the patrol car, eased its door shut, and started to climb the porch stairs. The climbing sent stabs of pain through his groin and made him wince.

The screen door of the house was off its hinges. The main door stood ajar. From inside came the television sound of a sports announcer. '. . . the two and two pitch. High and outside, ball three.'

Rusty knocked on the door frame.

'It's the sheriff,' he called.

'Come in if you want,' called a woman's raspy voice. 'I ain't gettin' up.'

Rusty pushed open the door and entered the front room. The woman looked at him over the top of an upraised beer can. She took her time about emptying the can, then set it on the couch beside her. It tipped over. Rusty saw a few drops spill out, darkening the faded green fabric.

'What you up to, law man?' She grinned. Her teeth were crooked and yellow.

'I'm looking for Blake White.'

'Come to the wrong place.' She took a deep breath that made her T-shirt pull tight across her enormous breasts and belly.

'Where is he?'

'Working over by the wharf. At the boat rental? Want a cold beer?'

'Thanks, but I can't drink on the job.'

'Don't say I didn't ask.' She lifted her foot off the coffee table, stood, and hitched up her jeans. 'Keep an eye on the game, law man.'

When she walked to the kitchen, Rusty kept an eye on her. She jiggled as she walked, but she looked powerful. As if plenty of muscle might be hidden somewhere under the layers of fat.

He turned his eyes to the television screen. The Budweiser frogs were waiting to ambush a beer delivery truck.

'What'd Blake go and pull this time?' the woman asked.

Her breasts swung and bounced as she walked back from the kitchen with a can of beer in one hand. She dropped onto the couch and fixed her eyes on the television.

'I'm not sure he pulled anything. What's your relationship to Blake?'

'He married me. Best move he ever made.' She popped open her can and took a swig.

'Do you have children?'

She swallowed a few more times, then lowered the can and swiped her mouth with the back of her hand. 'Only just the four.'

'Four kids?'

'Yep. Ya ask me, that's enough. How about you?'

'One son.'

'Well, one ain't enough. Yer wife die on you?'

'No, she's fine.'

'Better get yerselfs some more kids while ya got the chance. Just one, it ain't hardly worth the bother.'

Enough of this, Rusty thought. 'Is one of your children using the pick-up truck today?' he asked.

'Who knows? Who can keep track? All I know is, the baby's here.'

'Who has the pick-up?'

She drank some more beer, then wiped her mouth again and asked, 'It ain't out front?'

'No.'

'Must be Trinket has it.'

'Trinket?' He'd assumed the truck belonged to *Bill*'s family, not Trinket's.

'One of my girls.'

'I guess she's the one I'm looking for.'

The woman narrowed her eyes. 'What'd she go and do this time?'

'She might be able to identify a man I'm looking for.'

And socked me in the nuts.

'Bawsh,' the woman said.

Rusty wasn't quite sure what she meant by that. And he didn't quite care. 'Do you have a recent picture of your daughter?' he asked.

'How recent like?'

'Within the past year or two.'

'Not that I can lay my hands on.' Her head snapped toward the television as the crowd exploded with cheers.

The announcer's voice was quick with excitement. 'It's a hard line drive over second! Purnelle scoops it up, fires! Not in time! And the Yankees open the fifth inning with a man on first!'

Rusty waited while Trink's mother took a long pull at her beer and slid the back of her hand across her mouth.

'Who's the boy she goes with?' he asked.

'He see your man, too?'

'He may have. I need to talk to him. To both of them.'

'That'd be Bill,' she said.

'Bill what?'

'Mason. Snotty little so-and-so. Comes from over on the north end.'

'Do you know where Trinket might be?'

'Right now?' she asked, not looking away from the television.

'Right now.'

'You know Indian Point?'

Rusty nodded.

'Might try up there. They go up there a lot.' She drank some more beer. 'You a Yankee fan?'

'You bet,' Rusty said.

Grinning at him, she said, 'You're all right for a law man.'

'Thank you.'

'You gonna bust Trinket?'

'I might.'

'What'd she do? Besides all this bawsh about seeing some fella?'

'She broke half a dozen laws from indecent exposure to battery. I'm the guy she battered.'

'How come that don't surprise me?' she asked, and laughed. 'My Trinket, she's a mean one. Mean as a snake. Takes after her father. You bust that child, don't let on I told you nothin' or she'll hurt me. She come at me once with a fork. Look here.' Standing, she lifted her T-shirt over a roll of flesh as white and dimpled as biscuit dough. 'Look here. Come and get a good look.'

Rusty stepped closer. Her smell was sour, so he took shallow breaths through his mouth.

'See here? Got me with a fork.' One of her stubby fingers poked the skin to the right of her navel and Rusty saw a neat row of four red marks. And another row, and another. 'Five times. She stuck me five times, the little wad. Then I lambasted her in the bread-basket and she wasn't up and around for near a week.'

'How'd she manage to stab you so many times?'

'I was trying to reason with the child. Can't reason with her. She bites, too, you know.'

'Does she?' he asked, remembering the way she had nipped his shoulder.

'Hell, yes. Last spring she bit one of my lungs so hard she brought blood. I had to get it stitched up like an old sock. Still got scars to prove it. Look here.' She started lifting her T-shirt higher.

'That's fine. I believe you.' Rusty turned away.

'Don't you wanta see?'

'I have to get going.'

'Look at you!' She laughed. 'I made you red.'

'Thanks for your help, Mrs White.' He went out the door. As he shut it, he heard her call out to him.

'Come back here some time, law man!'

He climbed into his car, trying to stifle a groan as pain radiated from his testicles. At least the girl had confined the biting to his shoulder.

Could've been worse, he thought. A lot worse.

Chapter Eleven

THE CLASS OF 1990

'Walter? Walter?' Sitting up in bed, Merton listened to footsteps coming up the hallway. They stopped outside his door. 'Get it in here, Walter.'

The door opened and the lanky man stepped inside. Though he still wore only a robe, he was clean shaven now, his black hair combed and shiny.

'Are you done washing my clothes?' Merton asked.

'If you don't require me to iron them.'

'Bring them in here.'

'Let's hear the magic word.'

'*Now?*'

'Ha ha ha.'

'All right, all right. *Please.*'

'That's much better.'

'Walter?'

He lifted his eyebrows. 'Yes?'

'Let's not have any more of this "magic word" shit. Know what I mean?'

'I won't be treated like a slave.'

'That so?'

'Yes, that's so.'

'I don't treat you like a slave.' Merton grinned. 'I treat you like the mother you are.'

Walter frowned, looking puzzled. As if he couldn't make up his mind whether to be flattered or insulted. After a few moments, he said, 'Up yours.'

'You wish.'

Whirling around, Walter left the room. When he came back, he was carrying jeans, a plaid shirt and white socks.

'Bring them here.'

'A little politeness?'

'Bring them here, *please*.'

'I'd think you might be a bit more appreciative,' he said, walking toward the bed. 'After all, I'm taking an awful chance by having you here in the house.'

'How's that?'

'I could be arrested as an accessory. I could go to prison.'

'Accessory to what?'

'Merton, there were bloodstains on your clothes. I do know bloodstains when I see them, you know. I'm not blind.'

'That could be remedied.'

'Oh, very funny. Pardon me while I forget to laugh.'

'Did you get them out? The stains?'

'What did you do?'

Merton grinned. 'Sit down.'

Walter sat on the edge of the bed, holding the bundle of clothes on his lap.

'So you want to know what happened last night?'

'I most certainly do.'

'All right,' Merton said, and told him.

Walter stared with wide, horrified eyes as Merton

explained, lingering on every detail. At the end, Merton reached up and massaged the back of Walter's neck. 'You wanted to know.'

Half an hour later, Merton said, 'Get me your keys.'

'You're not leaving?'

Merton gripped a handful of black hair and pulled, lifting the weight of Walter's head off his chest and looking into his eyes. 'Get me your keys.'

'Where are you going?'

'Home.' He let go of the hair.

Walter sat up. 'You can't go home. What if they've identified you? The sheriff might be there waiting.'

'I'll just have to be careful, won't I?'

'You shouldn't take such chances.'

'It's no big deal. I'll be in and out. Won't take me two minutes.'

'I don't see why you have to go home at all.'

'Just give me your keys.'

'You're being so foolish.'

'You're being a fucking nag. Get them.'

Walter climbed out of bed. When he was gone, Merton got up and dressed. He was washing his face in the bathroom when Walter returned.

'I'll go with you,' Walter said.

'No.'

'I don't see why not.'

'Because I don't want you with me, that's why not. If you give me any more trouble, I won't be back.'

'You'll be back.'

'Don't press your luck.' Merton held out his hand and

took the keys. Then, without another word, he left.

His one-room house was on Pine Street, less than five miles away. When he got there, he drove past it at the maximum thirty m.p.h. speed limit, watching both sides of the road. Long ago, he'd made a point to become familiar with the vehicles belonging to all his neighbors. With the exception of a U-Haul van in front of the Willis place across the street from his house, everything fit. The U-Haul worried him. It would provide a fine cover for a surveillance team.

At the end of the block, he made a left turn. Then he cruised down the unpaved alley behind his house. The alley checked out. He headed up Pine again. This time, he saw Frank and Irma Willis wrestling a sofa across their front yard. The U-Haul was safe.

He drove down the alley and parked, not directly behind his house but close to a twisted stockade fence two houses down.

No fence, but an overgrown hedge enclosed his own back yard. He pressed through it, hands raised to protect his face. A stray branch scratched the back of his hand. It left a white mark like chalk, but brought no blood. When he was free of the bushes, he ran to the back of his house.

He climbed four stairs to the rear porch. The screen door came open easily, silently. He unlocked the wooden door and stepped into his kitchen.

Nothing seemed out of place.

In the living room, he went to a book shelf above his television set. There were seven matching volumes, each dark green, twelve inches high and half an inch in thickness. The spines were embossed, *Sierra Log*. They spanned the years from 1984 to 1990. Merton pulled down the last four.

Carrying them under his arm, he hurried into his bedroom.

His shotgun case lay across the shelf of his closet. He found its handle and pulled it down. He swung it onto the bed. Leaving the books beside the gun case, he knelt and pulled open the bottom drawer of his dresser. He took out a red and white cardboard box of Winchester and Western Super X shotgun shells. He flipped up the lid. The box was full. He carried it, the shotgun and the four yearbooks out the back door.

Not wanting to squeeze through the thick wall of bushes again, he ran to the end of the hedge and ducked through an open space.

As he stumbled out into the alley, a black retriever regarded him casually. Then it sniffed a garbage bin and lifted a hind leg.

Merton walked swiftly to Walter's car.

'I knew you'd be back,' Walter said.

'Give me a hand.'

Walter took the shotgun case out of Merton's grip. 'Where do you want it?'

'On the couch.'

Merton dropped the box of ammunition next to the case and sat down. He put three of the Sierra High School yearbooks next to him. The fourth, he placed on his lap.

It was his latest yearbook, and his last. It covered 1990. He riffled through its pages until he found the individual photos of the senior class.

So many familiar faces. Dumb, slow-smiling faces. Cruel faces. Smirky faces. Bored faces. Faces so lovely they made him ache.

There was Doug Hawkins, the emaciated, red-nosed boy who wrote him notes bleating of unrequited love. Biff Krasner, the class tough guy who hungered for pain. Jerry Miller, who thought he was straight and never let Merton close to him. And that damned Andy Tarver. Andy the Flit. The bitch who wanted it so badly, then panicked and snitched and ended it all.

Well, he'd fixed Andy pretty good. Pretty damned good.

Flipping pages to the center of the yearbook, he found the group photo of the varsity football squad. The players all stood in full uniform, but didn't wear their helmets. Each held his helmet against his side, tucked under one arm like the head of the Headless Horseman.

Merton drew his forefinger across each row, carefully studying the faces.

Wrong year.

He picked up the 1989 *Log* and turned directly to the football picture.

Fierce eyes scowled out at him from a boy standing next to the coach.

The same eyes glared at him from an individual shot lower on the page. There, a helmet hid his dark crew-cut. The boy was scowling toward the camera, crouched and ready to charge. The print beneath the photo read, 'Bass Paxton, Team Captain.'

'Get me your phone book,' Merton said.

Walter, standing motionless at the end of the couch, nodded and moved away. He returned a few moments later with the directory. Merton took it from him, fingered through its pages, then drew his forefinger slowly down a column of 'P' listings.

'Paxton, Bass,' he read aloud.

'He's the one?'

'That's him.' Merton smiled. 'He's gonna die tonight.'

Chapter Twelve

THE CALL

Pac took the call from Birkus. 'This is Deputy Hodges,' she said. 'What've you got for us?'

'We've finished up with Alison Parkington.'

'Good. What turned up?'

'I think we picked up a few interesting items. Cause of death was drowning. Her head was severed post-mortem. Also, there's evidence of sexual activity. That also took place post-mortem.'

'That's about how we figured it.'

'Our boy's a charmer.'

'Anything else?'

'He has A-positive blood. He's a secreter. We typed him from semen we picked up with a vaginal swab. We also got some interesting combings from the pubic area. The victim's hair was blonde, but we found a few strands of black mixed in. It's possible that they came from our suspect.'

'What about her husband?' Pac asked.

'We did a little checking. He has brown hair.'

'So our man has black hair and A-positive blood.'

'That's how it looks. If you get a suspect, we can pin him

down with a DNA analysis.'

'Right. Was there anything else?'

'That's about it. We'll send over a written report, of course.'

'Thank you very much.'

'Pleasure's mine.'

Chapter Thirteen

INDIAN POINT

Rusty didn't hurry. He drove at normal speed to the Indian Point turn-off, made the left turn, and took his time steering up the twisty, narrow road. At the top, he drove across the paved parking area toward the low stone parapet in front of the cliff. He passed five parked vehicles: two camper vans, a Jeep, a Toyota and a gray Chevy pick-up truck. The Chevy's license plate was the one he'd seen at the Sweet Meadow roadhead. Trink's mother had been right.

He saw half a dozen people. Three of them, a father and his sons, were taking turns viewing Silver Lake through a pay telescope. A pair of lovers stood facing the lake, arms around each other's shoulders. A lone man sat on the parapet, facing the parking lot as he bit into a sandwich. Trink and Bill were nowhere to be seen.

Rusty parked beside their pick-up and climbed out of his patrol car. He looked into the bed of the truck. No Trink, no Bill, only a couple of filthy, rumpled blankets. He glanced at his wristwatch.

Pac should be getting here pretty soon, but she might not arrive for another five or ten minutes.

'You're Sheriff Hodges,' said the man with the sandwich. The wind off the lake blew his white hair forward. He fingered a few strands out of the corner of his mouth and kept on chewing. 'Voted for you.'

'Thanks. I appreciate it.'

'Tough but fair, that's how I like 'em. Up here on a case?'

'That's right.' He stepped over to the man and shook his hand.

'I'm Voss. Harry Voss.'

'Good to meet you, Harry.'

'Same here. You like it up here?'

'As long as I don't get too close to that ledge. A mighty long way down to the lake.'

'Did you know the Washoes used to fling their chiefs off the cliff here?'

'I hope they were dead first.'

'Oh, yes.' The old man laughed. 'I reckon they were dead, all right. Know how come they'd get the old heave-ho?'

'Not off hand. If I ever heard, I've forgotten.'

'Water's a thousand feet deep right off the point here. *Over* a thousand feet deep. Know how cold it gets down there?'

'Pretty cold, I imagine.'

'Awful cold. Down in the thirties. Near freezing. A hundred years, those old chiefs are as fresh as the day they died. That's sure something, huh?'

'Sure is,' Rusty said.

'And they stay down there, too. Never come up. Never. Being an officer of the law, you can probably figure out how come that is.'

'Right. If they aren't decomposing, there's no gas build-

95

up. No gas in the bodies, they stay down.'

'You nailed it right on the button there, Sheriff. Glad I voted for you.'

'Now I have a question for *you*, Harry. If the chiefs never come up to the surface, how are you so sure they've stayed so fresh and nice?'

'Oh, now and again one of 'em washes up. Changes in the current, mostly.'

'That hasn't happened recently, has it?'

'Last I recall it happening was some thirty years back. That would've been around sixty-seven, sixty-eight, around that time. Sure had the sheriff going. That was Sheriff Rawls, back then. He thought sure he had a homicide on his hands. You eat yet? I've got another sandwich here.' He flicked a finger against the top of a grocery bag resting between his feet. 'Turkey, lettuce, and mayo on Wonder Bread.'

'Thanks, Harry, but I'll have to turn you down on that. I just finished my lunch.'

'Suit yourself. More for me. Can't get enough of that Wonder Bread. Must be the softest bread they've ever made, don't you think so?'

'It's nice and soft,' Rusty said.

'Stays that way, too. Stays that way a long time. Nice and fresh, like those chiefs they threw in the lake. Know what I think, Sheriff? When my time comes, I wouldn't mind going off the edge here. Suppose I might get that arranged?'

Rusty thought about the lake's strict pollution controls, but decided not to mention them. 'You might check with some of the mortuaries about something like that.'

'I might do that, Sheriff. Yes, I just might. Or I might just get some of my buddies to give me the old heave-ho in the middle of the night. I don't suppose anybody'd likely catch them at it. Nobody up here at night except a few sweethearts, and they pretty much got their hands full, if you catch my drift.'

'Speaking of which . . . Did you happen to notice the people who belong to that pick-up over there?'

'Nope. It was already here when I showed up.'

At the sound of an engine, Rusty looked toward the entrance of the parking area. A patrol car appeared. 'Well, that must be my deputy. Good talking to you, Harry.'

'Same here, Sheriff. You take care, now.'

'You, too.' As Rusty turned away from the older man, Pac climbed out of the car. The wind parted her blond hair. She looked into the wind, squinting, and took a deep breath. Then she waved at Rusty. He went to her.

'You find our witnesses?' she asked.

'I found their truck.' He pointed at the gray Chevy. 'The kids must be down on the trails somewhere. Maybe they hiked down to the lake.'

'We going after them?'

'It's either that or stake out the truck. But there's no telling how long we might have to wait.'

'I wouldn't mind a little hike.'

'Well, go and grab your baton.'

While Pac went for her night stick, Rusty opened the hood of the pick-up. He took off the distributor cap, reached down and removed the rotor. With the rotor in his pocket, he shut the hood.

He met Pac on the walkway near the telescope. The man with the kids had gone away. The lovers were walking slowly, holding hands, their heads close together. Harry Voss, still sitting on the low parapet, bit into his second sandwich as he watched a diving gull.

'We found the saw,' Pac said as they walked toward the main footpath.

'A hacksaw?'

'That's right. No fingerprints, but lots of blood. O-negative, same as the victim.'

'Did the saw look new?'

'Very new. It looks as if it'd never been used before. Jack's ringing up all the hardware stores in the area.'

'Fine. What about the autopsy? Did Birkus call in before you left?'

'He called. Mrs Parkington died by drowning, just like we figured.'

'Anything on the killer?'

'Maybe. Either the killer, or whoever last had sex with her. Might not be the same person.'

'Might not be, but probably is.'

'Well, it looks like a male with black hair. And he's A-positive. They typed him by his semen.'

'Anything else from the autopsy?'

'That's about it.'

'Anything more from Bass and Faye?'

Pac shook her head. 'Nothing new came up in their statements. They didn't get a make on anyone in the mug shots, either.'

'Well, maybe my friends Bill and Trink can give us something.'

'How'll we find them?' Pac asked.

'Stoned, more than likely.'

Grinning, she poked the head of her night stick against Rusty's side.

'No way to treat your boss,' he grumbled, smiling. 'Or your father-in-law.'

The trail, wide and well marked, led downward from the south end of the parking lot at a steep angle with many switchbacks. It never came close to the sheer face of Indian Point. Though the squeals of gulls were a constant reminder of the lake's presence, nothing was visible except pine forest.

Each step touched off an ache in Rusty, but he tried not to let his discomfort show.

'What now?' Pac asked when they reached the trail sign at the bottom.

The trail on the right would take them to the Silver Lake Picnic Grounds, while the trail on the left led to the cove. The picnic grounds were a quarter of a mile away; the cove was a mile.

'Let's try the picnic area first,' Rusty suggested.

'You don't want to split up?'

'I don't think so. That Trink's a real mean little bitch.' He grinned. 'She might hurt you.'

'Not like she hurt *you*.'

He grinned at Pac. 'You mean it ain't true what they all say about you?'

'What do you think?'

Rusty suddenly found himself blushing. 'I think this'd be a fine time to change the subject.'

After a few minutes of brisk walking, they reached the picnic area. The lakeside clearing looked deserted except for a squirrel sitting upright on one of the green tables, gnawing something it held in its forepaws.

As they crossed the clearing, the squirrel stopped eating. It sat motionless, alert, looking away as if it didn't want them to realize they'd been spotted.

Just ahead of them, the ground dropped off sharply. They walked toward the slope. After a few strides, they found themselves looking down at a woman.

She was on her back, hands folded under her head, her bare feet only inches from the lapping water of the lake. Sunglasses hid her eyes. She wore a white bikini. Her skin was glossy with oil and had a smooth, mellow tan.

She reminded Rusty of Ursula Andress in the first James Bond movie, *Dr No*.

'Think she's asleep?' Pac whispered.

'Might be.'

'Should we . . . ?'

'Wake me?' Smiling, the woman twisted her head awkwardly and looked up at them. 'May I help you?' she asked.

'I'm Sheriff Hodges. This is Deputy Hodges. We're . . .'

'A lovely couple,' the woman said.

Again, Rusty blushed. 'She's my daughter-in-law,' he said, and felt embarrassed about explaining.

'You have a very fortunate son,' she said. Then she introduced herself. 'I'm Amanda Lane.'

'Nice to meet you, Miss Lane,' Rusty asked. 'We're down here looking for a couple of teenagers who may have witnessed a crime we're investigating. A boy and a girl, both about seventeen.'

'What do they look like?' Amanda asked.

'Pin cushions,' Rusty said.

Amanda laughed softly. 'Actually,' she said, 'I haven't

seen anybody at all. Only the two of you.'

'Okay,' Rusty said. 'Well, thank you. Have a good day, now.'

'I'm having an *excellent* day, thank you.'

With a final look at Amanda's tanned, sleek body, Rusty turned around.

'That was a surprise,' Pac said as they walked away from the slope.

'A pleasant surprise.'

'Don't forget you're married, Pop.'

He looked at her, surprised she'd called him Pop. He couldn't recall Pac ever calling him that before. It was a term used mostly by Harney, and sometimes by Millie. Unlike 'Dad,' it carried a hint of playful derision.

This time, too.

'Kid,' he said, 'I *never* forget I'm married.'

'Glad to hear it.'

Chapter Fourteen

NIGHTMARES

As they crossed the picnic grounds, Pac looked up at Indian Point. 'Scary,' she said.

Rusty saw it through a break in the trees. The bleak, stone face of the cliff loomed over the lake, probably a hundred feet high.

'No wonder the Washoes held it sacred,' Pac said.

'You know that story?'

'Sure. They used to toss their dead chiefs off the top.'

'A fellow was just telling me about it.'

'You'd heard about it before, hadn't you?'

'If I did, I forgot.'

'Did you ever take the Cruise Queen tour?'

'That's for tourists.'

'Snob.'

He shook his head, still staring up at the cliff. 'When we were kids,' he said, 'we called it Loser's Leap. A fellow named Barth lost his shirt over in Reno. Next day, they found his car parked up there. His wallet and all his clothes were in a neat pile right at the edge of the cliff.'

'You said he *lost* his shirt,' Pac reminded him.

'Give a guy a break, huh?'

'Okay, okay. Sorry.'

'Anyway, Barth was never seen again. Most people figured he committed suicide by leaping into the lake, but I always had my doubts. Maybe he only wanted it to look that way so he could pull a disappearing act.'

'What gave you that idea?' Pac asked.

'I'm just naturally suspicious, I guess.'

'I guess we all know that.'

He laughed softly. 'But you know, taking a leap off that damn cliff never seemed to me like a hot way to commit suicide. It's high, but it's not *that* high. You might live through it. And if you *did* survive, you'd be within about a half a minute's swimming distance from shore.' He pointed across the picnic area. 'You could wade out right over there. Maybe that's what Barth did. And maybe he had a boat waiting for him down here. Or he could've hiked back up to the parking lot and met someone . . . A lot of possibilities.'

'Maybe he didn't take the leap, at all.'

'That's also possible. Nobody saw him do it.'

'Obviously, the body never turned up.'

'Nope. If he took the leap . . . if it killed him, I guess he's still down there.'

'Fresh as a daisy,' Pac said.

'Gives me the creeps. It *always* gave me the creeps, thinking about him down there. I didn't *need* any stories about Indian chiefs to give me nightmares, I had Barth. But *I'd* be the one falling off the edge, you know, and . . .' He shook his head again. 'It'd feel like I was falling forever, and I knew Barth was waiting for me. I might survive the fall, but he'd come swimming up from way down deep and grab me by the ankles . . . God! I used to hate those dreams.'

'I bet you always woke up before you hit the water.'

'Damn straight I did. How can you sleep through a thing like that?'

'You can't,' Pac said. 'They say if you hit, you die.'

'Wonderful.'

'But I've heard that's an old wives' tale.'

'Glad to hear it.'

They walked in silence for a while. Then Pac said, '*My* nightmares started when I got into competition. In those, I'd lose my grip on the uneven parallels and take a header for the mat. I actually saw that happen to a girl during my senior year in high school. It was like watching my nightmare happen in real life. She broke her neck and went into convulsions.'

'Die?'

'Almost. The coach gave her CPR until the ambulance arrived. She saved Julie's life. Then Julie's parents sued the school *and* the coach for negligence.'

'Grateful sons of bitches.'

'Everybody sues everybody.'

'Wonderful world.'

Coming to the signposts, they took the trail toward the cove.

'How was it when *you* fell?' Rusty asked.

'Not nearly as bad as my nightmares, that's for sure. All I thought about was trying to land right. The fear wasn't the same. I think maybe dreams are always worse than the real thing.'

'Or better.'

'I knew you'd have to drag sex into this.'

'According to Millie, it's at the root of all things great and small.'

'I wouldn't go—'

'*PRICK!*' Trink's voice shrieked in rage.

'For cry-sake . . . !' Bill's.

'Asshole! Goddamn two-timing fucking asshole!'

Rusty and Pac, standing side by side at a bend in the trail, braced themselves as the rushing footfalls thudded closer. From the sound of things, the two witnesses were chasing each other up the trail.

'I'm sorry, Trink!'

'Sorry my ass!'

Trink's head turned as she raced around the bend. Rusty and Pac leaped apart to make a gap for her.

Pac trailed a leg to trip her.

Rusty grabbed Trink's shoulder and shoved it forward to help her along.

She flopped, striking the ground hard and grunting as it knocked out her wind.

'Cuff her,' Rusty said.

Bill had time to slow down before rounding the bend. He staggered to a halt in front of Rusty. His eyes looked frightened. He panted for air.

'Just relax,' Rusty told him.

'Hey, man . . . I didn't . . . do nothing.'

'Put your hands on top of your head.' He reached to the back of his belt for his cuffs.

'Hey, we can . . . work something out? Right? I can . . . put you onto something.'

'Like what?'

'Wanta bust a dealer?'

'Right now, I'm more interested in busting a murderer.'

'Hey, man, I can put you onto him. I promise. Don't bust me and I'll put you onto him.'

Stepping behind the boy, Rusty reached up with the cuffs. He flicked one open and hit its hinge against Bill's right wristbone. The curve of steel whipped around, clamping Bill's wrist and latching.

'What did you see last night?' Rusty asked.

'When?'

Rusty pulled Bill's cuffed arm down, then the other. 'Last night when you were parked at the Sweet Meadow roadhead.' He clamped the other cuff around Bill's left wrist.

'I don't know, man. If you're gonna bust me . . .'

'Tell me what you saw, then we'll decide.'

As he frisked Bill, he watched Pac help Trink to her feet. The girl's hands were safely cuffed behind her. 'Take Trink up the trail a bit while I have a talk with Bill. And arrest her for battery on a law enforcement officer.'

'You bet,' Pac said. She led Trink up the trail, and they disappeared around a bend.

'Okay,' Rusty said. 'Let's hear it.'

'Okay. Yeah, sure. Last night, right?'

'And this morning.'

'And you won't bust me?'

'We'll see.'

'Okay. Sure. Okay. We drove in like at midnight? Or maybe later, I don't know. Maybe it was one or two, something like that.'

'When exactly?'

'Hey, who knows?'

'Where were you before you came to the roadhead?'

'The drive-in.'

'You came directly from the drive-in?'

'Yeah.'

'Did you stay till the end of the movie?'

'Sure. You think we'd leave in the middle? That's crazy.'

'What movie was it?'

'At the drive-in. Like I said.'

There was only one drive-in theater left in the region. 'It's playing a triple feature,' Rusty said. 'Which show did you leave after?'

'Christ, who knows? I think we left after the one about the prison. Yeah, a woman's prison where the guards were all a bunch of rednecks and sadists.'

'All right.' Rusty made a note to check with the theater and get a fix on the time the prison movie let out. 'Now, tell me what you saw when you got to Sweet Meadow.'

'A van. A VW van.'

'Color?'

'Blue, I guess.'

'What year?'

'Who knows? I don't know. They all look alike. But it wasn't real old. I mean, it looked like it was in pretty good shape.'

'Was it occupied?'

Bill shook his head.

'How do you know?'

'We had a look. Christ, you know, you can't be too careful.'

'Did you look in the windows?'

'They had curtains. Couldn't see inside. But we knocked on the doors. Nobody home.'

'Maybe someone was inside and just didn't answer you.'

'No way. We looked, man.'

'You said there were curtains.'

'We went inside. One of the doors wasn't locked, so we just climbed in.'

Rusty tried to keep the excitement out of his voice. 'What did you find inside?'

'Nobody.'

'Was it furnished?'

'Had a bed, table, sink. You know. The usual stuff.'

'Anything unusual about it?'

'Sure. You want to take these cuffs off me?'

'No.'

'They hurt, man. You ever been cuffed?'

'I'll loosen them a bit.' Using his key, he opened each cuff a single notch. 'How's that?'

'Better.'

'What did you see?'

'He had this mirror on the ceiling. This big mirror. Over his water bed.'

'A *water bed*?'

'Yeah. Cool, huh?' Bill smiled, shaking his head. 'Plus, he had red lights. Man, what a turn-on.'

'Did you use the bed?'

'That illegal?'

'I'm not looking to bust you on this stuff, Bill. I just want the truth.'

'So what do you want to know?'

'Right now, tell me more about the van. Did you use it?'

'Sure, man. Wouldn't you? I mean, a water bed with a fucking *mirror* up there so you can watch the action? Plus, you never know if maybe the guy's gonna come back and catch you at it? I mean, what a rush!'

'How long were you there?'

'Who knows? An hour, maybe more.'

'You had intercourse on the bed?'

'Man, did we ever!'

'Do you know your blood type?'

'My what?'

'Blood type.'

'You mean like my DNA? Like with O.J. and all that shit?'

'It's like A, B, O . . .'

'Huh? No. I don't know.'

'Let's find out.' Rusty removed the cuffs. 'I'm not inclined to arrest you, but I want you to come with us so we can get a blood sample and take your fingerprints.'

'What if I don't?'

'I'll bust you right now and drag you in.'

'Oh, okay. Hey, I'll come along.'

'Walk ahead of me.' Rusty followed him up the trail to where Pac was waiting with Trink. The girl was cuffed. Her eyes were red and she was gasping for air.

'*You hurt me, you prick!*' she yelled at Rusty.

'You shouldn't have been running,' he told her. To Pac, he said, 'Did she give you much trouble?'

'Not a bit.'

'All right, let's get up to the parking lot. You take the lead, Pac. Bill, you go next. Then Trink. I'll take up the rear.'

'Behind me?' Trink asked, scowling at him.

'Yep.'

'Well, don't try no funny stuff.'

'With you? Now why would I want to do that?'

'Fuck you.'

'Let's go.'

'You couldn't get it up if you wanted to, you old fart.'

'You'll never know. Now, get moving.'

'You better not touch me.'

'I wouldn't dare. Might get pricked.'

'You *are* a prick.'

'Move.'

The four of them started up the trail. They continued steadily, without trouble, almost to the top of the slope. Then Trink dropped to her knees and fell forward, hitting the trail shoulder-first.

Rusty knelt beside her. 'What's the matter?'

'These handcuffs.'

'What about them?'

'They hurt.'

'They're supposed to.'

'Take them off.'

'Not a chance.'

'That ain't fair! You don't got Bill cuffed!'

'Bill's not under arrest, you are. Now let's get up.'

'Not till you take off the cuffs.'

'I'll take one off. How's that?'

She didn't answer.

Rusty unlocked the bracelet on her left hand. He loosened the other one enough to reverse the direction of its chain, then clamped it tight again. 'Let's go.'

As he helped Trink to her knees, she swung her left fist toward his groin. He turned away, catching the blow on his thigh. She cocked back her arm for another punch. Before she could deliver it, Rusty drove his fist into her stomach. Her breath burst out. She sagged, gasping.

'Sorry, Trink.'

She kept on gasping.

More than a minute passed before her breathing calmed. Then she stood up, holding herself below the ribs. She couldn't stand up straight. 'Motherfucking prick bastard,' she said.

'Let's go.'

'I'll *get* you.'

'You already did.'

Chapter Fifteen

A SHOPPING TRIP

'Oh, I just bet *he* was a devil,' Walter said, leaning close to Merton and pointing at the photo of a twelfth grader with messy blond hair, an impish grin and a wide gap between his two front teeth.

'Doesn't look familiar,' Merton said.

'Oh, look at this one.'

Merton didn't bother to look. 'I need a few things from the store,' he said.

'I could have told you that. Oh, I just bet this one broke a lot of hearts.'

Merton glanced at the photo. 'Turner? He didn't break hearts, he broke maidenheads. He used to brag that he'd balled every gal on the cheerleading squad. I think Sav-on will be okay.'

'You should've picked up your toothbrush when you stopped by your house. I was intending to mention it at the time, but it slipped my mind.'

'I'm not going for a toothbrush.'

'Well, you should pick one up none the less.'

'Want to come along? You can choose the color.'

'I think blue. A translucent aqua, don't you think?'

'Sure. Ready to go?'

'In a jiff. Let me piddle first.'

As Walter headed for the toilet, Merton stepped into the kitchen. Draped over the faucet spout was a pair of rubber dishwashing gloves. He tried one on. The fit was too loose. The orange fingertips, protruding beyond his own, collapsed when he pressed them against the counter. These wouldn't do.

He pulled off the glove. His hand felt powdery and smelled of orange blossoms. He washed with soap, then met Walter in the living room.

'I'm having second thoughts,' Walter said.

'About what?'

'About you. All this. Has it occurred to you that you might be caught?'

'Let it drop.'

'You're taking awful chances. It frightens me. I don't want to lose . . .'

'If Paxton or his girl get on the witness stand, it's all over. They've gotta go. No away around it. It's either them or me.'

'But killing them is so drastic.'

'Them or me, Walter, them or me.'

'Still . . .'

'Self-preservation. Simple as that.'

'But the morality!'

'Fuck morality. If some mental defective is running at you with a butcher knife, are you gonna have qualms about blowing his brains out?'

'Certainly.'

'You always were peculiar.'

'No need to get personal,' Walter complained.

'Are you coming to the store with me, or not?'

'I'm coming.'

'Then let's go.'

'What is it that you're planning to buy?' Walter asked as he pulled the door shut.

'A toothbrush. Aqua.'

At the Sav-on Drug Store four blocks from Walter's home, Merton did buy a toothbrush – a translucent blue one chosen by Walter. He also bought a pair of rubber dishwashing gloves, a squeeze bottle of Ivory Liquid detergent, and a pair of pliers. Walter bought a bottle of Excedrin and a *Good Housekeeping*.

While Walter drove out of the parking lot, Merton opened the lowest button of his shirt, reached inside, and pulled out three small packages.

'You didn't *pay* for those?'

'Are you kidding?'

'Why not? If you're short on cash . . .'

'It's not the money. I didn't want some dumb-ass cashier remembering who bought these things if the cops come around asking.'

'So you stole them. What if you'd been caught?'

'God, you're such a nag. Would you try shutting up for a change?'

'No need to get nasty, Merton. I was just asking you a simple question. You're so touchy, always so touchy.'

'You ask too damn many questions.'

'It's only because I care about you. I don't want you to end up back in jail . . . or *killed*! I wouldn't be able to stand it.' He turned toward Merton, tears in his eyes. 'Is that so dreadful?'

'God, you're a pain in the ass.'

Walter sniffed, wiped his nose and didn't answer.

Merton fastened his shirt button and picked up one of the stolen packages.

'What is it?' Walter wanted to know. 'Or am I not allowed to ask?'

'Ask away. It's a wall-fastener set.'

'A what?'

Merton read aloud from the package. 'Complete set for hanging pictures, mirrors, shelves, signs, etc. Twelve feet of picture wire, twelve eye screws, six wall fasteners, six screws.'

'What do you want that for?'

'For the same thing as this.' He picked up another small package. Like the other, it was a rectangle of printed cardboard with the contents displayed inside a clear plastic bubble. The bubble of this one held two spools. 'Handi-wire,' Merton said. 'And here we have a roll of Electrical Sealing Tape.'

'I don't understand why you need such things.'

'You don't have to.'

Chapter Sixteen

INA

That afternoon, business was lighter than usual at the Discount Garment Center, so Leon Jones accepted his daughter's request to leave work early. She started for home shortly after three o'clock.

Though Ina Jones worked at her father's store, she no longer lived at his home, having moved out a year earlier after an especially nerve-wracking night with Johnny Carpenter in her bedroom. Not that it hadn't been romantic. On the contrary, it still held honors as the most romantic night of her life: sneaking downstairs after midnight to open the kitchen door for Johnny; leading him through the dark house and into her bedroom; letting him pull the nightgown over her head, then slowly removing all of his clothes as they stood shivering in the moonlit room; lying carefully down on the bed and making silent, fantastic love. It had been beautiful, unforgettable, and fear of her father catching them in the act had scared the living hell out of her.

The next day, she'd told her parents that she wanted a place of her own. They agreed at once. They not only agreed, but they helped her find a pleasant, three-bedroom house a mile away from home and they loaned her enough money for the down payment. After several months living alone except for occasional overnight visits from Johnny, Bob, Stu or Herb, she advertised in the *Sierra Evening News* for a roommate. Of the six women responding, she chose a friendly blonde named Faye Everett.

Her choice of roommate had absolutely nothing to do with the fact that Faye's steady boyfriend was a hunk named Bass Paxton.

Sure it didn't.

And her decision to leave work early on this particular Saturday afternoon had absolutely nothing to do with the possibility of catching Bass in a delicious position with Faye. A remote possibility, but it could happen.

They would probably be back from their canoe trip by now. After all, they'd taken off early in the morning, and it wasn't *that* far down the lake.

If she knew Faye at all – and she knew her very well – Faye would return from such an excursion feeling filthy and exhausted. Her first order of business would be to take a shower. Maybe Bass would get into the shower with her. Maybe they would even make love there. Probably not, though. Faye would probably make him wait so they could do it comfortably on the bed.

Ina wouldn't be surprised at all to find them asleep in Faye's room.

That might be a very nice thing to find.

She imagined Bass sprawled naked on top of the sheets, his body lit by rays of sunlight from the window.

Her spirits fell when she drove up to her house.

Bass's red Pontiac was nowhere to be seen.

Still, what did that really prove? Maybe he'd parked it in the garage, or something.

Hardly likely, Ina thought.

She parked in the driveway, eased her car door shut, then walked quickly but silently to the front door of her house. Carefully, she unlocked the door and opened it.

The living room was deserted.

She shut the door, stepped out of her shoes, and walked to the hallway. All three bedroom doors stood open.

Oh, let them be here. Please. Asleep in Faye's room.

And maybe let Bass wake up and see me and smile.

And come to me.

She walked slowly down the hall, heart thudding hard as she looked into each doorway.

Nobody.

Disappointment gave her a hollow ache.

It's all right, she told herself. *I beat them home, that's all. They might show up any second.*

She entered her bedroom. Leaving the door open, she took off her clothes. Naked, she hung up her skirt and blouse in her closet. Then she carried her panties and bra down the hallway.

They could show up right now.

And here I'd be.

Bass'd sure get himself an eye full.

But the front door didn't open. She entered the bathroom and dropped her bra and panties into the clothes hamper.

Out in the hall again, she listened for the sound of the front door opening. She could almost hear it. But not quite.

She was excited. Awfully excited, and awfully nervous

because she suddenly knew that she wasn't returning to her own room.

She walked into Faye's bedroom.

Its carpet was cool and soft under her bare feet, warm where a patch of sunlight lay across it. The closet door stood open. The bed was neatly made. She went to Faye's dresser.

In the mirror above it, she looked at herself. Her eyes seemed flat and blank, the way they often looked when she was aroused. Her lips were parted. She licked them. Then she lowered her eyes to the dresser top. To the polished-oak jewelry box. She opened its lid.

There were plenty of rings and earrings, a single brooch, a few necklaces. Ina didn't care about them. She lifted out a shelf loaded with earrings and found, in what Faye called her 'not-so-secret compartment,' the silver and turquoise necklace that Bass had given her.

Ina picked it up. She held it to her chest. Its cold weight felt exciting against her skin. Had Faye ever modeled it for Bass naked?

Fastening the clasp behind her neck, she stepped back from the mirror for a longer view. Her fingertips touched the smooth stone, the intricate silverwork. Then they strayed over her breasts, brushing against her nipples.

If Faye and Bass walked in the front door right now, there probably wouldn't be enough time to take off the necklace and put it back where it belonged.

Not enough time to get out of Faye's bedroom.

Ina would be caught, humiliated.

The thought of it frightened her – and heated her desire.

She stepped close to the dresser. Without taking off the necklace, she began to open the drawers. She found Faye's panties, folded and neatly stacked. Brassieres. Panty hose. Not quite as many pairs as Ina might have expected, but enough. One drawer held several nightgowns. One held only sweaters. There were six drawers in all. She searched every one of them, being careful not to disturb the neat arrangement of the contents.

She didn't know what she hoped to find – something belonging to Bass, maybe. Something personal. Something intimate.

Her hands trembled as she searched, and continued to tremble as she went to the closet.

There was something wrong about the closet.

Ina was puzzled. Her arousal diminished. She flipped through the hangers, no longer searching for an object to link her with Bass but trying instead to discover what made her nervous about the closet.

On tiptoes, she scanned the length of the shelf above the clothes bar.

Crouching, she let her eyes roam the dozen pairs of shoes on the closet floor. The shoes were set up in a single neat row near the back wall, but there were three gaps along in the row.

Three pairs of shoes were gone.

Abruptly, Ina stood up straight. The hangers! The hangers were wrong. Of course.

Flicking through the suspended clothes, she found nine empty hangers.

Proud of her systematic approach to life, Faye never kept spare hangers in her closet. 'Extra ones only end up on the floor,' she'd explained.

She'd done her laundry and ironing after work yesterday.

How could there be nine empty hangers?

Ina rushed over to Faye's bed, dropped to her knees and lifted the edge of the bedspread. The dark space between the box springs and the carpet was empty.

Suitcases are gone.

She went somewhere.

Without telling me.

On her feet, Ina hurried over to the dresser. With trembling hands, she reached behind her neck and unfastened the clasp of the necklace.

Where the hell did Faye go?

It was just supposed to be a little canoe trip, not a weekend at a motel or something!

Jealousy made a painful twist inside Ina's belly. She shut the jewelry box hard. After a quick look around to make sure she'd left no signs of her snooping, she lurched into the hall and ran to her bedroom.

Chapter Seventeen

PEPSI BREAK

Rusty sat alone in his office. He turned a cold Pepsi bottle slowly with one hand, staring at it, thinking.

He'd hoped that Bill would somehow crack open the case. 'Oh, sure, it was Joe Blow's van, I'd know it anywhere.' Or, 'I happened to take down the license number.' Or, 'I snapped a photo of it for my scrapbook.'

No such luck. There rarely was.

But the van *was* unusual. There couldn't be too many with a mirror above a water bed. Not in an area the size of Sierra County.

Who says the van's local. Might've been passing through.

The killer had almost certainly known Alison Parkington, though. A lone woman driving through the mountains at that time of night – in her nightgown, no less – would have to be nuts to pick up a stranger.

She'd have to be nuts to be out there at all like that.

Maybe she went out in hopes of finding a stranger to pick up.

Feeling horny.

But it was certainly possible – even likely – that the

rendezvous had been arranged in advance. A lover's tryst. Except the guy didn't exactly love her, not if he'd brought along a hacksaw.

Guys don't just wander around with hacksaws.

Any way you slice it, this was premeditated.

Slice it. Good one.

What about special circumstances?

He saw a dab of amber fluid at the bottom of his Pepsi bottle, so he raised the bottle and let it dribble into his mouth. Warm, but good and sweet.

Special circumstances?

Not likely. The victim wasn't a law enforcement officer. She'd already been dead before the decapitation took place, so it didn't look like there'd been any torture to speak of. No multiple murder involved . . .

That we know of.

Could've been a killing for hire . . .

Not my concern, anyway. Let the DA worry about whether it's a capital crime. My job's to catch the guy.

But how?

He'd have to take a closer look at Alison Parkington, find out if she was seeing anyone.

Check out all our local sex offenders too. See if we've got any necrophiles on record.

Find that van.

Chapter Eighteen

WAKE-UP CALL

Ina raised her face out of the pillow, stretched until her bare skin felt taut and sensitive against the sheet, then reached over to the nightstand and picked up the ringing telephone. 'Hello?' she asked, her voice husky from sleep.

'Ina?'

The voice sent a surge through her. Trying to sound casual, she said, 'Oh hi, Bass. How are you doing?'

'Not too bad, all things considered.'

Expecting his next words to be a request for her to call Faye to the phone, she quickly asked, 'How was the canoe trip?'

'Didn't Faye tell you?'

'No.'

'We found a body this morning.'

'A body? You mean a *dead* body?'

'As dead as they come,' he said.

'Jeez.'

'Yeah.'

'Where'd you find it?'

'At the Bend.'

'No kidding? Man, what a way to start your day.'

'It was pretty weird,' Bass muttered.

'What sort of . . . How did the person die?'

'Somebody cut off her head.'

'Eh!' Ina jerked the phone away from her face as if a repulsive bug were crawling on its mouthpiece.

'Ina?' the faint voice asked. 'Ina? You still there?'

She brought the phone closer. 'Yeah, I'm here.'

'Sorry. I shouldn't have been so blunt about it.'

'It's okay. God. The head was cut off?'

'Like with a saw or something.'

'God. And *Faye* saw this?'

'She saw what was left.'

'God. Poor Faye. Is she all right?'

'She took it pretty hard at first. But she seemed quite a lot better by the time I dropped her off.'

'Must've been awful.'

'It wasn't very pleasant. Faye didn't even want me to come in. She said she wanted to take a sleeping pill and forget the whole thing.'

Just like Faye, Ina thought.

'If she's still asleep,' Bass said, 'don't bother waking her up. But maybe you could take a look for me. The ringing might've woken her. But if it didn't, just wait till she wakes up and tell her I called. I only called to make sure she's okay.'

'She isn't here, Bass.' Ina wiggled. The rub of the sheet felt good against her bare skin, like a caress.

For a few seconds, Bass said nothing.

Then, sounding confused, he said, 'What do you mean, she isn't there?'

'She isn't in her bedroom. She isn't in the house.'

'Where *is* she?'

'I don't have any idea. I figured she was with you.'

'No. I dropped her off at the house a long time ago. Around one forty-five?'

'Well, hang on a second. Let me check around. I just woke up from a nap. Maybe she came in while I was asleep.'

'Okay, would you?'

'Sure.'

'And if she's not there, would you check to see if her car's gone?'

'Sure. I'll be right back.'

Ina set down the phone on her pillow and climbed out of bed. Not bothering to put on any clothes, she hurried down the hallway to the kitchen. The linoleum floor felt cool under her feet, and a little sticky in places. At the far end of the eating area, a door led into the garage. She opened it. Faye's Volvo was gone.

Though certain that nobody'd come into the house while she'd been asleep, she did a quick search before returning to her bedroom. She flopped onto the bed and picked up the phone. 'Bass?'

'Yeah.'

'Faye's not here. Neither is her car.'

Bass was silent for a while. Then he said, 'Maybe she went to the store or something.'

'No, I don't think so.'

'Why's that?'

Squirming against the sheet, Ina asked, 'Why would she take her suitcases to the store?'

'Her suitcases are gone?'

'That's right. And so are a bunch of her clothes. There's a lot of stuff missing from her closet. There're empty hangers, missing shoes.'

'My God. Where'd she go?'

Ina grinned. 'I have no idea. I thought she was with you, Bass.'

'No. Huh-uh. I wonder . . . Do you think she might've gone to see her parents?'

'That's possible,' Ina said. 'She's done it before.'

'Maybe that's it,' Bass muttered. 'But you'd think she would've told me . . . or you . . . *somebody*.'

'You'd think so. But, you know, Faye didn't tell anyone last time she took off, either.'

'No, she didn't.'

Thinking about the last time Faye had pulled a disappearing act made Ina feel good. The long wait with Bass, the quiet talking, the sharing. That vigil was the closest she'd ever been to him. If only Faye had piled into a bridge abutment or taken a flying leap off the Golden Gate Bridge or simply decided to *stay away* . . .

'Burlingame's a good six hour drive,' Bass said. 'That's if you don't stop to eat or anything.'

'How'll we know?' Ina asked.

'Know what?'

'Whether that's where she went?'

'I guess we won't. Not for . . . Let's see, I dropped her off at about a quarter till two. Give her about an hour to pack and get ready, she probably didn't leave till two-thirty or three. It's almost five now.' Ina heard a quick mumble of numbers as Bass counted. 'She shouldn't get to her folks' place much before nine o'clock.'

'That's a long time to wait.'

'Yeah. It sure is.'

'Want to do your waiting over here?' Ina asked. 'That way, you can be right here in case she shows up or calls. And we can give each other some moral support.'

'Thanks, but I'd better stay. She might call here.'

'Well . . . if you think that'd be better.' Ina tried to keep the disappointment out of her voice.

'At nine,' Bass said, 'I'll give her folks a call. Will you be home?'

'Sure.'

'Then I'll give you a ring as soon as I've talked to them, and let you know.'

'What if Faye's not there?'

Sounding a little lost, Bass asked, 'Where else would she go?'

Ina said nothing. She let the silence speak for her.

'She wouldn't go there,' Bass said. 'She's finished with him.'

'I hope so.' Ina made herself sound doubtful. 'It's just that, if she was so upset and everything . . . maybe she needed a shoulder to cry on.'

'She could've cried on mine. Besides, she couldn't go over there even if she wanted to. What would they do about the asshole's wife, put her in the guest room?'

'It was just a thought. I'm sorry. I shouldn't have mentioned it.'

'I guess they could've gone to a motel,' Bass muttered. Then he said firmly, 'No, she's through with him. She promised me.'

'I'm sure she is,' Ina told him in a voice heavy with doubt.

'I'll call you after I've talked to her parents.'

'Fine. See you later.'

'Yeah. So long.'

Ina heard him hang up. She reached over to the nightstand and hung up the phone.

And smiled, pleased with the job she'd done.

She wished she'd been able to lure him over. Somehow, though, she felt certain that she would see him before the night was done.

This time, maybe they would get to know each other a lot better than before.

And this time, maybe Faye wouldn't come back.

An awful thing to wish. She liked Faye. But she liked Bass more.

She headed down the hallway.

First, she would take a nice long shower and wash her hair. Then she would dress herself in something special for Bass.

Chapter Nineteen

WHERE, OH WHERE CAN SHE BE?

'Are you sure there's nothing else I can do?' Pac asked, hoping Rusty would let her leave.

'Nothing that can't wait. Go on home and celebrate your anniversary.'

'We'll see you and Millie tomorrow morning at our place, right?'

'Barring unforeseen misfortunes . . .'

'Come over around eleven. We'll start with Bloody Marys.'

'Get out of here.'

'*Adios*, Pop.'

Outside, the heat was bad. As Pac walked toward the station's parking lot, the late afternoon sun felt burning against her face and the backs of her hands. It made an oven of her uniform blouse. A drop trickled, sliding between her breasts. Another drop glided down her side. Her bra stopped both, absorbing them.

At her car, she stood in the V of the open door and rolled down the window before climbing in.

How great it would be to get home, get out of these hot

sweaty clothes, take a cool bath, then have a vodka tonic so loaded with ice that the glass would fog up and drip onto her as she drank. They'd have a couple of hours before leaving for the Fireside. She could have a drink or two on the porch with Harney and still have time to get dressed and take off for the restaurant.

Or maybe we could skip the drinks, she thought, *and spend an hour in the sack.*

Smiling, she pulled out of the parking lot.

But she suddenly remembered the last time they'd been at the Fireside. They'd gone with Bass and Faye to celebrate Faye's birthday.

What a shock for poor Faye, walking into a body that way.

She'd seemed to take it fairly well, though. Shocked, terribly upset, but at least the experience hadn't unhinged her.

Maybe I oughta drop by and see her.

Pac sighed.

She *really* wanted to get home.

But it's not every day one of your best friends stumbles onto a headless stiff. Won't kill me to stop in for a couple of minutes.

When Pac arrived at the house where Faye lived, she saw Ina's car in the driveway. She swung in behind it, shut off her engine, and climbed out. On her way to the front door, she tried to remember whether the house had air conditioning.

She sure hoped so.

She knocked on the door. Before she could knock again, it swung open.

Ina Jones gazed out at her, looking surprised at first, then alarmed. 'Pac! What's . . . ?'

'Nothing's wrong,' she said. 'I just thought I'd drop by and see how Faye's doing.'

'You'd better come in.'

'Is something the matter?' Pac asked, stepping inside. The house was cool. She shut the door and followed Ina into the living room.

Ina faced Pac, then lowered her eyes. She lifted a hanging end of her robe belt and studied it. 'Faye isn't here,' she said.

'Did she go off with Bass?'

'No. I talked to him on the phone a while ago. He doesn't know where she is. He thought she'd be here.' Shaking her head, Ina sank onto the couch.

'Do you have any idea where she might've gone?' Pac asked.

'I don't know. She took her suitcases and some clothes. We think she might've driven home – to her parents' house.'

'They're in the Bay Area.'

Ina nodded. 'Burlingame, I guess. Bass said he'll phone them tonight after nine and see if she's gotten there yet.'

'Her car isn't here?'

'No.'

'A green Volvo, right?'

Ina nodded.

'Do you know the year?'

'Not really.'

'I think it's a ninety-four.'

'Maybe,' Ina said. 'I don't know.'

'Would you know the license plate number?'

'I don't have a clue.'

'What time do you think she left here?'

'Well, I got home from work a little after three. She was gone by then. Bass said he dropped her off her at a quarter till two.'

'Okay if I use your phone?' Pac asked.

'Yeah, sure.'

Pac placed a call to the station. Deputy Lincoln answered and put her through to Rusty.

'It's Pac,' she said. 'I'm over at Ina Jones's house, where Faye lives. She's gone. Faye's gone,' Pac quickly explained the details she'd learned from Ina. 'What do you think?' she asked.

'I like the theory that she's on her way to Burlingame. A girl sees a murdered body, it can knock the props out from under her. Nothing like Mom and Dad to put the props back where they belong.'

'If that's the case, why didn't she tell somebody where she was going?'

'Could be she didn't think anyone would miss her. Not this soon, anyway. Or maybe she wanted people to worry.'

'People like Bass?' Pac asked.

'Happens all the time. A gal feels neglected so she pulls a disappearing act. Either to get attention or revenge.'

Pac nodded. 'Might be something like that,' she said. 'On the other hand, maybe someone *took* her. Maybe the *killer* took her.'

'It's possible,' Rusty said. 'But the fact that her suitcases are gone . . .'

'He could've followed her home from the station. Or

maybe he recognized her this morning and already knew where she lives.'

'If he knew Faye, she must've known him, too. She probably would've mentioned the fact.'

'Most likely,' Pac said.

'Gives us a few interesting possibilities, doesn't it?' Pac could easily imagine Rusty nodding, his eyes narrow with thought, his teeth clamping a cigar.

'One,' Pac suggested, 'is that she might know the guy but didn't get a good look at him this morning.'

'Or she didn't recognize him,' Rusty said, 'because he *looked* different. Maybe he'd changed his appearance, somehow.'

'Or,' Pac added, 'she *did* recognize him but chose not to tell us.'

'Can of worms,' Rusty said.

'Pandora's Box,' said Pac.

She heard him laugh. 'Don't talk dirty,' he said.

'Hey.'

'Sorry,' Rusty said. Then, 'If Faye did recognize him, why would she keep it from us?'

'To protect him?' Pac suggested.

'Or to extort him.'

'In either case,' Pac said, 'she'd need to get in touch with him.'

'Which might explain her disappearing act.'

'It might,' Pac agreed. 'But I can't see her taking suitcases along for the ride.'

'To hold the money?'

'They're apparently full of clothes and shoes.'

'I just hope she *is* on her way to Burlingame. If she isn't,

I'd have to say there's a good chance you're right about the killer putting the snatch on her. He could've forced her to pack her bags to make it *appear* that she went off on her own.'

'If that's what went down . . .' Pac couldn't force herself to finish the sentence.

'I'll get her car description onto the air,' Rusty told her. 'You said Bass is going to phone Faye's parents at nine tonight?'

'Right. And then he'll call Ina.'

'Let me know what he finds out.'

'Will do.'

'Now go on home, Pac. You don't want to miss your big night on the town.'

'Yeah. I'll take off right now.'

'Have a good one, honey.'

'You, too, Russ.' She hung up.

Ina, shaking her head, muttered, 'Good God. You think the killer kidnapped her?'

'She'd only have to say "That's the man" in front of a jury, and it'd just about be over for him.'

'But Bass could say the same thing. Bass saw him, too, didn't he?'

Pac nodded.

'So he'll want to . . . get rid of Bass too, won't he?' Her eyes pleaded with Pac, cried out for a denial of her logic.

'Maybe we should get in touch with him,' Pac said.

Ina glared at her as if betrayed, lurched past her and picked up the phone. She tapped in a number, then listened for nearly a full minute before lowering the phone. 'He doesn't answer,' she said. Her voice held disbelief. She shook her head slowly, frowning. 'He said he'd stay home.' Tears began to shine in her eyes. 'Oh, my God!'

'Maybe he just stepped out for a minute.'

'No!'

'Take it easy, Ina. He might've just gone for dinner or something. There's no reason to think anything's *happened* to him.'

'I'm going over there.'

Chapter Twenty

ILLEGAL ENTRY

Merton rang the doorbell of the house at 432 Malfi, and waited. He rang it again, again. Then he knocked hard with his fist. It didn't surprise him that nobody answered the door. He'd expected the house to be empty, counted on it. But he had to be certain.

Shaking his head and trying to look disappointed for the sake of any neighbors who might be watching, he walked back to his car. He drove up the block, counting houses, then turned. Like most of the blocks in town, this one had an alley. He drove down it, counting houses again, and stopped behind the green one belonging to Bass Paxton.

A chain-link fence surrounded the back yard. He climbed out of his car, took out what he needed, and went to the gate. It was latched shut, but not locked. He opened it and crossed the neatly mowed lawn, swinging his shotgun case in a carefree way. The screen door of the back porch wasn't locked. Nor did it squeak.

A nice porch. It had a couch, a portable television, even a miniature refrigerator. A door led into the house. He looked through one of its glass panes into a small, shadowy kitchen. Nothing moved inside.

He propped his shotgun case against the refrigerator and pulled a pair of dishwashing gloves from his pocket. After pulling them on, he tried the door knob. It didn't turn.

With a quick upward swing, his elbow smashed the window. The sudden sharp pop of glass was loud, but it ended quickly. The clink and clatter of shards hitting the floor, however, seemed to last forever.

When silence finally came, Merton continued to wait. He listened carefully, but heard nothing. Reaching through the broken window, he found the inside knob and opened the door.

Glass crunched under his shoes as he crossed the kitchen. Bits of it embedded in his soles and scratched the hardwood floor of the dining room. The living room was carpeted. He wiped his feet on the green shag as if it were a welcome mat, then hurried across it to the front door.

He glanced upstairs. A pretty decent house for a guy Paxton's age.

Merton unzipped the case and pulled out his Browning 12 gauge shotgun. He pumped a shell into the chamber, then climbed the stairway.

He searched quickly.

A bathroom, two bedrooms and a study.

All were empty.

As he'd hoped.

He hurried back downstairs.

Chapter Twenty-one

THE OPEN ROBE

Pac watched Ina turn away, hands tugging open the belt of her pink robe as she hurried toward the hall.

'Ina?'

She stopped, turned and sniffed, not seeming to care that the robe hung open. Its wide gap showed the inner slopes of her breasts, her tanned belly, the neat round hole of her navel, the sudden pale skin where her tan ended, the kinky black thicket of her pubic hair, the tan that started again high on her thighs.

The sight shocked Pac, made her stomach leaden and cold.

Ina, blushing, pulled her robe shut.

'I'm sorry,' Pac said. 'I was just . . . I'll go with you to Bass's.'

Ina frowned. 'What were you staring for?'

'Nothing. Just surprised me, I guess.'

'What did?'

'Nothing. Never mind. Go get dressed and I'll wait for you.'

Still frowning, Ina turned around and rushed down the hall.

Pac sat down. Leaning back in the chair, she shut her eyes and folded her hands across her belly.

She probably thinks I'm a lesbian.

What a shock, though, seeing Ina that way. Like looking at Alison Parkington's body all over again.

Ina was taller, thinner, with smaller breasts and dark pubic hair instead of blonde – and she had a head – but the similarities were still strong enough to remind Pac of the corpse and make her feel sick.

Just because they're both women?

She wondered how she would feel the next time she saw herself naked.

Maybe I'll have to give up baths.

The idea of it made her smile. Then she turned her thoughts to Bass. Was he really in danger? It seemed possible. Odd how Ina had reacted, though.

Almost like she's got a thing for him.

Almost?

At the sound of footsteps, Pac opened her eyes. What she saw didn't surprise her.

Ina had changed into sandals, cut-off jeans with sides split nearly to her belt, and a clinging halter top.

'Let's hurry.' Ina picked up her purse and rushed past Pac, leaving a heavy scent of perfume in her wake. 'I'll take my own car,' she said.

'Just a second. Phone him once more, first.'

Ina nodded. She picked up the phone, hit redial, and waited. 'Still no answer,' she said.

'He lives on Malfi, doesn't he?'

'Four three two,' Ina said.

'If you get there first, wait for me.'

140

Chapter Twenty-two

BOOBY TRAP

In Bass's dining room, Merton picked up two straight-backed chairs. He carried them into the foyer. There, he set one chair down – its back about five feet in front of the door – the other chair directly behind it.

After making sure the safety was on, he set his shotgun across the back rails of the chairs. With a roll of electrical tape from his pocket, he fastened it securely into place.

He stepped behind the second chair, crouched, and sighted. He nudged the chair half an inch to the right, then took another look up the sighting ramp.

The shotgun was lined up with the door knob, but a few inches higher.

'That'll do the trick,' he muttered.

The phone rang.

Merton stood motionless until it stopped.

Then he twisted an eye screw into the door frame adjacent to the knob.

He peeled eight feet of galvanized steel Handi-wire off its spool and snipped it with pliers. Then he fastened one end to the door knob and ran the length of the wire sideways through the metal eye on the door frame.

Pulling the wire along with him, he stepped to the rear of the chairs. He twisted his second eye screw eye into the shoulder stock of the shotgun, passed the wire through it, pulled in most of the slack, and drew the wire forward.

Carefully, he wound the wire around the shotgun's trigger.

He took one more glance down the barrel.

Then he flicked the safety to OFF and left Bass's house through the back door.

Chapter Twenty-three

THE SHOT

Rusty stepped into his house, breathed the air and sighed with pleasure at the tangy aromas. 'I'm home,' he called. He removed his gunbelt and set it on a nearby table.

Millie stepped out of the kitchen, grinning. In her skirt and white blouse, she looked fresh and cool. A real achievement in the heavy hot air of the house.

'Is that Bratwurst I'm smelling?' he asked.

She nodded and stepped into his arms. 'Only the best for my injured hero.'

They kissed, and he put his hands under the hanging tails of her blouse. Her back was warm and smooth.

'Did you get your man?' she asked.

'Not the killer.'

'But someone?'

'I busted the bitch who decommissioned me.'

'Very good. Did you stomp her?'

'Not exactly,' Rusty said, smiling at Millie's eagerness. 'But let us say that she didn't come through the experience unscathed.'

'I hope you scathed her good.'

'Oh, I think Pac and I both scathed her about equally.'

'Well, I'll have to thank Pac. We're still going over tomorrow, right?'

'That's the plan.'

'I guess they're having dinner at the Fireside tonight,' Millie said.

'That's what I heard.'

'How's your injury?'

'Improving, I think, but I still hurt like hell sometimes.'

'Maybe some beer will help.'

'It's helping already. That smell!' Rusty moaned as if the odor were so pleasant that it made him ache. 'I hope you didn't pour it *all* on the Brats.'

'I saved a little for you.'

They went into the kitchen. Rusty opened the refrigerator and looked down at a shelf loaded with cans of Budweiser. 'I trained you good,' he said. 'Want one?'

'Sure, why not?'

He took out two cans. As he snapped them open, Millie brought him two glass steins. He poured, then picked them up. 'Patio?' he asked.

She nodded.

Outside, he waited for Millie to sit on a patio chair. Then he handed a stein to her and sat on the lounger. 'Here's how,' he said.

They raised their glasses and drank.

'Just to set your mind at ease,' Millie said, 'Harney's in charge of the food tomorrow.'

'In charge?'

'He's barbecuing chicken.'

'Oh, thank God. That Pac's a hell of a cop, but her cooking is the shits.'

Rusty took another long drink of beer. He sighed with pleasure and noticed how the house threw its shadow across the patio and half the enclosed yard. The chimney's shadow stretched like a dark walkway to the fence. The whole yard looked cool – even the sunlit leaves of the aspen tree. A breeze came. Rusty took off his shoes.

'You ought to get out of that uniform,' Millie suggested.

'I can't move. Maybe after another beer or two.'

But the telephone suddenly rang and he had to move.

He rushed into the kitchen and picked up the phone before it could ring a third time. 'Hello?'

'Sheriff, this is Deputy Blaine.'

'What's up?' he asked.

'I'm catching tonight?' Blaine phrased it like a question. The man lacked self-confidence, but he'd improved a lot since joining the department last year. 'I just got a call from a Miss Yvette Young. She heard a gunshot next door?'

'Has a unit been despatched?'

'Yes, sir. Deputy Osgood? He's en route to the scene.'

'Well, is there a . . . ?'

'The reason I called you, sir – I thought you might want to know about this one right away. I hope I didn't catch you at an inconvenient time?'

'It's all right.'

'The thing of it is, this Young woman, this Yvette Young, she lives at sixty-six Cove Road? The gunshot came from next door.'

Rusty concentrated.

Cove Road?

A connection, but he couldn't quite make it.

Maybe if it weren't for that beer . . .

'The gunshot,' Blaine said, 'it came from the Parkington condo. The one they're staying in for the summer? Or were? Alison Parkington, the dead lady? And her husband, the professor? That's where the shot happened.'

Chapter Twenty-four

GOING IN

Pac pulled to the curb across the street from Bass's house.

Ina's car was already parked in the driveway; she must've violated the speed limits like mad to arrive so fast. She was standing at the front door.

Pac climbed out of her car. Rushing across the street, she unsnapped the safety guard of her holster. 'You were supposed to wait for me,' she said.

'I couldn't.' Ina jabbed the doorbell button. 'He's not answering.' She pounded on the door. 'Bass?' she called. 'Bass, are you there?' To Pac, she said, 'What'll we do? He said he wouldn't leave. What if he's dead?'

'Do you have a key?' Pac asked.

'A key? No. Why would I? Faye's got a key, I don't. Can't we break the door down or something? He might be hurt. He might be *dying*! For God's sake, can't we break it down?'

'Let's see if there's an easier way, first. I'll try the back door.'

'Go ahead.' Ina pounded on the door again and yelled, 'Bass!'

'Why don't you come with me?'

'You go ahead.' Ina quickly opened her purse. Pac waited long enough to see her take a Visa card out of her wallet.

Seen too many movies.

'You'll ruin your card,' she warned, and started for the back of the house.

On the way, she passed three windows. None was open. The view through each was blocked by heavy curtains. She glanced to the right at the garage: he wouldn't be in there. Not unless he was tinkering with his car or cleaning fish, and then the door would be open for fresh air.

She hurried to the gate, pushed it open, and entered the back yard. She rushed up the stairs to the porch. Its screen door wasn't locked. She jerked it open and crossed the porch to the back door.

A single pane of the glass was broken. The one on the lower right. The one just above the knob.

Pac's heart started to race.

She drew her pistol and jacked a round into the chamber. The action of the slide shoved the hammer back into its cocked position.

The knob wouldn't turn. Carefully, Pac reached her left hand through the broken window and twisted the knob. The latch popped. She withdrew her hand, then eased the door open and stepped into the kitchen.

She saw no one.

So much glass was scattered on the floor that she couldn't avoid it. She went ahead and started to cross the kitchen. With each step, glass crunched under her shoes.

He's gonna hear me coming.

But maybe he's already gone.

148

Don't count on it.

As she made her way across the kitchen, she heard Ina struggling to force open the front door.

The door bell suddenly rang with a startling jangle that made Pac flinch.

Then came a harsh thud. Ina must've kicked the door.

Ina cried out, 'Bass! Are you in there? Are you okay?'

Then came the strange scraping sounds of her credit card as she tried to spring the lock.

Pac stepped into the dining room. Her eyes swept it from side to side.

Nobody here.

The carpet silenced her footfalls as she circled the large round table.

The last time they'd had dinner at this table – St Patrick's Day? – they'd gotten into the whiskey after dinner and Harney and Bass had started singing duets. 'Danny Boy' and 'My Wild Irish Rose,' and Harney had talked Pac into doing her famous rendition of 'The Wearing of the Green.' They'd tried to get Faye to join in for a round of 'When Irish Eyes Are Smiling,' but she'd refused and said, 'You guys wouldn't be singing, either, except you're all shit-faced.'

Ina pounded on the front door.

The noise was unnerving in the silent house, but Pac appreciated its value as a distraction; if an intruder was still in the house, his attention would probably be focused on Ina, not on Pac.

The credit card started scraping again.

Pac stepped into the living room.

And saw the shotgun rigged on the chairs.

Then came the metal sound of the door's lock tongue slipping back.

'*INA!*'

Chapter Twenty-five

GRANT'S DOOM

Grant Parkington, dressed in brown slacks, a white shirt and a tan corduroy jacket with elbow patches, lay sideways on the couch.

Rusty stepped closer.

Just above the back of the couch, where the man's head would have been if he'd been sitting up straight, the wall was splattered with a shiny pattern of gore. At the center of the pattern, Rusty saw a hole.

Grant's right hand was still clutching a .32 automatic. His thumb was trapped inside the trigger guard.

'Looks like he ate it,' Osgood said.

Rusty nodded. He'd seen this sort of thing before. 'That's the best way,' he said, 'if you want to make sure.'

'He left a note.' The lanky, ashen-faced deputy pointed at a sheet of paper on the coffee table.

Rusty knelt and read the note.

> When I think, fair creature of an hour
> That I shall never look upon thee more –
> Then on the shore of the wide world

I stand alone.

Forgive me, Alison.
I killed not thee
With half so good a will.
                    Your loving,
                              Grant

The body of the note was typed, but the signature was longhand.

'It's his signature,' Osgood said. 'Or a damn good forgery.'

'I doubt it was forged,' Rusty said. 'This looks about as much like a suicide as anything I've ever seen.'

Chapter Twenty-six

CLOSE CALL

'Stop!'

As the door started to open, Pac threw herself against it. Though it was only open a fraction of an inch, her sudden impact slammed it shut with a loud crash.

'Stay out!' she shouted.

She hurried around behind the chairs.

Bending over the shotgun, she pushed its safety on. Then she twisted the steel wire loose and freed the trigger.

'What's going on?' Ina called.

'Just a second.' Pac hurried to the door and untwisted the wire around the knob. Sidestepping, she swung the door open wide and watched Ina flinch to find a shotgun muzzle pointing at her bare belly.

'Holy shit!' she gasped. The bent credit card dropped from her hand, did a single flip, and clattered against the wood of the threshold.

'Come on in,' Pac said, 'but don't touch anything.'

Keeping her eyes on the shotgun as if it were a sleeping snake that might awaken and strike her, Ina knelt to pick up her credit card. Then she stepped into the house. Once out of the shotgun's line of fire, she smiled nervously at Pac. 'He's not here?'

'I doubt it.' Pac shut the door. 'Nobody seems to be downstairs, but I haven't searched the second floor yet.'

'That.' Ina pointed at the strange arrangement of chairs and shotgun. 'Was that meant for Bass?'

'Apparently.'

'My God!'

'You'd better wait here. I'll take a look upstairs.'

Nodding, Ina lowered herself onto the couch. 'Don't take long, okay?'

'I'll hurry.'

Pac went to the stairway. She took the steps slowly and silently, her .45 ready and her eyes searching. Though much of the house was still light with the early evening sun slanting through windows, the stairs were obscured by shadow. She kept her left hand low, brushing the carpet of the higher stairs, hoping to feel an unseen tripwire if the stairway, too, was booby trapped.

She reached the top of the stairs. The bathroom door stood open. So did the door of the study across from it. Looking down the hall, she saw that the doors of both bedrooms stood open. She would search each room. The bathroom first; it was the nearest.

She shoved the bathroom door. It swung and bumped the rubber stop. Entering, she glanced into the tub.

Nobody.

She turned to leave.

'*Pac!*'

She rushed to the head of the stairs and looked down at Ina. 'What's wrong?'

'Someone's coming. I heard a car.'

'Get away from the door.'

Ina dodged out of sight.

Pac dropped to her knees. She heard footsteps on the front porch. Keys jangled. She lowered herself to a prone position that gave her a full view of the front door and an easy shot at anyone who might enter.

She heard the metalic ratchet of a key pushing into a lock.

The knob turned. The door opened. Bass Paxton started to step inside, then let out a startled gasp and lurched away from the shotgun.

'Bass,' Ina said. 'It's all right. It's safe. You can come in.'

'I'm not sure that's such a good idea.'

'The shotgun's disconnected,' Pac called down to him. 'And I put its safety on.'

'Who is that?' he asked, squinting up the stairs. 'Pac?'

'Right,' she told him. She stood, holstered her pistol, and started down the stairs.

'I don't suppose this shotgun belongs to either of you?'

'Somebody left it for you,' Pac said.

He stepped quickly past the muzzle and into his house. 'I've been needing a new shotgun,' he said.

'You told me you'd be here,' Ina blurted. 'We called and you didn't answer. We were so worried, Bass. We thought . . . something might've *happened* to you.'

'Something happened, all right – I got hungry.'

'You shouldn't have gone off.'

'I'm not so sure of that.' He gave the shotgun a glance.

Pac joined them in the living room. 'What time did you leave here?' she asked.

'About five.'

'After you left, someone apparently broke in through your back door and set up this booby trap.'

'The thing would've cut me in half.'

'Wouldn't have done you any good,' Pac said. 'Assuming it's loaded.'

'You don't know if . . . ?'

'I haven't touched it except to put on the safety. Didn't want to risk ruining any evidence. But it probably *is* loaded. Somebody went to a lot of trouble to set this thing up. Do you have any ideas who might've done it?'

He rubbed the back of his neck. 'I can only think of one person – the guy we saw this morning. The guy who killed that woman.'

'It's certainly a possibility,' Pac said.

'Excuse me,' Ina muttered. Her face looked pale. 'Where's your bathroom?'

'Upstairs and to your left,' Bass told her.

She nodded with a quick jerk of her head. Her shoulders were hunched. Pac saw goosebumps on her bare arms and midriff. Her stiff nipples pushed at the fabric of her halter top. Crossing her arms, she turned away and walked quickly to the stairs.

'That shotgun,' Bass said to Pac. 'If the killer left it for me . . . it means he knows who I am. If he found me, maybe he's *already* found Faye.'

'Yeah. Maybe so.'

'Do you think he . . . killed her?'

Pac grimaced, but shook her head. 'If he only wanted to kill her, why is she gone? Why didn't he kill her at the house? Why take her clothes and luggage and car? Doesn't make

156

sense. If he's got her, he's taking her someplace.'

'But where?'

'Any ideas?' Pac asked.

'I wish.'

'Is it possible that Faye knew the killer, recognized him this morning?'

'God, I don't know. No. She would've said something. She'd have told me.'

'He must've recognized her, then. I can't imagine him actually following her from the Bend to the station, then waiting around while she gave her statement and *finally* following her to the house. It just doesn't seem likely at all. So he must've already known who she was.'

'If he found out her name,' Bass said, 'he could've gotten her address from the phone book. She's listed.'

'Yeah. Or maybe he already *knew* where to find her. So this afternoon he paid her a visit and snatched her. Took her clothes and suitcases to make it look like she'd gone away of her own volition. And maybe took her car because he needed it for transportation.'

'But why would he do all that instead of . . . you know, booby trapping *her* door like he did mine?'

'Maybe he only had one shotgun. Or he was afraid he'd get Ina by mistake.'

'He could've just waited for Faye and killed her on the spot.'

'That's right,' Pac said. 'So maybe he took her away to buy himself some time. Nobody'll be looking very hard for Faye if they think she drove off to visit her parents or take a little vacation or something. That gives the killer time.'

'For what?'

'Maybe he wanted to get some information from her. Maybe your address.'

'My God.'

'Yeah.'

'So he could come over here and blow me away.'

Pac watched Bass's eyes, and she could see by his look that he knew what she was thinking: if the killer had taken Faye alive only to make her give up Bass's address, then maybe she'd served her only purpose and he'd killed her.

Bass dropped to the couch. Wearily, he rubbed his face. 'There's still a chance she really did leave on her own.'

Pac nodded. 'Sure. She might be zipping along on the Coast Highway even as we speak. There's a pretty good chance of it, really. We've got no *real* reason to think the killer grabbed her.'

Looking very tired, Bass said, 'If I don't hear from her by nine, I'll phone her folks and see if they know anything. Maybe she'll even be there . . .'

'Is it all right if I make a couple of calls right now?' Pac asked.

'Sure, go ahead. You can use the extension in the kitchen if you want.'

'Thanks.' She went into the kitchen and phoned her own house. After two rings, Harney picked up.

'Hello?' he asked.

'Hi, honey, it's me.'

'Hey, what's up?'

'Plenty, but I can't get into it right now. I just wanted to let you know I'll be a little late.'

'Should I cancel the reservations?'

'No! I'll be back in time. I hope. I *intend* to be. Barring unforeseen calamities.'

He laughed softly. 'Okay, Pop.'

'Speaking of which, I've already reconfirmed with him about tomorrow. Anyway, I'd better get back to business. See you soon, honey.'

'Okay, take care.'

'You, too. Bye.' She hung up the phone, then placed a call to headquarters. Deputy Blaine picked up the phone. Pac requested that a car be sent over to Bass's house with the crime-scene kit and camera. 'When she rains,' Blaine said, 'she pours.'

'What do you mean by that?'

'Means things don't happen one at a time, they happen in bunches. Haven't you ever heard the expression before?'

She laughed, more out of frustration than amusement. She was tired. She wanted to get home. And here was Blaine acting like a dimwit. 'Can you have the stuff sent over?' she asked.

'It'll be a spell, I'm afraid.'

'Why's that?'

'Sheriff Hodges has it. Over at the Parkington place? I guess you know about Dr Parkington, the professor? The fellow whose wife got herself killed?'

'Know what?'

'Well, looks like he shot himself this afternoon.'

'Is he dead?'

'Dead as it gets. Like I say, when she rains, she pours.'

'Let me have Parkington's phone number.'

When Blaine finally gave it to her, she called the

Parkington condo. Osgood answered. 'This is Pac. Is the sheriff there?'

'Sure is.'

'Put him on, would you?'

A moment later, Rusty's low voice said, 'Good news travels fast.'

'Everyone's got a saying tonight.'

'What?'

'Nothing. Doesn't matter. Was it definitely suicide?'

'I'm no coroner, but I'd say there's not much room for doubt. The pistol was still in his hand, no signs of forced entry or a struggle, and he left us a message with a signature that seems to match other samples of his writing. The note claims he killed his wife.'

'Did he?' Pac asked. 'Kill her?'

'I tend to doubt it. The way things look, he was just feeling responsible. He must've felt guilty about letting her out of the house last night. Natural enough way to feel.'

'I suppose.'

'I'd say it's a pretty definite suicide, Pac.'

'Well, we just had a pretty definite attempted murder over here.'

'Where?'

'I'm at Bass Paxton's house. At four three two Malfi. Ina and I came over here to check on him. She'd phoned him from her place and he didn't answer, so we wanted to make sure he was okay. He didn't come to the door, so I looked around back and found evidence of a break in. So I entered. He wasn't here, but somebody had booby trapped his front door with a shotgun. Five minutes after I disarmed it, Bass walked in.'

'Looks like this is his lucky day.'

'I'd say so.'

'Sure is starting to look like our killer might be out to eliminate the two who saw him this morning.'

'That's how it looks to me,' Pac said. 'I'd like to take some photos and dust the place for latents.'

'Fine. We're about done over here.'

'I'll be waiting.'

'We don't want this to mess up your dinner at the Fireside,' Rusty said. 'If it looks like things are taking too long, give me a call. I'll rush over so you can take off.'

'Well, thanks.'

'No problem.'

'Bye for now,' she said. She hung up and returned to the living room.

Nearly half an hour passed before Deputy Osgood arrived with the crime-scene kit and camera. Pac took photos of the back door. Dusting its inside knob, she found a latent thumb print. Though she doubted it belonged to the man who'd broken in, she lifted it with cellophane tape, smoothed the tape across an index card, and labeled the card.

At the front door, she snapped photos of the shotgun trap. The door knob held several good prints. She lifted them. She also took partials off the backs of the dining-room chairs used to support the shotgun. The painted doorjamb had prints, too.

The shotgun was absolutely clean.

She cut it loose and opened the chamber. With Bass and Ina watching, she plucked out a bright red 12 gauge shell.

Bass turned a little pale.

Pac took the shotgun out to her car along with the tape,

wire, and the eye screw from the door frame. Then she returned to the house.

'That about takes care of it,' she said.

'I'm sure glad you dropped by when you did,' Bass told her. To Ina, he said, 'You, too.'

Ina smiled nervously. She had spent a long time in the bathroom, but seemed well recovered now.

Pac turned to Bass and said, 'It might be a good idea to go somewhere else for tonight. I wouldn't stay here if I were you. This fellow might come back for a second try.'

'You want me to go into hiding?'

'No point making it easy for him.'

'Well, I wouldn't do that. I'd make it very hard.'

'It's up to you.'

'You could come over and stay in Faye's room tonight,' Ina suggested.

'That's an idea,' he said. 'But I wouldn't want to be in your way.'

'I'm scared to death. I couldn't stay there by myself. Not after all this.'

'It's a deal, then.'

'If you hear anything about Faye,' Pac told them both, 'give me a call. You have my home phone number, Bass?'

'You kidding? I know it by heart.'

'I'll either be there or at the Fireside restaurant.'

'Ah!' he gasped as if he suddenly remembered. 'That's right! This is your big anniversary dinner. Hey, congratulations.'

'Yeah,' Ina said, seeming a bit at a loss.

'And give my regards to the big Harn, huh?'

'Oh, I will. Thanks. Now both of you be careful, okay?'

'You bet,' Bass said. 'And you two have a great dinner.'
With a nod and a wave, she left the house.

As she headed for her car, she decided to drive straight home. Time was getting short. Morning would be plenty soon enough to take the evidence in, and if anyone needed the camera or crime-scene kit before then . . . well, they knew where to find her.

In the car, she sighed deeply. She rubbed her face and yawned. Though she'd been keeping track of the time, she looked at the dashboard clock anyway. Almost 6:15.

It'll be a rush, but we'll make it.

More than twelve hours on duty, she thought. *No wonder I'm wasted.*

It had been a long time since she'd put in a day like this. But then, they sure didn't have a homicide every day.

Well, she'd probably saved Bass's life. That made the extra effort worthwhile.

If only I could've saved Faye.

Hey, cut it out. Don't bury her yet.

Faye might still be alive, she told herself. She might be on the way to Burlingame, for instance.

But Pac doubted it.

Ina obviously doubted it, too. Ina, ready and willing to accommodate Bass. She'd probably been waiting for a chance like this for a long time.

Who could blame her, though? If it weren't for Harney, Pac might've been tempted to go after Bass, herself.

No. The guy's damn good-looking – hell, gorgeous – but somehow, he just didn't appeal much to Pac. He made a fine friend, but she couldn't picture him as a lover.

Too possessive, she thought. *He'd try to run my life.*

If Faye wants to subject herself to that sort of thing, good for her. But not me. I just want a nice, laid-back guy like Harney.

Wanta get laid by a nice, laid-back guy . . .

She laughed at herself, opened her eyes and wondered how long she'd been sitting there. Starting the car, she pulled away from the curb and headed for home.

Chapter Twenty-seven

THE WATCHER

Merton, sitting in Walter's car near the corner of Malfi and Granger Street, watched the car of the female deputy drive away. That left two of them in the house: Bass Paxton and the skinny brunette.

The brunette obviously wasn't the woman who'd seen him at the Bend. That one was blonde and had a much better figure.

He wondered where the hell *she* could be.

The brunette came out, climbed into her car and backed out of the driveway.

That left Bass alone in the house.

He could take Bass.

He could walk up to the door and ring the bell. Bass would open up. There would be a quick struggle, Bass under him warm and hard-muscled for a couple of minutes, then dead.

The images of it brought a smile to Merton's face.

Then the garage door swung up and Bass stepped out carrying an overnight bag. As the door lowered, he walked down the driveway and went to the rear of an old red Pontiac parked on the street.

Merton figured he was about to stow his bag in the trunk. But then Bass shook his head slightly, stepped around the side of his car and tossed his bag into the back seat.

Merton started his engine.

When the Pontiac pulled away from the curb, he followed it.

Chapter Twenty-eight

VICTORY

Ina arrived back at her house ahead of Bass. She parked in the driveway, leaped from her car and ran up to the front door. Remembering the shotgun trap, she stood aside as she unlocked the door and pushed it open.

Nothing happened.

She peeked around the door frame.

No trap. Nothing looked unusual.

So she entered, shut the door and hurried into the bathroom. After locking the door, she studied herself in the mirror. Her hair needed work. She brushed it. Her eyes and lips looked fine.

Stepping back, she turned to each side. She looked good in the halter top. It was loose on her, clinging slightly and showing a lot. The cut-off jeans were even better with the denim legs scissored away at the crotch, the sides slit almost to the waistband.

She watched one of her hands slide up the front of her thigh, lift the hanging denim and slip under it. Closing her eyes, she imagined that the hand was Bass's.

The doorbell rang. Her hand jerked away and she rushed to the door.

'Who's there?' she called.

'It's me.'

Recognizing Bass's voice, she opened the door.

And saw no one.

'Is it safe?' asked a voice from the side.

Before Ina could answer, Bass stepped away from the front wall. He glanced past her into the foyer. 'No booby traps?' he asked, grinning.

'I don't think so.'

He hurried through the doorway, brushing against her as he went by.

She shut the door and fastened its guard chain. 'Aren't you scared?'

'Not much.'

'You were almost killed.'

'Almost, but *not*. A world of difference there.'

'I'd be scared to death. In fact, I am scared to death and nobody's even *after* me.'

'Nobody that you know of.'

She laughed. 'Oh, thanks a heap.'

'Don't worry, I'm here. I'll protect you from any and all harm.'

'Thanks. Can I get you a drink?'

'I could go for that.'

'Whiskey on the rocks, right?'

'Exactly.' Bass smiled. He sat on the couch and watched her.

'I'll be right back,' Ina said. Walking to the kitchen, she could feel his eyes on her. She could feel them as if they were hands caressing the bare curves of her back, sneaking up her cut-offs, delving. The wall of the kitchen blocked the contact, making her feel suddenly abandoned. But the excitement remained.

Her hands trembled as she took two glasses down from a cupboard. She dumped a handful of ice cubes into each. Crouching, she felt the inseam of her cut-offs press into her. She moaned a little. Then she reached into a low cupboard and pulled out a bottle of Glenlivet.

On her way to the counter, she twisted off the bottle cap. The heavy fumes filled her nose as she poured. They smelled rich and sweet and woodsy. After capping the bottle, she picked up both glasses.

She carried them into the living room. The television was on. Bass looked away from it as she approached him. He grinned. 'I should go into hiding more often,' he said.

Ina, bending to hand him the drink, saw his eyes move down to her halter top. He was looking in. She waited, even after he had the glass, letting him take a good long look at her breasts before sitting down on the couch beside him.

Bass lifted his glass toward her. 'To you, Ina. For saving my neck.'

'Pac's the one.'

'To both of you.'

They clinked glasses and drank.

'Feels sort of strange,' Ina said, 'you being here without Faye.'

'Does it?'

'Sure. Don't you feel . . . a little odd about it?'

'Not very. I like it.'

'Me, too,' Ina said.

'Remember last time?' he asked.

'Sure I do.'

'Her *last* disappearing act. I think I would've gone nuts if it hadn't been for you.'

'Thanks.'

'You made it . . . bearable.'

'I was glad to help. I thought she was horrible . . . to do a thing like that. To you.'

'You were wonderful,' Bass said. 'I think about it all the time. How sweet and understanding you were.'

'Well . . .'

'The thing is, I'm through with Faye.'

Ina gazed into his eyes. Her heart pounded hard. 'Are you?' she whispered.

'Even if this . . . all this today . . . hadn't happened. It isn't about today. It's about everything.' Bass set down his drink. 'It's about you, Ina. You and me. It's about everything I've been feeling about you . . . Not just because of the day we were waiting for her. Even before that. I've always felt . . . very strongly about you. I've always wanted you.'

Reaching out with one hand, he stroked the side of her face. She pressed his hand. As she leaned forward to put her drink on the table, he caressed her back. She turned to him and they kissed. It was the way she had hoped it would be, gentle at first, then wet and open and crushing.

Too soon, his mouth went away. 'You won't feel bad about it later, will you?' he asked.

'Why would I?'

'Some kind of loyalty to Faye.'

She wondered briefly if this might be a trick, a test. She studied his eyes, but they held nothing. 'I don't want to come between you two,' she said. 'But if it's over anyway . . .'

'It is. One way or another, Faye and I are finished.

Either she's not coming back . . .'

'Oh, don't say that.'

'I don't *care* if she comes back. She's run out on me once too often.'

'Oh, Bass.'

'You're not like that,' he murmured.

'No, I'm not. I'm sure not. I'd be true to you forever.'

'I know, I know.' He reached out to her.

'We'd be more comfortable in my room,' she whispered.

'More exciting here,' he said.

Ina leaned back on the couch and watched his hand move up her leg. So much like before, in the mirror, but now it was real. Now it was *his* hand warm and strong on her leg.

His hand under her cut-offs.

His fingers slipping into her.

Soon, she was naked under him and it was his penis inside her, big and hard, filling her, thrusting.

Chapter Twenty-nine

DORIS'S TALE

From a coin-operated newspaper display case in front of Patty's Cafe, Rusty bought a copy of the *Evening News*. He glanced at it as he entered the cafe.

The Parkington murder didn't make the headline – an earthquake in China held that spot – but it made the front page. The bold print read, WIFE OF PROFESSOR SLAIN.

Rusty scooted across the red vinyl cushion of a booth and started to read the news story:

> The naked body of Alison Parkington, wife of Sierra College visiting lecturer Grant Parkington, was found early this morning at a beach area of the Silver River known as the Bend.
>
> According to a source close to the Sheriff's Department, the victim's head, arms and legs had been severed from her torso . . .

'Crap,' Rusty muttered. Where the hell do they get this crap? *What* source did they have for such garbage?

He folded the *News* and slapped it down on the table.

A paper mat, napkin and silverware were placed in front of him. Rusty looked up at the waitress, embarrassed to be caught with his anger showing.

He didn't know her.

She set a glass of ice water at the corner of the mat. 'Are you ready to order?' she asked.

'Sure am. I'll have a patty melt and coffee.' Hardly the brats and beer that he'd hoped for. But after the call about the shooting, he'd told Millie to go ahead and eat without him.

'With or without onions?' The waitress laughed softly. 'The patty melt, not the coffee.'

Rusty smiled. 'With.'

She nodded, writing it down. She was young, maybe just out of high school. Soft blonde bangs draped her forehead. She had the sort of face that probably kept the boys awake half the night with dreams of kissing her. And her figure . . . Rusty tried not to stare, but it wasn't easy. The yellow blouse of her waitress uniform was too tight, the skirt too short.

He looked at her hands as she slipped the note pad into a pocket at the front of her skirt.

On her left hand, she wore a class ring with a blue stone.

When she walked away, he watched her buttocks and the high backs of her thighs. But he quickly lifted his gaze to her head. Her ponytail swished and bounced.

Where'd *she* come from? he wondered.

Wherever – they oughta patent it.

When she brought the coffee, Rusty saw the front of her hand. White tape was wound around the band of the class ring to help it fit. He smiled. Millie had done the same thing to the class ring he'd given her, so it wouldn't fall off.

The girl started to walk away, then turned around and looked at Rusty with a frown. She came back to his booth. 'That's really something about Professor Parkington's wife, isn't it?'

'It's something,' he agreed.

'Do you mind if I talk to you?'

'Sure.'

'I mean, you're the sheriff, right?'

'That's right. Sheriff Rusty Hodges. And you're Doris?'

'Right!' She seemed surprised that he knew her name. Then she glanced down at the red plastic name tag above her left breast. She gasped, 'Ah!' and slapped the tag, making her breast give a small hop. 'That's how you knew! You had me going there for a second. I forget I'm wearing the darn thing. This is just my first day, you know.'

'I figured you were pretty new.'

'You're a regular, aren't you?'

'I get in here now and again.'

'Do you mind if I sit down?'

'Not at all.'

She slid into the booth across the table from him. 'I don't want to interrupt your dinner or anything,' she said, sounding uncertain of herself.

'It isn't here yet.'

'It won't be ready for a while,' she said. 'Five or ten minutes, maybe. I'll bring it when it's ready.' She eyed his glass of ice water. 'Do you mind if I have a sip of that?'

'Help yourself, Doris.'

'Thanks.' She lifted the glass to her mouth. When she set it down, half the water was missing and a pink lipstick print had been added just below the rim. 'I'll bring you another with your meal, okay?'

'Fine,' Rusty said.

'Anyhow, here's the thing.' She leaned forward until the edge of the table stopped her. Gazing into Rusty's eyes, she said, 'I have Professor Parkington.'

'You *have* him? What do you mean?'

'Romantic Lit. It's a morning class. You know, just a summer session thing.'

'How is he?'

'Romantic.' She smiled, turned red, and lowered her eyes. 'Not in the sense of Romantic literature. That's something different, you know. That's like praising poverty, the simple life, nature and all that. You know. But he wasn't romantic that way, he was romantic *horny*. That's why I think he killed his wife.'

'You think *he* killed her?'

'Oh, sure.' She drank the rest of the water. 'Him and maybe his girlfriend. I think maybe they collaborated on it.'

'Why?'

'Why'd he kill her? He was screwing around, that's the thing. So maybe she was causing him some kind of grief about it. Maybe she found out about his girlfriend and made some kind of threat. You know. Like she might blow the whistle on him. Something like that.'

'What do you mean, blow the whistle?'

'You know. *Tell* on him. Snitch. Like to the college administration, for instance.'

'Would that present a problem for him?'

'It might. I mean, it's probably against the rules to mess around with your students. To, you know, screw them?'

'Was he doing that?'

'You bet he was.'

'Are you sure?'

'Sure, I'm sure. Are you kidding?'

'Was he that obvious about it?'

'He was pretty obvious if you were one of the girls he liked.'

'Did he like you?'

'What do you think?'

Rusty blushed. 'I'm sure he must've. How could he not?'

She grinned. 'You got it right, there. I must've been his first. I mean, he's a real operator. It was only like the second day of class and he asks me if I'll stay after the bell. So the bell rings and I stay in my seat till everyone's gone. Then he starts coming on to me like he thinks he's God's gift to everything with a . . .' Frowning, she shook her head. 'Anyhow, I let him know I wasn't interested, you know? Not that there's anything much wrong with the guy except for the fact that he happens to be married – *was* married. But I'm already sort of going with someone else, you know?'

'I noticed the ring.'

'Yeah? You like it?'

'It's very nice.'

'The fit's not too great, but who cares? I don't. Robby and I aren't exactly engaged. Not yet. But I'm not in the market for a guy, and if I *was*, I wouldn't go around messing with someone who's *married*.'

'That's a very good policy.'

'Don't I know it? But a lot of girls do, you know. I've got *tons* of friends who go around with married guys. Which is totally stupid, if you ask me.' She narrowed her eyes.

'There's no future in it. Only heartache.'

'And sometimes murder,' Rusty said.

'That's *exactly* what I mean. Hey, hang on a second, I'll go see if your food's ready.' She scooted out of the booth and walked toward the counter.

Rusty watched her go.

No harm in looking. She's not into married guys.

Or old guys, probably.

Good thing.

When she returned, she had a plate in one hand and a glass of water in the other. She put them down in front of Rusty. 'Let me warm up your coffee,' she said, and hurried off again. She came back with a coffee pot, poured, took it away and returned with another glass of ice water. Scooting into the booth, she said, 'I got Lucy to take my tables just in case.'

'Good idea.'

'So anyhow, where was I?'

'Staying after class with Parkington.'

'Oh. Right. So that was that. I told him no dice, you know? But I was nice about it. I don't believe in being nasty, especially about that kind of stuff.' She grinned. 'Besides which, I've gotta see this guy in class every day. He's still my teacher, so I don't want him any more . . . ticked off at me than is like absolutely necessary. So I tried to let him down gently. And you know what?' She raised her eyebrows and waited.

'What?' Rusty asked.

'The very next day, he starts in on *other* girls in the class. You could always tell who he had his eyes on just by the way he acted. You know, the tone of his voice, the way he'd stare at them, that sort of stuff.'

Rusty bit into the grilled rye of his patty melt, but his attention was so focused on Doris that he was hardly aware of eating.

'After me, he went after this tacky brunette – Hester something. She was a real snorter, though, if you know what I mean.'

'Not especially attractive?'

'Yeah, and then some. Anyhow, I think he went after her just because he knew she'd put out. Girls like that always do, you know. That's because they're so desperate. A guy just has to give them a second look, and they'll drop . . . they'll give in. So I'm *sure* he made it with Hester. But as soon as he got her, he didn't want her any more. That's the way guys like him operate, at least when they go after someone like her. Anyhow, he started picking on her in class, calling on her with impossible questions, really giving her a tough time. She broke down crying one day and ran out of the room and never came back. I guess she dropped the class.'

'Professor Parkington doesn't sound like a very nice fellow,' Rusty said.

'Oh, he can be very sweet when he wants to be. You know. But he can be really cold and cutting when he feels like it, too. A real . . . jerk. I think he's insecure. Insecure people always get a thrill out of putting other people down and hurting them and stuff.'

'I've noticed that, too,' Rusty said.

'Yeah. Well anyhow, after he dumped Hester, Dr Parkington finally made a play for this really hot blonde. I mean, this gal was drop-dead gorgeous. She'd been in class from the start, so God knows why he went after me first instead of her. Maybe she was *too* gorgeous, you know? Maybe that's how come he waited. Maybe he felt like he had to work his way *up* to her, or something. Who knows? Maybe he was waiting for a signal from her. But when he finally did make his play, she came across. As far as I know, they're still at it. What I think is, maybe she helped him kill his wife.'

'Who is this gorgeous blonde?'

Doris grinned. 'Her name's right there.' She nodded toward the newspaper on the table beside Rusty's plate. 'She's the one who found Mrs Parkington's body down by the river this morning. Faye Everett.'

'*Faye?*'

Doris grinned.

'*Faye Everett* was having an affair with Grant Parkington?'

'You better believe it.'

He tried to believe it.

It wasn't easy.

Faye? Bass's fiancee, Faye? Harney and Pac's friend, Faye? Faye, who'd gone to the Bend this morning to start a canoe trip with Bass and happened to find the headless corpse of a woman who happened to be the wife of her secret lover?

Faye, who vanished this afternoon?

What the hell?

Rusty felt astonished and disoriented. He rubbed his face. Then he took a drink of coffee. Then he asked Doris, 'Are you sure? Do you know it for a fact that Faye was having an affair with Parkington, or are you just assuming . . . ?'

'Oh, it's not an assumption. I just sort of assumed things

about him and Hester, but I *know* what he was up to with Faye.'

'How?'

'About a week ago, I needed to see Dr Parkington about an assignment. I wanted to do this paper about how Coleridge got interrupted when he was writing "Kubla Khan." I wanted to find out where I could get my hands on certain source material . . .' She laughed and shook her head. 'Which is all besides the point, right? I mean, Coleridge smoleridge. The deal is, that's how come I needed to see Parkington. Anyhow, it was pretty late in the afternoon, but he was scheduled to have office hours so I went up to drop in on him. Well, his door's shut, so I knock on it. Right? But nobody answers. I figure maybe he's out for a little break or something, so I'll just hang around and wait for him to come back. So I park myself on a chair right outside his office. It's really quiet in there. I mean, the whole building is as quiet as a tomb. And kind of spooky. I keep sitting there, but I'm starting to get the creeps. Finally, I've had enough, so I'm just about to leave when all of a sudden his office door swings open. It scared the *life* out of me. But then I see it's only Faye. She just gives me this snotty smile and keeps walking.'

'Parkington was in his office?'

'He was in there, all right. I waited a couple of minutes after Faye left, then I knocked and he said, "Come in." So I went in, and he was all red and huffy like he'd just finished running a marathon or something.'

'And you think they'd had sex in his office?'

'I'd bet a million dollars on it.'

'That's a lot of money.'

'I'd win. See, the good professor hadn't done a very good

job of cleaning up. I don't think he even *tried*. I mean, the carpet in front of his desk . . . Well, you know.'

Chapter Thirty

SWEETHEARTS

When they finished, they lay side by side on the couch. Ina's fingers smoothed the hair above Bass's ear.

'If I'd known it would be like this,' Bass said, 'I wouldn't have waited so long.'

'Serves you right.' Lightly, she brushed her lips against his mouth.

'I guess I'm just slow sometimes.'

'You wouldn't even be here now,' Ina said, 'if that guy hadn't booby trapped your house.'

'We need to send him a thank you.'

'Even with Faye missing, you didn't have the least intention of seeing me, did you?'

'Well . . .'

'You would have stayed in that house, all alone, just waiting to hear from her. After everything she's done to you.'

'All of which you were good enough to tell me about.'

'Faye had no right to hurt you that way. She was *cheating* on you, honey.'

'We weren't married. She had the right.'

'She shouldn't have done it.'

'I guess they've both paid, haven't they?'

Ina's skin grew prickly with goosebumps. She pressed herself tightly against Bass, then felt the comfort of his arms wrapping around her back. 'You should've told me sooner who the body was.'

'Does it matter?'

'Of course it does.'

'Why?' he asked.

'I don't know, because. It makes it all so *close*.'

'You don't think *I* killed Parkington's wife, do you?'

Ina shook her head. She felt one of his hands move slowly down her back. 'You wouldn't have much reason,' she said. 'You might kill what's-his-name. Him.'

'Grant?'

'Right. Grant. And I wouldn't blame you for it if you did. But you wouldn't have any reason to kill his wife, would you?'

'I shouldn't think so.'

'*She's* not the one who slept with Faye.'

'Not that we know of,' Bass said, and smiled.

'You're terrible.' Braced on her elbow, Ina rubbed Bass's chest. She watched her hand. Her skin was darker than his. She wished vaguely that he wasn't so hairy, and imagined the mess his dark curls would make in the bathtub.

'Do you think it was a coincidence?' he asked. 'Me and Faye finding that body?'

Ina shook her head.

'Then what's the connection?'

'Do you want me to guess?'

'Give it your best shot,' Bass urged her.

'Do you know?'

'How should *I* know?'

'I don't know,' Ina said.

'So, what do you think?'

She slid her hand down his belly. 'Welllll.' Lightly, she fingered his penis. It stirred and began to grow. 'Maybe either Grant or Faye decided to kill Mrs Parkington. Or maybe they . . . did away with her together.'

'Possible,' Bass said. He sighed with pleasure as she stroked him.

'I guess they could've even hired someone else to do it,' Ina suggested, watching him rise and thicken in her hand.

'Hired a killer?'

'Right. The man you saw this morning. And they needed to have you there as a witness so you could testify that he wasn't Grant.'

'I guess it's possible,' he said.

''Cause, you know, the husband's *always* the first guy they suspect.'

'Yeah.'

Ina climbed onto Bass and eased herself down, moaning as he slid into her.

They were finished and sweaty and trying to catch their breath when the doorbell rang.

'Oh, shit,' Bass said.

'I'd better see who it is,' Ina whispered.

They both sat up. As Ina pulled her cut-offs up her legs, Bass started picking up his clothes.

The bell rang again.

Bass hurried for the hallway.

Ina, standing, buttoned and raised the zipper of her shorts.

She lifted her halter top off the couch.

The bell rang again.

'Just a minute,' she called. She put on her halter as she walked to the door. 'Who is it?'

'Sheriff Hodges.'

Though Ina had seen him on the news and she knew he was Pac's father-in-law, she had never met him. She took off the guard chain. Turning the knob, she realized with a sudden jolt of fear that he might be bringing news of Faye. She jerked the door open.

The man on the front step didn't look at all like Sheriff Hodges. He was lean and bald – not a husky redhead.

He held something against his leg.

A tire tool.

'You aren't . . .'

His arm swung the black steel rod.

Chapter Thirty-one

THE VISITOR

Merton wished he'd aimed higher. Instead of smashing her temple, the tire tool caught her across the cheek and ear. But the effect pleased him; her legs folded.

She dropped to the floor.

He shut the door, locked it and stepped into the living room.

Nobody there.

Two glasses remained on the coffee table, though. Not much had been drunk from either one, but the ice cubes were melted to nothing.

The ice had probably done all that melting while he'd been sitting outside listening to his car radio, smoking and waiting.

Waiting for what? For the other woman, the blonde, to show up? For Bass to leave and drive over to the blonde's place so he could follow. Maybe for the blonde to drive up, herself, and knock on the door. But you can only wait so long. The time it takes for a few ice cubes to melt in booze.

Besides, the radio news had finally given him the blonde's name, so finding her address shouldn't be any great trick.

He could do that after finishing Bass.

He looked in the kitchen.

Nobody.

The hallway was too dark. He turned on a light and started walking quietly. He opened a door. A closet. The door made a soft bump when he shut it.

'Ina?' asked a voice.

Just ahead of Merton, a door opened and Bass Paxton looked out. Merton lunged. The door crashed shut, slamming like gunfire a moment before his tire tool struck, burying its head in the wood.

Merton grabbed the knob and twisted. Locked. He backed off and threw himself against the door, his shoulder driving against it.

The door didn't give. Instead, it threw him backward. Raging, he squared his back against the wall across from it, raised his right leg and shot his foot forward. His heel crashed against the wood beside the knob. The door exploded open, throwing splinters, slamming the wall behind it.

The bathroom was empty. Above the tub, the dusky evening sky looked cool and empty through the open window.

Chapter Thirty-two

ANNIVERSARY DINNER

'A cocktail before dinner?' The waiter, a slim man with slicked-down black hair, bent forward to listen.

'Two margaritas on the rocks,' Harney told him. 'Better make them doubles.'

The waiter snapped his head toward Pac. 'And for the lady?' His friendly smile made her forget his hair trouble.

'That's one margarita for each of us,' she said.

'With or without salt?'

'With,' said Pac.

'Without,' said Harney.

'Excellent.' The waiter jotted down the order. 'I'll be right back with your drinks,' he said, then left.

'That's the guy who waited on us last time,' Harney said.

'You're right.'

'He's very good.'

'I like him.'

'Remember Faye kept calling him *hombre*?'

'Yeah.' Pac couldn't keep the worry out of her voice.

'Are you sure you want to be here?'

'It's all right.'

'Are you sure?'

'It's fine. A lot better than sitting at home waiting.'

'We could put this off for another night.'

'Another night isn't our anniversary. I'm fine with staying. Really. Anyway, it's not like she's dead or something.'

The waiter arrived with the margaritas on a tray. He set them on the table in front of Pac and Harney. 'Would you care to order now, or would you like a few minutes?'

'We're not quite ready,' Harney told him.

'Very good.' He left.

They lifted their glasses and Harney toasted, 'To my favorite wife.'

'To my favorite husband,' she said, grinning.

They clicked their glasses together. A few chunks of wet, grainy salt fell off Pac's rim into Harney's glass. Other crumbs sprinkled the back of her hand.

The margarita tasted fine to Pac.

As she took a few sips, Harney said, 'And to your most spectacular dress.'

She grinned.

'And to the body inside that gives it the spectacle.'

She laughed.

She had bought the dress especially for tonight – as a treat for Harney.

Back at the house, when she'd stepped out of the bedroom wearing it, Harney's eyes had gotten wide and his jaw had dropped. 'Whoa,' he'd said.

'Like it?'

Smiling stupidly, shaking his head and blinking, he'd said,

'That's a *great* slip. Where's the dress?'

'This *is* the dress, genius.'

'Whoa.'

'Should I change into something else?'

'No!' He'd started coming toward her.

She'd held up a hand. 'Freeze, buster. You can look, but you can't touch. Not till later. That has to wait for after dinner.'

'Oh, you're cruel.'

'Oh, yes.'

She'd slowly turned around for him. The backless blue gown, held up in front by a cord that tied behind her neck, flowed against her skin like warm water. She'd already seen, in the mirror, how it clung to every curve and how it left her sides bare all the way down to her hips. Viewed from either side, if she moved an arm out of the way, a slope of breast could be seen rising from her ribcage. The skirt was long enough to hang below her knees and loose enough to sway lightly, drifting against her body, caressing her.

In Harney's eyes, she'd seen stunned delight. 'Happy anniversary, honey.'

'Yeah. Good God.' Shaking his head, he'd asked, 'What are you wearing under that?'

'Just me.'

He'd moaned. He'd swallowed. 'That's what I thought.' Laughing softly, he'd asked, 'So, where's your gun?'

'Wouldn't *you* like to know?'

'I can *see* you're not wearing it anywhere. You're not, are you?'

'That's for me to know.'

'And for me to find out?'

'Like I said, no touching allowed.'

'Would you like to lift your skirt?'

'No, I would not, you lech.'

Now, as Pac sipped her margarita, Harney set down his glass. He stared into her eyes. 'There's something I need to talk to you about,' he said.

The words pounded fear into her. They shriveled her insides, sucked her breath out, made her heart pound painfully hard and quick.

'What?'

'Don't take this the wrong way, okay?'

Oh, my God! I don't want to hear this.

'What?' she asked again, feeling weak and sick.

'It's in your purse.'

'Huh?'

A wide, mischievous smile split Harney's face. 'Your gun. It's in your purse.'

She gaped at him.

'I've had plenty of chances to look you over. Especially getting into and out of the car. I can now say with complete certainty that you're wearing the gun nowhere on your body. Since you're required to carry it, I can only conclude that it's concealed in your purse.'

'You . . . !'

He laughed.

'You scared the hell out of me.'

'I know. I'm terrible.'

'You'll get yours, buster.'

'I'm counting on it.'

'Or maybe you won't.'

'Aw, come on. I was just trying to cheer you up, take

your mind off the *other* situation for a while.'

'Well, you succeeded. I thought you were about to dump me or confess to an affair or something.'

'Never.'

'Never say never.'

'Never.'

The way he said it, Pac suddenly felt her throat tighten and tears rush to her eyes. She reached across the table. He took hold of her hand and squeezed it gently.

'I love you so much,' she whispered.

'How could you not?'

She laughed. 'Jerk.' She tried to pull her hand away, but he wouldn't let go.

'I love you, too,' he said.

They stared into each other's eyes. Since Harney still clutched her right hand, she used her left to wipe away her tears. 'I wish we were home right now,' she said.

'Want to leave?'

She thought about it for a few moments, then said, 'We'd better not. I mean . . . we'd better go ahead and order dinner. We reserved the table and everything. Besides, we've got to eat.'

'I suppose so.'

'The restraint will be good for our souls.'

'Ah, very true.'

Pac slipped her hand out of his, took another drink of margarita, then picked up one of the menus. She read the list of *à la carte* items, then the lists of dinners. It came down to a choice between a *carne asada* plate and a *tostado de chorizo*. She pictured each in her mind, and thought about how they would taste.

Harney, sipping his margarita, hadn't picked up the other menu.

'Aren't you going to look at the menu?'

'I already know what I want to eat,' he said, and wiggled his eyebrows.

Pac scowled at him, but his words had triggered a surge of heat. 'Let's not be crude, darling.'

His eyebrows flew up. 'Huh? Crude? I was speaking of enchiladas.'

'Sure.'

'I *always* have enchiladas, you know that. What are you going to have?'

'I feel like having some pork,' she said.

'Oh! *Now* who's being crude?'

'Or maybe some tongue.'

'Jeez, Pac.'

She lowered her eyes to the menu. 'There it is right there, *taco de lingua*. That's tongue taco, isn't it?'

'I dare you to order it.'

'Double dare me?' Pac asked.

'Think you're married to an idiot? I know darn well that double-dares go first.'

'*Cobarde*.'

'I'm having the cheese enchilada dinner.'

'You *always* order that. Why don't you live a little dangerously for a change?'

'I like enchiladas. If I like something, what's wrong with sticking to it?'

'You get in a rut,' Pac said.

'Let's not talk about ruts,' Harney said.

'There you go, getting crude again.'

'Me crude?' Leaning forward, he whispered, 'You're the one sitting there without any panties on.'

She frowned down at her menu. 'I think maybe I *will* have the tongue.'

Harney squirmed, glanced around to make sure nobody was paying attention, then dropped his fork on the floor.

'Oh, no you don't,' Pac said.

Harney ducked underneath the table.

Pac took a quick look around. The booth enclosed them on three sides, and nobody at any of the nearby tables was in a position to watch.

She slid her skirt up above her knees, swung her legs wide apart and slowly brought them back together.

A few seconds later, Harney sat up. He looked a little flushed.

'Is everything okay?' Pac asked.

He swallowed, nodded, gave her a shaky smile, and held up his fork. 'Found it.'

'Find anything else of interest down there?'

'Oh, man,' he said. 'Yeah.'

'And what might that've been?'

Grinning, he raised his other hand and showed her a shiny coin. 'Found me a penny.'

As they both laughed, the waiter returned. Pac asked for the *carne asada* plate, and Harney ordered the cheese enchilada dinner.

'Would you care for more margaritas?' the waiter asked.

Harney met Pac's eyes. She gave him a nod. 'Sure,' he said. 'Why not?'

He waited for the waiter to leave, then said, 'I thought

you wanted the tongue taco, darling.'

'Maybe later,' she said. 'If I still have room for it.'

Chapter Thirty-three

THE BAG MAN

When he heard the distant truck, the man stood up. He brushed pine needles off his jeans. As he hurried down the wooded slope, the weighted bottom of the plastic garbage bag bumped against the side of his knee.

He stopped at the edge of the four-lane highway. Only darkness in both directions.

The truck's diesel engine grew louder, but he knew there was plenty of time. With the steep grade of that approach, the truck would be powering upward at a crawl until it reached the crest a hundred yards to his left. Then it would start gaining speed. He would be able to see the light of its headbeams, but the truck itself wouldn't appear until it rounded the curve about fifty feet away.

By then, it wouldn't stand a chance of stopping in time.

Or swerving quickly enough.

If it came down in the slow lane – and they nearly always did – it wouldn't be likely to miss. Not likely at all.

He stepped out into the lane, lowered the plastic bag onto the pavement, and reached inside.

Chapter Thirty-four

ON THE ROAD

Judy Billings didn't like driving at night, especially on these dark mountain roads. 'Why can't they put up streetlights?' she asked.

'Out here?' Larry sounded as if he questioned her sanity. 'This is the *boonies*. Boonies haven't got streetlights.'

'I don't see why not.'

'Would you like me to take over the driving?'

'Oh, you'd like that.'

'I'm hell on wheels.'

'You'd kill us both.'

'Me? Not I. I'm hell on wheels.'

'You're smashed.'

'Me? Not I.'

'Oh yes you are. You must've drunk at least ten beers.'

'Me?'

'If not more.'

'Me?'

'You're drunk as a skunk.'

'Stinking drunk?' he asked, and laughed.

'If you hadn't been such a hog . . .'

'Not a hog, a skunk. You said skunk. Can't you make up your mind?'

'If you hadn't made such a *hog* out of yourself, they wouldn't have run out of beer and Dad wouldn't have sent us out here in the middle of the night . . .'

'He needs ice cubes, too,' Larry pointed out. 'I did not hog ice cubes. Or skunk them, either. Not I. I am entirely innocent in the matter of the missing ice cubes.'

'Where is this liquor store supposed to be?' Judy asked.

'Just a couple of miles.'

'It'd better be open.'

'It's always open.'

'I'll bet.'

'Never fear, we'll buy the beer.'

'Cute.'

'Thank you. I'm a poet and my feet show it.'

'They're Tennysons.'

That broke up Larry, and he laughed so hard that he fell sideways against Judy. She shoved him away with her elbow. 'Cut it out! You'll get us killed.' As if to prove her point, she found herself suddenly barreling down on the rear of an eighteen-wheeler.

Her foot jumped to the brake pedal. 'Shit!'

'Go around it,' Larry said.

Chugging up the hill, the truck moved so slowly that it almost seemed motionless.

'Go around it!' Larry repeated, this time urgently as they rushed toward its tail.

Judy swerved into the fast lane just in time to miss the left rear corner of the truck.

'Jesus H. Christ on a rubber crutch!' Larry cried out, his

voice filled with fright and relief. 'You damn near got us killed!'

'Not I,' Judy said, and smiled nervously. 'I'm hell on wheels.'

With the truck behind her, she swung in front of it. For a moment, its headbeams filled her rear-view mirror, their brightness hurting her eyes. Then the glare disappeared. She was over the crest of the hill.

'Congratulate me?' she asked.

'For what, almost getting us killed? Holy jumping Jesus, this'll teach me to ride with a goddamn . . . *What's that?*'

Judy shook her head. She didn't know what it was: a rock, maybe, or some sort of ball. But she knew she didn't want to run over it.

Suddenly, Larry cried out as if frightened awake by a nightmare.

In the headlights, Judy saw that the thing on the road had blonde hair. Its wide eyes looked up into hers.

She screamed and jerked the steering wheel.

Larry reached over, grabbed the wheel, and wrenched it from her hands.

'*No!*' she yelled.

The head looked about to scream as the car bore down on it.

Judy waited, horrified, for the bump.

It didn't come.

Her eyes lifted to the rear-view mirror. In the brief red sweep of her brake lights, she saw the head untouched on the pavement.

'We missed it!' she blurted.

'Passed right over it.'

'Should we stop?'
'Are you kidding? Anyway, the truck's gonna nail it.'
'Oh my God.' Judy stepped on the gas.

When he saw the hair-draped face looking up at the headbeams of his tractor-trailer rig, Charlie Farrow muttered, 'Oh shit oh shit oh shit oh shit' until he felt a subtle change in the smoothness of the pavement and knew that his right front tires had mashed the head.

Chapter Thirty-five

AFTER DINNER

'Could you use some dessert?' Harney asked.

Pac groaned. 'Don't mention food. Please.'

'How about some coffee?'

She smiled. 'That's another story.'

'Here or somewhere else?'

'Here would be fine. What time is it?'

Harney glanced at his wristwatch. 'Almost nine-thirty.'

Pac suddenly felt a little sick. 'Excuse me, okay? I'd better go and call about Faye. You can go ahead and order the coffees, okay?'

'Sure.'

Pac scooted out of the booth. She straightened her dress as she stood up, then walked toward the back of the restaurant.

The public telephone was located in an alcove near the restrooms. She slipped the directory off its shelf under the phone and looked up Jones. There were two listings for Jones, I., and neither listing included the street address.

Though Pac had phoned Faye several times in the past, she'd never bothered to memorize the number.

She considered calling directory assistance.

Only two numbers. I've got a fifty-fifty chance of getting it right on the first try.

So she dropped in a quarter and dialed the first Jones, I. After a couple of rings, a man said, 'Hello?'

'Bass?'

'What?'

'Is this Bass?'

'Nope, it's Trout.'

'Is this the home of Ina Jones?' Pac asked.

'Nope, Irene.'

'I must have called the wrong number. Sorry about that.'

'We all make mistakes, honey pot.'

Very nice.

'Goodnight,' Pac said, and hung up.

She tried the second Jones, I. This time, the phone rang eleven times but nobody answered it. She hung up, collected her coin, then searched the directory until she found the number for Paxton, Bass.

Nobody answered there, either.

'This can't be good,' she muttered.

On her way back to the table, she saw Harney watching her. She tried to smile for him. From the look on his face, however, he could tell that she was upset.

She scooted into the booth.

'What's wrong?' he asked.

'I couldn't get Ina. Or Bass. Nobody's home at either place. Either that, or they chose not to pick up the phone.'

'Why would they do that?'

'If they're in bed together, for instance.'

'Hey.'

'Wouldn't surprise me. You should've seen Ina tonight. She's on the make for Bass. In a big way.'

'I don't think he'd go for something like that.'

'Of course not. That's because *you* wouldn't do it, honey. Underneath it all, though, Bass is really sort of a jerk.'

'Hey, come on. He's our friend.'

'I know. But he's still sort of a jerk.'

'Even if he is, he wouldn't jump into the sack with Ina. He loves Faye too much for that. I bet there's some other reason why nobody answered the phones. Maybe they went somewhere.'

'Bass was planning to phone Faye's parents at nine o'clock. That was more than half an hour ago. Then he was supposed to call me here at the restaurant.'

'Maybe they found out something and took off.'

'Can we drop by Ina's house on the way home? Just to make sure nothing's wrong?'

'I don't know, honey.'

'It won't take long.'

'It's not that. I mean, we don't want to barge in on anything.'

Raising her eyebrows, Pac asked, 'And what could we *possibly* barge in on? Bass, the paragon of virtue, would *never* betray his dear Faye.'

'Well. He might. You never know.'

The waiter brought two mugs of steaming coffee. 'Will there be anything else?' he asked.

'That should about do it,' Harney said.

'If I may inquire?'

'Yes?'

'I recall a blonde *señorita* when I served you last time – oh, several weeks ago.'

'Yes?'

'I hope she is well.'

Harney nodded and said nothing.

'If I may inquire, is the *señorita* married or otherwise disposed of?'

'Disposed of?'

'Taken? Engaged?'

'She's engaged,' Harney told him.

'A pity.' His smile was touched with disappointment. 'I hope your dinner has been satisfactory.'

'It's been great,' Harney said.

'Terrific,' Pac added.

'Excellent,' said the waiter. 'Shall I bring you your check?'

'Please,' Harney said.

'That's Ina's car,' Pac said.

Harney swung into the driveway behind it.

'You can wait here,' Pac told him. 'I'll probably just be a second.'

'Why don't *you* stay here and I'll check?'

'Because I'm the fuzz.' She smiled at him and opened the door.

His door opened at the same instant.

Together, they walked toward Ina's house.

On the way, Pac reached into her purse and took out her off-duty pistol, a .380 Sig Sauer. She opened the screen, put her head close to the wooden door, and listened. 'The TV's on,' she said. She pressed the doorbell button and waited.

When nobody came, she pushed it five times, pausing a while between each ring.

'Now what?' Harney asked.

'Let's give them a couple more minutes.'

'What for?'

'To get decent?' She said it like a question, grinning over her shoulder at Harney.

He stepped up close behind her, slipped his hands through the open sides of her dress, and gently cupped her breasts. As he caressed them, he nibbled the side of her neck.

Pac squirmed. 'Stop that!' she whispered.

'Are you sure?' he asked, circling her nipples with his thumbs.

'They might come to the door.'

'If they do, I'll stop real fast.'

'Hey, come on. This is serious.'

'So is this,' Harney said. 'God, I love the feel of you.' One of his hands slid down from her breast, down her ribs and belly, and pressed between her legs.

She squirmed. 'Don't, hon. Please.'

'You sure?'

'I'm sure.' She felt a finger slide in. Harney's other hand squeezed her left breast. She gasped and writhed.

'I think you like it,' he whispered.

'Of course I like it.'

'But I'll stop if you insist.'

'You rat.'

'Do you insist?'

'How am I supposed to think straight?'

'I'll stop,' Harney said, and took his hands away from her.

'Thanks.'

'Now let's see if we can arouse *them*,' he said. Stepping in front of Pac, he lifted the door's heavy knocker and brought it down hard. 'That oughta wake the dead.'

'Let's hope it isn't necessary,' Pac said. Then she yelled, 'INA! BASS!'

Harney brought down the knocker two more times.

'Try the knob,' Pac suggested. While Harney attempted to turn it, she stepped to the side and pressed her face close to the frosted glass of a high, narrow window. She could see nothing through it except the brightness of a living-room lamp.

'Locked,' Harney said.

With the butt of her pistol, Pac smashed the window. She waited for the glass to stop falling, then reached through the hole, found the knob, and turned it.

After she pulled her arm clear, Harney pushed open the door.

Suddenly, he caught his breath and rushed inside.

Pac followed, Sig ready, and saw him kneel over Ina. The young woman's face was torn and swollen. Blood streaked it. But she was alive. Pac could hear her harsh, labored breathing.

'Harney, call for an ambulance.'

'I'll call Dad's office while I'm at it.'

She stepped over an outstretched arm, taking a long step to avoid the blood. Her foot came down on something hard like a pebble. It rolled under her shoe, and her foot slipped. Shifting her weight to her trailing foot, she avoided a fall. The pebble skittered across the hardwood foyer and stopped in the carpet. Pac went to it. She picked it up, saw that it was a blood-stained molar, and dropped it in disgust.

She scanned the living room, noticing the two glasses on the coffee table. Both glasses were half-full. She bent over them and touched one with the back of her hand. Still cool, but far from cold. The drinking had been interrupted some time ago.

She hurried into the kitchen, gave it a quick look, and headed for the hallway. As she walked up it, pistol ready, she heard Harney on the phone.

Halfway up the hall, she looked into the dark entrance of the bathroom and saw its splintered door frame. With the muzzle of her Sig, she flicked the light switch.

Nobody in the bathroom.

She let out a deep, shaking sigh.

Seeing the open window, she suspected she would find nobody in either of the bedrooms. She searched them, anyway. Then she returned to the living room. Harney, done with his calls, was again kneeling beside Ina.

'Did you find Bass?' he asked.

Pac shook her head. 'It looks like he made it out through the john window.'

'Brave son of a bitch.'

'That's your good buddy you're talking about.'

'Buddy or not, sometimes he can be a jerk.'

'I'd better have a look outside.'

'No way.'

'He might be out there, Harn. Just because he made it out the window doesn't mean . . .'

'Stay right here, okay?'

'It's my job.'

'Fine, but if you go out there, I'm going with you.'

'No, stay with Ina.'

'Then you stay here.'

A knock on the glass startled Pac. Spinning around, she saw a face at the hole she'd knocked in the window.

'Don't shoot.' The face grinned. It belonged to Deputy Joe Shepherd.

Pac unlocked the door and the deputy pushed it open.

'That was quick,' Harney said.

'Sorry. We were pretty far out when we caught the squeal. Made it here as fast as we could.'

'How long did it take?' Pac asked.

'Just under ten minutes, I guess.'

'That wasn't my call,' Harney said.

Chapter Thirty-six

HAIRY PIZZA

'What can I do?' the truck driver wanted to know. But he didn't wait for Rusty to answer. 'There she is, staring up at me like something out of a fuckin' nightmare. What can I do, swerve? Lay on the brakes? Hey, I'm not gonna take no chance of jackknifing my rig over some gal that ain't gonna know the difference anyhow, you know what I mean? Besides, it wouldn't of done no good. I mean, I'm gonna hit her, no way out of it. Not a fucking chance in hell I'm gonna miss her.'

'Don't worry about it,' Rusty told the man.

'Don't worry. Sure. You ever run over a fuckin' head? How do you think it feels, squashing something like that under your wheels? Did you *see* her?'

'I saw her.'

'Flat as a fuckin' pizza. A *hairy* pizza.'

'Did you see anyone?'

'Sure I saw someone – used to be a cute blonde.'

'You mean the head?'

'You're goddamn fuckin' right I mean the head. I shouldn't of taken this run, that was my big mistake. I should've stayed home with the wife and kids. How'm I gonna sleep, huh? Answer me that. Christ, I'm never gonna sleep another fuckin' wink the rest of my life.'

'Did you see anyone by the side of the road?'

'I didn't see nothing but the head.'

'How about a car? Did you notice a car parked along the roadside?'

'No, like I said . . . No, wait, there *was* a car. Only it wasn't parked. It passed me on the grade. A Mercedes.'

'What year?'

'Looked like new, but how can you tell with those things? It passed me, must've been doing sixty.'

'Did you notice the occupants?'

'There were two of them. That's all.'

'Did you catch the plates?'

'You kidding?'

'The head. Was it moving when you saw it?'

'Sure, it was tap dancing. What the fuck're you talking about, was it moving?'

'Rolling?'

'Oh, Jesus. No, it wasn't rolling. You think they tossed it outa the Mercedes? Not a chance. It was just sitting there staring up at me. Sorta like the rest of her was buried under the pavement and she was looking for a hand to pull her out.'

Chapter Thirty-seven

THE RETURN

The stretcher carrying Ina was being rolled out to the ambulance when a big red Pontiac Grand Prix pulled up to an empty length of curb across the street. Pac watched its driver's door swing open. Bass climbed out and crossed the street.

'Bass!' Pac called.

He ran up the lawn and met her at the front door.

'How's Ina?' he asked, glancing from Pac to Harney.

'Alive,' Harney said. 'Where were you?'

Bass ran a hand through his dark hair and shook his head. 'Running. My God, running, hiding, trying to lose that son of a bitch.'

'How did he get in the house?' Pac asked.

'He knocked. Ina went to the door. I don't know what he did to her.'

'He hit her with something.'

'The tire tool, I bet. He had a tire tool. I was in the crapper, though. I didn't know what was going on. I came out and there's this guy in the hall. The guy we saw this morning. I got out through the john window, but he came after me out

211

the back door. Chased me through all these yards, over hedges and fences. Jesus! Finally, I thought I'd lost him so I circled back to get my car.'

'You didn't go inside to see about Ina?' Harney asked, sounding annoyed.

'You're kidding. I figured that crazy bastard might be in there.'

'With Ina.'

'I'm gonna take him on by myself? The guy's a goddamn killer! What am I supposed to do, *wrestle* with him?'

'What did you do after you got your car?' Pac asked.

'I figured I'd drive someplace and call you guys. What happened, though, he was waiting for me. In *his* car. He started after me. Took me forever to lose the bastard. I finally did, though. Must've been twenty minutes ago. Suddenly, he's gone. So I pull into the first gas station I see and call the sheriff.'

'What kind of car was he driving?'

'Jesus, I don't know. Who knows? It was dark as hell . . . I don't know. Where'd they take Ina?'

'County General.'

'Is she gonna be all right?'

'We don't know.'

'That crazy bastard's gonna kill us all.'

Chapter Thirty-eight

THE SPAT

Merton unlocked the door and entered the house.

Looking up at him from the couch, Walter said, 'And where have *you* been?'

'Out.' Merton tossed the key ring underhand.

'I suppose my car is now so hot I'll have to bury it in a hazardous waste dump.'

'I don't think so.'

'Are you going to tell me what happened?'

'Nothing much.'

'Nothing much? You go hunting a man with a shotgun and claim nothing much happened?'

'He got away.'

'Well, thank heavens for that.'

'They all got away: Paxton, the bitch he was with this morning – hell, I never even saw *her*. And some other one. They *all* got—'

'What other one?'

'I don't know. Paxton had some skinny brunette bitch with him tonight. I nailed her pretty good, but I didn't get a chance to finish the job. Least I don't think so. If she lives, she'll be able to put me away all by herself.'

'Good heavens.'

'So I guess I'll be hitting the road. See you around, Walter.'

'You're not leaving again?'

'I just came back to pick up my van.'

'You *can't* leave.'

'Ah, sure I can. Thanks for the help today.'

Walter got up from the couch, pulling his robe tight across his white chest. 'Just stay here,' he said. 'Please. You'll be safe here.'

'Not gonna take any chances.'

'Where'll you go?'

'Far away.'

'No!' He reached out a long-fingered hand and stroked the side of Merton's cheek. His eyes glistened with tears. 'Don't leave, Merty. Please.'

'If I stay, they'll get me. Do you want that? Do you want me to get sent back inside?'

'Of course I don't want that. But . . . even if they find you, it doesn't mean you'll be convicted. People are *always* getting off. Even *guilty* people.'

'Not me. With my record? And two eyewitnesses to place me with the body? And the brunette bitch? Not to mention whatever kinds of evidence they might pick up on me from going after Paxton and that bitch tonight.'

'So you're just going to . . . run away?'

'That's about the size of it.'

'Can't you . . . do away with them?'

Merton shook his head. 'Hell, yeah. I could kill their asses. Only problem is, I've already given it a try. They'd be ready for me next time. So there ain't gonna be a next time. Just isn't worth the risk. I'll have to pull a disappearing act.'

'For how long?'

'Just till the twelfth,' Merton said, and grinned.

'The twelfth of September?'

'The twelfth of never.'

'You . . . how can you *joke* about it?' Walter threw his arms around Merton and wept. 'You can't leave me. You can't.'

'Afraid I've got to. I'll get in touch with you when I can.'

'When you *can*?' Walter's voice was suddenly bitter. 'When you *can*?'

'Yeah, when I can.'

Walter stepped back. 'Isn't *that* wonderful. Isn't that just *ducky*?'

'Take it easy.'

'Easy? Take it *easy*? You dirty shit!'

'Hey.'

'You treat me like shit! You always have, Merton! What've you ever done for me? Always, "I want this, I want that, let me use your car, wash my clothes." But what have you ever done for *me*? Would you move in with me after prison? No no no, you've got to have your freedom. Did you ever once ask me over to your place? No no no, only when you wanted something from me. It's always on your terms. It's always what *you* want. You never give a *thought* to how much you're hurting me. All you do is *use* me. I'm nothing more than a *convenience* for you. And you can't even be *faithful*! Is that asking too much? Always have to be going out in that obscene van of yours, picking up everything in pants. How do you think *that* makes me feel?

I have feelings, Merton! I can be hurt. And now you're planning to just *leave*? I won't have it!'

Merton smirked. 'Sure, you will.'

'I won't!' Walter stomped his foot on the floor.

'Oh, knock it off. You're an old woman. Always have been.'

'*Old woman!*' Walter shrieked and lunged at Merton, fingers spread like claws.

Merton's fist caught him in the belly.

He folded at the waist and dropped to his knees.

'An *ugly, whiny* old woman,' Merton said. 'You disgust me.' Shaking his head, he left.

'Hello? Is this the Sheriff's Department? My name is Walter Fern. I'm calling in regard to the dead woman they found this morning at the river. The one without any head? Well, I know exactly who killed her.'

Chapter Thirty-nine

SWEET MEADOW

Merton steered his van over the rutted dirt road and came to the Sweet Meadow roadhead. He parked in the same spot as the night before, killed his lights, and climbed into the back of the van.

Sitting on the bed, he sank deeply into its soft cushion of water. The water rolled under him as he pulled off his shoes.

Then he lay back.

The water slowly settled, rocking him gently.

Soon, he fell asleep.

Chapter Forty

TATTLETALE

Rusty knocked on the door of Walter Fern's house. The pale man who opened it wore a grey, pinstriped suit, a white shirt and a black bow tie. His short hair was wet and neatly combed. A white tuft of shaving cream hung below his left ear lobe.

'Mr Fern?' Rusty asked.

'Yes, I am.'

'I'm Sheriff Hodges.'

'Yes. Please come in.' Mr Fern offered his hand. Rusty shook it. The hand was cold. 'May I get you some coffee, Sheriff?'

'That sounds real good,' Rusty said.

'Have a seat, please. Do you take cream or sugar?'

'Just black, thanks.'

'I'll only be a sec. Please make yourself at home.'

Rusty sat on an easy chair next to the couch. Though he'd never met Walter Fern before, he'd made up his mind that he didn't like the man. Fern was something pale that might be found crawling in the moist dirt if you suddenly rolled aside a heavy rock. Probably not dangerous, but vaguely repulsive and sinister.

Rusty realized he was tense. He made an effort to relax his shoulder muscles.

'*Voilà!*' Walter said, entering with a serving tray. The white porcelain cups clinked on their saucers as he lowered the tray in front of Rusty.

'Thank you.' Rusty felt clumsy lifting the delicate cup and saucer. He was used to drinking coffee from mugs or cups of heavy china. This dainty thing looked tiny in his big hand. But he managed to take a drink and gently return the cup to its saucer without a mishap.

Walter sat on the couch. He sipped his coffee and said, 'Well. I imagine you must wonder why I've decided to, shall we say, "Blow the whistle"?'

Rusty nodded.

'The man who murdered this Alison Parkington woman is a friend of mine. A very dear friend. I'm afraid for his life, Sheriff. Can you understand that?'

'I think so. You'd like to see him taken into custody without any violence?'

'Exactly.' He smiled quickly in appreciation. 'This is a very difficult task for me, as you may well understand.' He sighed and sipped his coffee. 'I hope I'm doing what's best for him.'

'Who is your friend?'

'Merton LeRoy.'

'*Whoa!* Merton *LeRoy*?'

It hardly seemed likely.

But you never know, he told himself.

'I believe you're the man who sent him to prison,' Walter said.

'A jury did that. But I'm the guy who arrested him. What makes you think he was involved in the killing of Alison Parkington?'

'He told me so. He came to me this morning. I even washed his clothes for him.'

'What kind of clothes?'

'Oh, let me think. There was a pair of blue jeans, quite old and faded and filthy, with frayed cuffs. In their state, they should have been incinerated, but Merton would never have forgiven me.'

'Bloody?'

'Who could tell? Really, they were such a disgrace.'

'What else?'

'No underwear, of course. Merton never wears underwear. Rather primitive of him, in my opinion. He says they inhibit his freedom of movement.'

They slow you down when you're raping kids, Rusty thought. But he kept the opinion to himself and said, 'What about his shirt?'

'Plaid flannel. I'd given it to him myself, just last Christmas. It was *très* bloody this morning, but I got most of the stains out. Spray 'n Wash absolutely works marvels.'

Nodding, Rusty said, 'The clothes do fit our description pretty well.'

'Certainly they do. Merton was there. He did it. He's the one those two people saw this morning.'

'But they said the man was bald,' Rusty explained.

'You haven't seen Merton lately?'

'It's been a few years.'

'He started shaving his head while he was in prison.'

And his mug shot shows him with a full head of hair. No

wonder Bass and Faye couldn't pick him out.

'I keep telling him to let his hair grow out, but he won't hear of it. I'm afraid he equates a hairless scalp with virility. I, personally, think it's utter nonsense.'

'What kind of car does Merton drive?'

'A blue Volkswagen van.'

'Do you know the tag number?'

'The tag?'

'The license?'

'Why would I know that?'

'It would be helpful, that's all.'

'Well, I haven't a clue.'

'Is there anything unusual about the van?'

'In what way?'

'What about its interior?'

'Oh! Well, it certainly does have something a bit odd, there. For one thing, Merton has a water bed. I'm sure you don't find water beds in vans every day of the week.'

'Probably not.'

'He also has an enormous mirror attached to the ceiling above the bed so he can watch . . . himself, I suppose. And whatever creature he happens to be *stumphing*. He's *such* a degenerate.'

'Did he tell you why he killed Alison Parkington?'

'Oh, certainly. He told me everything, absolutely everything.'

'What did he say about his motive?'

'He's been having a thing with her husband, of course.'

'A *thing*?'

'An *affaire de coeur*.'

'A what?'

'An affair of the heart. A love affair. Merton, of course, is gay. He makes no secret of that. After all, how *could* he after all the publicity about his seamy school-yard seductions and rapes? So. He's having an affair with the good professor, and made up his mind to eliminate the man's wife.'

'Did he tell you what prompted him to cut off her head?'

'Oh, yes. Certainly. This morning, Merton offered it as a gift to Professor Parkington.'

'Jesus,' Rusty muttered.

'I know. Shocking. Disgusting. Might I get you some more coffee?'

Rusty nodded. As Walter poured more steaming coffee into his cup, he asked, 'Was the professor in on the murder?'

'I really shouldn't say. After all, I only know what Merton told me. I wouldn't want to slander the man.'

'He won't care.'

'But of course he will. He might even sue me if I should make any accusations against him. *Everybody* wants to sue.'

'Not Professor Parkington. He's dead.'

'Dead?'

Rusty demonstrated by pointing toward his own open mouth, then bringing down his thumb like a pistol hammer.

'Oh, my heavens!'

'He's in no position to sue you or anyone else. So tell me. According to Merton, was the professor involved in the murder of his wife?'

'Why yes, he was.'

'In what way?'

'He helped with the planning, among other things.'

'Which other things?'

'Well, it was the professor's job to see that his wife drank quite a lot of liquor last night. In other words, he was to get her drunk. That way, she wouldn't be able to put up much fuss when Merton came for her.'

'He came for her?'

'Certainly. First, he drove over to the professor's house. Then the two of them grabbed the woman and forced her into the car. The professor drove her to the river, and Merton followed in his van. Afterward, they both came back together. Merton and the professor, that is. In the van.'

'With Alison's head?'

'Oh, no. Merton cut her head off later.'

'When?'

'Much later. First, they went back to the professor's house and had a few drinks to celebrate. Then . . .' Walter scowled down at the floor. 'He was *such* an unfaithful bitch.'

'Who?'

'Merton, of course. He made love with the professor that night – while the wife's body was lying down there in the cold sand by the river.' He shook his head furiously as if to dislodge the thought. 'Only after he'd finished satiating his lust with the professor did he return to her body.'

'Did he say why he went back?'

'For her head, of course.'

'Why didn't he take it in the first place?'

'It was an afterthought,' Walter explained. 'You see, while he was at the professor's house, they danced. Merton is such a fine, graceful dancer. Well, somehow one of them brought up John the Baptist. And Salome? The Dance of the Seven Veils? Apparently, Merton danced his version of it for the professor. That's when he got the idea.'

'And he just happened to have a hacksaw handy?'

'He found it in the professor's garage.'

'I see. What did he do with the arms and legs he cut off?'

The lines of flesh between Walter's eyebrows deepened to dark grooves. 'What do you mean?'

'Didn't Merton tell you about cutting off her arms and legs?'

Eyes narrowing, voice turning bitter, Walter said, 'You're trying to trick me. Merton didn't cut off any arms or legs. You know he didn't. *I* know he didn't. Only those fools at the *News* think he dismembered her that way. You're trying to trick me, Sheriff, and personally I find it quite unnecessary and offensive.'

'Sorry you feel that way.'

'If you don't believe what I'm telling you, there's no point in wasting any more time. I'd appreciate it if you would simply leave.'

'I'll be glad to leave,' Rusty said, 'as soon as you've told me the truth.'

'I did tell the truth.'

'You lied about Grant Parkington's involvement. He didn't drive his wife to the river.'

'Of course he did.'

'Afraid not. We know who drove her car there, and it wasn't her husband.'

Looking slightly befuddled, Walter said, 'I only know what Merton told me.'

'Did he tell you about having intercourse with Alison Parkington?'

'Having what?'

'Sexual intercourse. With Alison Parkington.'

'You're trying to trick me again.'

'He did, you know.'

'Impossible.'

'What's so impossible about it? Just because he prefers men and boys doesn't rule out—'

'He wouldn't *touch* a woman. Impossible!'

'Someone did.'

'Not Merton!' he snapped. 'Merton wouldn't do such a thing.' Walter shut his mouth tightly, pressed his trembling lips together and turned his face away.

'Tell me the truth, now,' Rusty said. 'What is Merton's involvement with the murder?'

'He killed her.'

'Are you sure?'

'Yes, I'm sure!'

'Then start talking. This time, give me the whole truth. If you try any more lies on me, I'll take you to the station and book you as an accessory.'

Walter turned his face toward Rusty. His eyes were red, his cheeks shiny with tears. 'Okay! If you're going to be that way . . . I was lying about it all! I know nothing!' He sniffed. 'Nothing at all. I made up all those lies to hurt Merton, the despicable unfaithful bitch!'

'Where'd you get your information?'

'From the news. And . . . I made up the rest.' With a neatly folded white handkerchief, Walter wiped his face dry. 'My imagination is quite fertile, Sheriff.'

'I don't doubt it, but I said I wanted the truth this time.'

'And the truth is what I've given you. The whole truth, and nothing but the truth . . .'

'Horse shit, Walter. You know the paper was wrong about the dismemberment. You're under arrest. You have the right to remain silent. If you choose to give up the right to remain silent, anything you say can and will be used against you . . .'

Chapter Forty-one

THE SALE

A rapping sound woke Merton from a dream of changing tires in the rain. With his eyes still shut, he wondered where he was. He could tell that he was naked and in a hot place. Sweat was trickling down his skin, and the sheet felt sodden underneath his body.

I'm in my van, he thought.

Then he remembered driving over to the Sweet Meadow roadhead after leaving Walter's house.

Opening his eyes, he saw his reflection in the mirror overhead. He couldn't see much. The interior of the van was dark except for a mist of moonlight coming in through one of the windows. His image in the mirror appeared to be a dim, pale smudge against his blue satin sheet.

Someone knocked on the door again.

'What do you want?' Merton called.

A clear, youthful voice answered, 'I'm looking for Mister In-Between.'

'Yeah, okay, hang on a second.'

Merton rolled to the edge of his water bed. Sitting up, he reached down to the floor and found his jeans where he'd dropped them. He put them on, then got up and walked in a crouch to the side window. He opened it, and a cool night breeze eased in, chilling the sweat on his body. It felt great. He took a deep breath, then stepped to the rear of the van. He opened one of the doors.

In the darkness, he could see that his visitor was a young man, tall and slim with straight dark hair hanging to his shoulders. Less than twenty feet back, an old convertible waited in a patch of moonlight. 'You alone?'

'Yeah. It's just me.'

'Do you want to come in?'

'Are you Mister In-Between?'

'That's right.'

'Well, I'd like to buy some stuff from you.'

'Some stuff, huh?' Merton sank down slowly to his knees. 'We'll see about that,' he said. 'Maybe I don't know what you're talking about. What's your name?'

'Steve.'

'Pleased to meet you, Steve. Let me ask you something. Are you aware of the house rules?'

He shrugged. 'Maybe.'

'Well, rule number one is that you can't come in with your clothes on. Is that your car?'

'Yeah.'

'You can leave them in your car if you want. You can't bring anything in here except yourself. I gotta know you're not wired.'

'Okay.'

Merton watched his visitor walk back to the convertible.

Standing beside the car, Steve removed his T-shirt and tossed it onto the driver's seat. Then he took off his shoes and socks and dropped them over the side of the door. He turned away before pulling down his jeans. He stepped out of them, then draped them over the door and turned toward Merton.

He was slender and pale in the moonlight. His bikini style underwear was so white that it almost seemed to glow.

'Okay?' he asked.

'Not quite, my friend. How do I know you don't have a bug in your shorts?'

'Do I have to take them off?'

'It's the only way you're getting in here. I don't do business with people who might be wired for sound.'

'I'm not . . . It's just . . . embarrassing, you know?'

'I'm sure you knew what to expect.'

'Well, yeah, I guess so, but . . .'

'And you came anyway, didn't you?'

'Yeah.'

'Well, then . . .'

'Okay.' Steve turned away.

'Oh, stop being coy.'

He looked over his shoulder, then turned to face Merton.

'That's much better,' Merton said.

Thumbs hooked under his elastic waistband, Steve bent over and drew his shorts down. He stepped out of them. Holding them in his right hand, he covered his groin with his left as he stood up straight. He dropped the shorts into the driver's seat of his car, then walked toward Merton.

A few strides from the rear of the van, he stepped into a bright patch of moonlight.

'Stop right there,' Merton said.

Steve stopped.

'Now, raise your arms. Reach for the sky, as they say.'

Steve raised only his right arm. His left arm stayed down, hand cupping his genitals.

'Both,' Merton said.

Steve brought down his right arm and lifted his left.

'Both at the same time,' Merton said.

'Do I have to?'

'No, you certainly don't have to. You're free to go back to your car and get dressed and drive away. But if you want to *buy* something, you'd better do what I say.'

'Okay, okay.' Steve raised his other arm.

'Very good,' Merton said, gazing at him. 'That wasn't so tough, was it?'

'I guess not,' Steve said, his voice trembling.

'You have nothing to be embarrassed about. Nothing at all.'

'Thanks.'

For a while, Merton simply stared at him in silence, relishing the view. His own mouth was dry, his heart beating quickly. Sweat slid down his face and neck and bare torso, tickling him as it dribbled. He was already hard, but still growing, rising and pressing against his jeans.

Finally, he said, 'Now turn around very slowly.'

Keeping his arms high, Steve turned around until he again faced Merton.

'I don't see any wires,' Merton told him.

'There aren't any.'

Merton rubbed the back of a sweaty hand across his mouth. 'Now we're sure, aren't we?'

'I guess.'

'Climb in.'

Merton stood up, stepped aside and watched Steve climb in. Then he shut the door, locked it and turned on a dim red light.

Steve's mouth hung open as he scanned the interior of the van. 'Hey, this *is* pretty cool,' he said. 'Awesome mirror. Is that really a water bed?'

'Check it out for yourself.'

In a crouch, Steve made his way toward the bed.

Merton was tempted to reach out and caress his flank as he passed. But he resisted the urge. The kid was nervous enough about all this. The wrong move might send him running.

Steve sank down onto the bed. He bounced on it a couple of times. The water inside the mattress rolled and quietly sloshed. 'Awesome,' he said.

'How did you find out about me?' Merton asked.

'Phil Dobson,' he said.

'What did he tell you?'

'He said I could, you know, score some stuff off you.'

'What kind of stuff?'

'You know. Like weed, crank, acid.'

'What did you come for?'

'Just some weed, I guess.'

'Fine, fine. We should be able to arrange that. Did you bring money?'

Steve's brow rumpled slightly. 'Yeah. But I haven't got it on me.' He let out a nervous little laugh. 'I can go get it, though. It's in my car. How much?'

'That'll depend, won't it?'

'I've got twenty bucks to spend. Want me to go get it?'

'Later. Dobson sent you, did he?'

'Yes.'

'Did he tell you about the arrangement I have with him and some of the other guys?'

'Sort of.'

'Would you like an arrangement of that sort?'

'I . . . I don't know. Maybe.'

'It'd mean a fifty percent discount on every purchase.'

Steve nodded.

Merton reached out a hand and patted his knee. 'There's nothing to be nervous about.'

'I guess.'

'You aren't afraid of me, are you?'

He shrugged slightly and shook his head. 'I guess not.'

'Have you talked to Dobson about what we do?'

'Not really. He . . . he didn't say much.'

'He *loves* it. He comes around even when he doesn't want any stuff.'

'Really?'

'Sure.'

'Dobson?'

'Dobson.' Merton glided his hand lightly up the top of Steve's thigh. Though he met no objections, he felt the leg trembling slightly. He stopped midway up, and let his hand drift back toward Steve's knee. 'Did you like that?'

'I don't know.'

'Phil does.'

In a shaky voice, Steve said, 'But Phil . . . he isn't . . . he goes out with one of the . . .'

'Oh, I know. One of the hottest babes on campus. Judy Thompson.'

'You *know* about her?'

'Of course. Phil's told me all about her. But he prefers me for certain activities. I know that must be hard to believe. Considering Judy.'

'Yeah, sure is.'

'But there are some things that she doesn't do very well, and other things she refuses to do at all . . . or can't.' Merton slid both his hands slowly up Steve's thighs. 'I give Phil pleasures that he'll never be able to get from someone like Judy. I can give those pleasures to you, too.'

'I don't know,' Steve said. 'I've never . . . done anything like this.'

'With someone like me?'

'Yeah. Never.'

Merton eased his hands higher. His thumbs slid against the moist heat of Steve's groin.

Steve flinched and caught his breath, but didn't protest.

'I bet you've thought about it,' Merton said. 'Haven't you?'

'Not really.'

'Sure you have. You've wondered what it would be like, haven't you?'

'I mostly just . . . think about girls. You know. I'm not sure I want to do something like this.'

'You want to.'

'I'm not so sure.'

'I am. Look what we have here. You're rising to the occasion.'

'Yeah, but . . .'

'The cock never lies.'

'I really don't think . . .'

'I'll make you a deal, all right?'

'What sort of deal?'

'Lie back. Feel the waves under you. Close your eyes, or watch in the mirror, whichever you prefer. But just lie still, relax, and I'll do things that'll make you feel *so* good. The minute I do something you don't like, just say so and I'll stop. I'll give you the discount, no matter what. How's that?'

'Uh . . . I don't know.'

'Just lie back, Steve. You'll love it.'

'You promise to stop if I tell you to?'

'I promise.'

He'll never ask.

Not our lovely Steve.

He wants it bad. He's scared, but he wants it.

'Now, lie back. Yes, yes, that's it. Doesn't that feel good? Oh, look at you. Look at you.' He slid his hands down to Steve's knees and gently spread them wide apart. Steve didn't resist at all. 'God, you're gorgeous,' Merton said. 'And so *big*. Just *look* at yourself.'

As Steve gazed up at the mirror, Merton reached down and quickly unfastened his jeans. The trapped, tight feeling went away. Letting the jeans fall down around his knees, he eased forward.

'Do you mind if I do this?' he whispered.

'Huh?'

'This.'

Steve groaned.

'That doesn't hurt, does it?'

'No.'

'I didn't think so. You like how it feels, don't you?'

'I . . . guess so.'

'I *know* so. How about this?'

'Mmm.'
'Do you want me to stop?'
'No. Don't . . . don't stop.'
'Are you sure?'
'*Yes*.'

Chapter Forty-two

HOSPITAL

A hand on her shoulder woke Pac and she looked up at the calm, serious face of Rusty Hodges.

'How's it going?' he asked. He sat down beside her on the waiting-room couch.

Pac shook her head. 'Ina? I don't know.' She rubbed her eyes and glanced at her wristwatch. It was nearly midnight. She'd been there an hour.

'I just spoke to the doctor,' Rusty said. 'Ina's probably going to make it.'

'When can we talk to her?'

'As soon as she wakes up.'

'Is she comatose?' Pac asked.

'Nope. She regained consciousness while they were setting her jaw. She's sleeping now, and the doctor doesn't want us to bother her for a while.'

'How long?'

'An hour or two. Do you want to stay?'

'I'll stay,' Pac said.

'They moved her up to room four-oh-four. It's a private room. You can wait in there if you'd like. I cleared it with the doctor. I let him know there might be another attempt on her life.'

'Do you think there might be?'

'It's possible. I'd say Bass is in a lot more dangerous situation than Ina, though. He can still put the guy at the scene of the murder. Ina can't do that.' Rusty slipped two mug photos out of his shirt pocket. He handed them to Pac. 'You can keep those. Show them to Ina and find out if this is the man who attacked her. He doesn't have any hair now.'

'Who is he?'

'The name's Merton LeRoy.'

Pac thought for a moment. 'You mean the bus driver?'

'That's him.'

'Harney told me about that guy. He drove for the high school and they found out he was seducing the boys?'

'Or raping some of them if they didn't cooperate. He finally beat one of them so badly the kid lost an eye.'

'He nearly killed the kid, didn't he?'

'Yeah. Bashed him with a tire tool.'

'Sounds like our man,' Pac said. She studied the mug shots: a full-face view and a profile. The eyes were close together, separated by a slim bridge of nose. The mouth, a grim line, seemed to have no lips. 'How did you get his name?' she asked.

Rusty grinned. 'Elementary.'

'Give.'

'He jilted a boyfriend. The boyfriend snitched.'

'Was the boyfriend in on it?'

'He aided Merton this morning, loaned him a car, even went with him to the store this afternoon for wire and things.'

'For the shotgun booby trap?'

'Apparently.'

'I've still got all that stuff in my car.'

'It can wait till morning. The main thing, right now, is to get a positive ID on these pictures. Did Bass go back home?'

'No. I didn't think it would be safe. He's supposed to be at the Lakeview Motor Hotel. He called there from Ina's place to make sure they had a vacancy.'

'Okay. I'll go over and check on him.'

They both stood. Pac saw Rusty's eyes lower to her dress. 'I guess your evening's been ruined.'

'We managed to squeeze in our dinner. Did you get a chance to eat?'

'I had a very interesting supper,' Rusty said, 'At Patty's Good Food Cafe between Parkington's suicide and the flattened head.'

'The what?'

'Didn't Shepherd tell you? An eighteen-wheeler found our missing head. Out on Forty.'

'My God.'

'Interesting that it finally popped up that way after so long. Makes me wonder what it was doing in the meantime.'

'I think I'd rather not know,' Pac said.

Rusty smiled. 'Don't let revulsion get in the way of your investigation. That's Rule Six.'

'You're terrible.'

'Part of my charm, honey. Okay, I'm on my way. If you want to run home and change while you're waiting for Ina to wake up, go ahead.'

'I might do that.'

'Do you have a car?'

'I have ours. I dropped off Harney at home before coming over.'

'If you go home, don't stay long. I think Ina'll be safe here, but you never can tell. And let me know what she has to say about the photos.'

'Right.'

'If you see Harney, give him my regrets.'

'For what?'

'Keeping you out of his arms on your anniversary, of course.' With a grin, he walked away.

Pac went to an elevator. She pushed the UP button. As she waited for the metal doors to slide open, she looked down the hallway. A man with a flower arrangement entered a far room. The minute arm of a clock on the wall made a quick jump sideways. She saw a drinking fountain and realized how dry her mouth felt. As she started toward it, the elevator door opened.

She wanted water worse than the elevator.

Ignoring the open door, she hurried over to the drinking fountain. The water tasted fine and cold, hurting her teeth.

When she was done, she headed again for the elevator. Halfway there, she walked past a telephone stall.

The clock thumped, its arm jerking.

She stepped over to the phone, set her purse on the metal shelf beside it, and took out a quarter. Then she stared at the phone. It took several seconds to recall the father's first name.

The local directory assistance operator connected her to an operator in the 425 area. 'I'd like the number of Elton Everett in Burlingame.'

Moments later, a recorded voice gave her the number.

Using her phone card, she placed her call to Faye's parents.

The phone rang seven times before someone picked it up.

'Hello?' answered a woman. The voice was much like Faye's, but more husky.

'Is Mr Everett there?'

'Just a moment, please.'

A few seconds passed, then a man said, 'Yes?'

'Mr Everett, this is Mary Hodges.' She waited, but he made no sound of recognition. 'I'm a friend of Faye's.'

'Oh?'

'I met you and your wife last Thanksgiving.'

'Oh, is this Pac?'

'That's right.'

'Well, how are—' Abruptly, he stopped. 'Oh Lord Jesus, you're the dep . . . Has something happened to Faye?'

'We don't know. Has she been in touch with you?'

'When?'

'Today.'

'No. Why? What's happened?'

'We don't know where she is. We thought she might've headed your way.'

'We haven't heard from her.'

'She and Bass found a body this morning. A murder victim.'

'Oh, sweet Jesus.'

'She seemed pretty upset about it. This afternoon, she disappeared. Apparently, she packed a suitcase before leaving.'

'Did she drive?'

240

'Her car's gone.'

'And Bass doesn't know where she went?'

'Nobody does. We thought maybe she'd decided to pay you and your wife a visit.'

'What time did she leave?'

'About two-thirty, we think.'

'Well, then she would've gotten here by now.'

'Unless she stopped somewhere,' Pac said.

'She always drives straight through. She won't even stop for a meal. Nothing. She likes to get the driving over with.'

'If she does show up, will you give us a call at the Sheriff's Department?' She gave him the phone number.

'You don't suppose anything's happened to her?'

'I sure hope not, Mr Everett.'

'Sweet Jesus, if anything's happened to her . . .'

'I'm sure she's just fine,' Pac said, and hoped the man couldn't detect the lie in her voice.

Chapter Forty-three

BASS FISHING

Rusty pushed open a glass door and entered the brightly lit office of the Lakeview Motor Hotel. The office was deserted. From an open door to the rear came the sound of television laughter.

He dropped his palm on the ringer.

A few seconds passed, then a white-haired woman appeared. She smiled at Rusty with lips like a bright, shiny heart. Up close, he saw that the lipstick had been applied with little concern for the borders of her lips.

'Sheriff. What can I do for you?'

'I'm looking for a man who registered to stay here tonight.'

'Oh, I bet I know just the one you mean. A handsome, dark-haired boy with a tongue as smooth as whipping cream.'

Rusty smiled. 'I never noticed about his tongue.'

'Oh, my yes. A real charmer, that boy. He put me in mind of my first husband. A real charmer he was, too. Charmed his way straight into San Quentin. Enough of *him*, says I. He won't drag me down to perdition with his fancy ways. No sir, not me. I divorced that man quicker than you can spit, you bet I did.' She plucked out a guest registration card. 'This'll be your boy.'

Rusty read the name: Bill Palmer. The wrong name, but the right initials. 'Was he in his late twenties, six-two, about a hundred and eighty pounds?'

'Oh, my yes. And he had the most fetching blue eyes. Who'd he bamboozle?'

'Nobody that I know of.'

'Now really,' she said, as if ashamed of Rusty for lying to her.

'He's just a witness.'

'I'd lay he's a con man or a card sharp, one or the other.' She winked.

'He sells boats at the Silver Lake marina.'

'A salesman! Ha! I knew it, a con man!'

'What room is he in?'

'Two-thirty. Upstairs and to your right.'

'Thank you.'

'My pleasure, Sheriff.'

He left the office, took the stairs two at a time, and hurried along the concrete balcony. The balcony, apparently supported by steel beams, rang each time one of his feet came down. He knocked on the door of two-thirty.

Nobody answered.

Light filled the room's window, but he could see nothing through the curtains. He knocked again, then hurried back to the motel office.

He hit the ringer four times.

The woman came in, blinking.

'Get me the key. Hurry.'

'Oh, my! Is there trouble?'

'Hope not.'

She put it in his hand. 'I'll come with you, if it's . . .'

'You'd better stay here.'

He ran from the office, slipping sideways past a man about to enter, and rushed up the stairs. Running along the balcony, he unholstered his Smith & Wesson. He shoved the key into the lock, turned the knob and threw open the door.

'Bass?'

No answer.

After a quick scan of the room, he stepped inside. Nothing moved. He flung open the sliding door of the closet. Empty. He hurried to the far side of the bed. Nobody. He entered the bathroom. Nobody there, either.

Holstering his revolver, he returned to the bed. He knelt and glanced under it, then sat on the side of the mattress. He was lighting a cigar when the powdered face with the heart-shaped lips appeared in the doorway, blinking.

'I take it he slipped through your fingers.'

Rusty nodded. 'Okay if I use the phone?'

'A local call?' she asked, coming into the room and looking nervously into corners as if she expected to find a corpse.

'It's local.'

'Be my guest. Dial nine for an outside line.' Craning her neck, she peered into the bathroom.

Rusty tapped the nine, then called directory assistance. With the number of the hospital, he placed a call to room four-oh-four. Pac answered after the first ring.

'I'm at the motel,' he told her, 'but Bass isn't. Do you have any idea where else he might've gone?'

'I don't know. Is he registered there?'

'A guy by the name of Bill Palmer is. He checked in at the right time and fits Bass's description.'

'He sure is being careful.'

'I guess I would, too, with somebody trying to kill me.'

The woman gasped, and Rusty looked up at her. Her red mouth hung open and her hand was pressed to her heart. 'Are you all right?' he asked her.

She whispered, 'Murder.'

'If you want me to,' Pac said, 'I'll go over and check at his house. He might've gone back for some reason.'

'No, you stay with Ina.'

'It isn't really necessary. She woke up a few minutes ago.'

'You show her the pictures?'

'I sure did. Merton LeRoy is the one who attacked her, no question about it.'

'All right!' He slapped his leg. 'We'll find Bass later. Let's pick up Merton. You want in on it?'

'I'm ready when you are.'

Rusty took out his notebook and leafed through it. 'Let's try his home, for starters. It's at six eight two Pine Street. Can you make it there by twelve-thirty?'

'I'll be there,' Pac said.

Chapter Forty-four

MERTON'S PLACE

Pac watched Rusty step away from the dark window of the garage and wipe a hand on his trousers. 'Damn spider webs. The van's not here.'

She felt disappointment like an emptiness in her stomach. 'Do we go in anyway?'

'We do.'

She followed Rusty toward the front door.

'He's a mean sucker, Pac, so watch out for yourself.'

'He's probably a hundred miles from here.'

'On the other hand, his van could be parked on the next block and he might be watching us from one of these windows.'

Three dark windows faced them. The curtains all were open. Pac's disappointment faded. She reached into her purse and pulled out her .380 Sig Sauer.

'We'll assume he's in there until we know otherwise. You cover the back.'

She ran along the side of the house to the rear. Four wooden steps led up to the back door. She rushed up them.

The door had glass panes. She could easily break one

and be inside in seconds. But she waited.

Through the glass, she could see only darkness.

A mosquito buzzed close to her ear. She didn't move. It landed on the side of her neck. With her left hand, she brushed it off.

A drop of sweat slid down her side. She wished she had taken time to go home and change into her uniform. She sure didn't want to ruin her brand new dress. And it was much too revealing. Fine for a nice restaurant, but she didn't much like the idea of chasing after suspects in it.

Not that a guy like Merton'll be interested, she thought.

A kitchen light came on, startling her.

She saw Rusty stride through the kitchen, the big .44 magnum in his hand.

He opened the door for her. 'Merton's not here,' he said. He glanced at her breasts, then quickly turned away.

She knew from their feel how they must look, but she checked as she stepped into the kitchen. Her nipples were erect under the light, clingy fabric. They stuck out like a couple of fingertips.

Just terrific, she thought.

'Let's have a look around,' Rusty said. 'You start with the kitchen.'

He went out, and Pac took a deep, trembling breath. She returned the pistol to her purse. Then she began to search. She started with easy places: the counter top, the oven, the refrigerator. In the vegetable drawer of the refrigerator, hidden under grapes and oranges, she found a stainless steel .22 caliber semi-automatic.

There's a felony, she thought. *A convicted felon in possession of a firearm.*

We'll have to come back with a warrant.

She removed the weapon's magazine, drew back the slide and ejected the round from the chamber. Then she thumbed the cartridges out of the magazine. As they fell into her cupped hand, she was surprised by how heavy they felt. The weight of ammunition, even little .22s, nearly always took her by surprise.

When the magazine was empty, she dumped all the rounds into her purse. She slid the magazine back into place, closed the action, and returned the pistol to its hiding place under the fruit.

'Come back for you later,' she muttered.

Continuing her search, she pulled a chair close to one of the counters, climbed onto it, and inspected the upper cupboards. They were bare enough to make the search easy. When she finished, she found a clean dish towel in one of the drawers, spread it on the floor to protect her dress, and knelt down to look through the lower cupboards.

She was reaching deep into a cupboard when someone walked into the kitchen. She pulled out, careful not to bump her head, and looked over her shoulder.

Rusty stood in the doorway, grinning. 'Look what I found in the john.' His arms were raised. From each hand dangled a glassine bag: one held white powder; the other held a dark chunk that looked to Pac like black tar heroin.

'Our boy Merton's doing a little business in illegal substances,' Rusty said.

'So it would seem,' Pac said, nodding and blushing. Except for the tie behind her neck, she couldn't feel the top of her dress touching her anywhere. It was obviously hanging well away from her front. She was giving Rusty a terrific view of her bare left side all the way down to her hip. Not just her side, but her left breast.

He seemed determined to keep his eyes on Pac's eyes, but he *had* to be aware of her problem.

He was blushing, too.

'Anyway,' he said. 'Come and have a look at his stash when you get done there.' He turned away.

'I'll come now,' Pac said.

When he was out of the kitchen, she stood up and straightened her dress. Then she found her way to the bathroom.

Rusty was waiting for her there.

The toilet seat was piled with socks and a wadded sheet. A white-painted wicker hamper lay on its side. Plastic bags littered the floor. Rusty toed one. 'More heroin.' The point of his boot touched another. 'Hash. And here's uppers, downers, speed, pot. That's probably angel dust in that one.'

'Quite an inventory,' Pac said.

Rusty set the hamper upright and began dropping the bags in. 'We'll have to come back with a search warrant.'

'When we do,' Pac said, 'there's a .22 semi-auto hidden in his fridge.'

Rusty frowned. 'I'm not sure we should wait on that one. Don't want him using it on anyone.'

'I took liberties with it.'

Rusty's frown changed to a smile. 'Good girl.'

'What next?' she asked.

'First we make this place look like we were never here. Then we split up. You try to dig up Bass.'

'I'll check at his house,' she said.

'And I'll drop in on one of Merton's customers. Maybe he can tell me where to find the guy.'

Chapter Forty-five

BACKTRACKING

No light showed through the windows of the old wooden house on Muir Road. Rusty's headlights flashed off its windows as he pulled onto the driveway. His car rocked on the pitted dirt. He climbed out, stepping carefully.

The screen door was still propped against the house wall. This time, however, the front door was shut and no sounds came from inside. He pushed the doorbell, but heard nothing. Probably out of order.

'Who're you?' came a boy's voice.

'Sheriff Hodges,' he answered, turning toward the window. The boy, looking out, rested his elbows on the sill. His hair was messy and he wore striped pyjamas, but he looked wide awake. 'Who're you?' Rusty asked.

'Sam. What do you want?'

'Is your sister here?'

'Which one?'

'Trinket.'

'Are you gonna take her back to jail?'

'Nope.'

'She was in jail today. They let her out.'

'I know.'

'You the guy she busted in the nuts?'

'I'm the guy.'

The boy nodded. He seemed sympathetic. 'She got my nuts, too.'

'Did you get her back?'

'She ain't got none, stupid. Girls don't. They got pussies.'

'Thanks for the tip.'

'You didn't know that?'

'Is Trink home?' Rusty asked.

Another child appeared in the window, this one a chubby girl no older than six, whose brown hair was cut like a boy's. She wore no top.

'Hi,' she said. 'Who're you?'

'I'm the sheriff.'

'I'm Lena.'

'Hi, Lena.'

'Hi.' She frowned. 'You're old.'

'Thanks.'

'Go to bed,' the boy told her.

'*You* go to bed.'

He shoved her away from the window. Her small fist swept past his face, barely missing. The boy's fist caught her hard on the shoulder with a sound like a hammer striking beef. For a moment, she was silent. Then she spread her mouth, squeezed her eyes shut and wailed.

'Shut up, damn it, or I'll sock you again.'

Fear sharpened her cry.

'Leave her alone,' Rusty said, seeing the boy make another fist.

'What the fuck's going on?' yelled a man from

252

somewhere inside the house. At that moment, a baby's cries joined those of Lena.

A voice Rusty recognized as Mrs Blake White's said, 'Goddamn it!'

Behind the boy and girl in the window, a light came on. Lena stopped crying.

'Sam hit me, Pa.'

'She hit me first.'

'Did not!'

'Did, too!'

Rusty moved in front of the window in time to see the hairy man in boxer shorts grab Lena's arm and jerk her across the room. She stumbled and resumed crying. The man grabbed Sam by the arm, dragged him away from the window, and cuffed his face. 'Get in bed, both of ya!'

'Mr White!'

He spun around. 'Who's that?'

'Sheriff Hodges.' Rusty stepped closer to the window until he was standing in the light from the room.

'What the fuck you doin' out there?'

'I came to see you about Trinket.'

'She's not here. See?' He pointed to the upper bunk bed. 'Not here. Bed's empty. Go bother somebody else.'

'I'd like a talk with you.'

'Who you talking to?' came the raspy voice of Mrs White. She entered the bedroom, waddling on her thick legs, her huge breasts swinging inside a sheer pink nightgown.

'It's your buddy the goddamn sheriff.'

'No shit?' She grinned, ducked to see him better, and waved. 'Hey there, law man.'

'I'd like to talk with you,' he said. 'Both of you.'

'Sure. I'll get the door. Come on, Biff.'

Rusty stepped sideways to the front door. He heard Biff warn the children to stay in bed and shut up. Then the door opened.

'Come right on in. Get you a beer?'

'No, thanks.'

'Tell him what he wants, Lida,' the man called. 'Leave me out. I need my sleep.'

'Okay?' she asked Rusty.

'I guess I won't need him.'

'He don't know doodle-squat, anyways.' She headed for the couch. 'Take a seat for yourself,' she said. She dropped to the couch and patted the cushion next to her.

Rusty turned a rocker to face the woman, and sat down on it.

'So, now, law man, you're back.' She lay an arm across the back of the couch. 'Sure I can't get you a cold one?'

'Thanks, but it'd probably put me to sleep.'

'You been up all day?'

'Since about six this morning.'

She yawned and patted her gaping mouth. 'Makes me tired just hearing.'

'I came about Trink.'

'Figured that. You should've kept her jailed where she belongs.'

'Couldn't do that. She's a juvenile.'

'She's a hell raiser. Oughta be penned up.'

'What sort of drugs does she use?'

'Dope?'

'Yes.'

'None I know about but weed. I took some off her, used

it myself.' She cackled. 'Wasn't half bad. Made her so damn mad she come at me, though. I thought she'd take a bite out of me, and I just wasn't up to that, so I give up and paid her good cash money for what I used. Girl's a devil. Takes after her Pa.'

'Do you know where she gets the marijuana?'

'Sure do.' Eyes turned downward, Lida gently pushed at her left breast. 'Did I tell you how she bit one of my lungs?'

'Yes, you did.'

'Still pains me some.'

'Have you seen a doctor?'

'Sure. Had to get me my rabies shots.' She laughed, holding the old wound.

'Where does Trink get her drugs?' Rusty asked again.

'The Mason boy. Bill. He's got himself a connection.'

'Do you know who it is?'

'Nawp.'

'Do you know *where* he gets the stuff?'

'All I know is, he gets it. Him and Trink go out driving. Sometimes they'll come back here, but mostly not.' Hooking a finger over the low neckline of her nightgown, she pulled downward and bared her breast. Frowning, she inspected the damage. 'Leastwise the girl's got straight teeth.'

Rusty studied the floor.

'They do a lot of balling, her and Bill. They'll do it on the sofa here if they figure nobody's gonna barge in. Or they'll head out into the woods. Over by the river, up on Indian Point. Anyplace they can get them some privacy, they'll park and get doped up and ball their asses off.'

'Where do you think they might be now?'

'Oh, Trink won't be *anyplace* with Bill. They had them a fight.'

'Do you know where *she* might be?'

'Is the pick-up out front?'

'I didn't see it.'

'Must be out cruising.'

'Do you . . .' Looking up, Rusty saw that the nightgown had dropped around Lida's waist. Her breasts hung like twin white loaves. He looked away from them and said, 'Do you know what Trink and Bill were doing last night at the river?'

'Where 'bouts?'

'Near the Bend.'

'Smoking dope and balling.' She grinned. She pulled up the skirt of her nightgown and spread her legs. 'How about it, law man?'

'I appreciate the offer,' he said, getting out of the chair. 'But it's late, we're both married, and I've got a busy night ahead of me.'

'Bawsh. Never heard of a man passing up some free nooky.'

'It happens.'

'C'mon, now. Don't rush off. We have to make sure Trink didn't do you no permanent damage.'

'I'll be fine,' he said. 'Thanks, though.'

'Please?' Lida's eyes were suddenly sad. 'Biff's such a bastard. I'll bet *you* know how to treat a lady.'

'I really have to leave. Sorry.'

At the Mason house on the north side of town, Rusty drove up a long, smoothly paved driveway. The upstairs windows of the house were dark, but a lamp in the living room's picture window was on. So was the porch light. Rusty moaned. The porch light was probably lit for a reason: probably, someone wasn't home yet.

Someone like Bill.

He pushed the doorbell button and heard chimes inside.

'Who is it?'

He recognized Bill's voice.

'Sheriff Hodges. I'd like to talk to you, Bill.'

Silence.

'Bill, open the door.'

'Okay, okay. Just a minute, okay?'

'Right now, please.'

'Okay. Christ!' The door opened three inches before its guard chain snapped taut. Bill's face appeared in the gap. It was red, the eyes quick and nervous. 'What do you want?'

'I want to talk to you.'

'Okay, go ahead.'

'Inside.'

'Why?'

'It's almost one-thirty. I'm not feeling very patient. Now take off the chain and let me in.'

'Look, I got company.'

'Good for you. In about ten seconds, your company can watch you get arrested.'

'For what?'

'Take your pick.'

'Okay, okay. Christ!' He shut the door. The chain rattled. Then the door opened wide. Bill stood just inside the entrance and crossed his arms. He'd changed clothes since the last time Rusty saw him. Barefoot now, he wore a clean white T-shirt and plaid Bermuda shorts. 'What do you want?'

Rusty stepped past him and entered the living room. A haze of smoke swirled in the air. He breathed its pungent odor. 'Where're your parents?'

'Out.'

'Looks like your company departed.'

'Thanks to you.'

'Anyone I know?'

'I doubt it.'

Rusty pressed the back of his hand against the couch. The fabric still held body heat. He moved his hand down the length of the cushion, smiled up at Bill and said, 'Cozy.' Then he sat down.

'What do you want?'

'Tell me where you buy your grass.'

Bill made a nervous gasp that struggled to sound like a cough.

Rusty slipped a photo from his shirt pocket and handed it to him. 'That's your source. His name is Merton LeRoy.'

Bill shook his head. 'Don't know the guy.' He reached out as if to return the photo, then dropped it.

The picture fluttered to the carpet in front of Rusty's right boot.

'Pick it up, Bill.'

'You pick it up.'

'I didn't drop it.'

Muttering, his face red with anger, Bill bent down. As he reached for the photo, Rusty darted his boot forward and trapped Bill's hand against the carpet.

'Now, Bill, where do you buy your grass?'

'Get off my fuckin' hand!'

Rusty put some weight on his heel.

Bill cringed. 'Cocksucker!'

'Where do you buy your grass?'

'I'm not telling!'

'No?' He applied more weight and Bill cried out. 'How about it, champ?'

'He'll kill me!'

'Who will?'

'*Him!* Merton!'

'He won't kill you. He'll be in prison.'

'Motherfuckin' asshole!'

'Where do you make your buys from him?'

'Get off my hand!'

Rusty twisted his boot. Bill's face puckered and his eyes squeezed out tears.

'Okay! Okay!'

Rusty let up the pressure. 'Where do you meet him?'

'By the river. Where you found us this morning. At the roadhead. He deals out of his van.'

'What happened last night?'

'Take your foot off!'

'Tell me,' Rusty said and began pressing down again.

'Okay! I made a buy from him.'

'What time?'

'I don't know, midnight. He gets there about eleven and stays. So, yeah, probably around midnight.'

'How long does he stay?'

'Depends on the action. Till one or two, sometimes all night.'

'Is he there every night?'

'Where? Sweet Meadow? Just Tuesdays, Fridays and Saturdays.'

'So he should be there now?'
'I don't know. Maybe.'
'Let's go see.'

Chapter Forty-six

POSITIVE ID

Pac stood at the front door of Bass's house. Though no lights showed through the front window, she pushed the doorbell button half a dozen times. Then she rapped the wood hard, making her knuckles sting.

A moist breeze chilled her bare back. It drifted the thin fabric of her dress against her buttocks and the backs of her legs.

Waiting, she remembered how Harney had been standing behind her on Ina's porch, reaching through the open sides of her gown and caressing her.

She wished she could be home with him now.

The sooner we get this over with . . .

Turning away from the door, she started down the walkway toward the street. She was nearly to her car when a sound came from somewhere behind her: a quick, low thump like a car door shutting.

A new chill scurried up her back. This one wasn't caused by the damp night air.

She opened her purse and pulled out her pistol.

Dew spattered her feet as she ran across the grass. She

headed directly for the garage wall nearest the house, where moonlight made a window shine.

As she crouched next to the window, her bare shoulder touched the wall. The wet cold startled her. She rubbed her shoulder, then rose out of her crouch and peered through a low corner of the glass.

Only darkness.

But the darkness was strange.

Standing up straight, Pac leaned closer until her forehead and nose pressed the glass. At the far edge of the window, she saw a vertical, broken thread of light.

Someone, she realized, must've covered the inside of the window with a sheet of opaque material, maybe cardboard.

Someone who wanted privacy.

Pac stepped away from the window. She looked down the wall toward the back of the garage and saw a door. Leaving her purse on the ground near the wall, she walked silently to the door.

She tried to turn the knob, but it didn't move.

She knocked gently on the door.

'Bass? Bass, are you in there?'

'Is that you, Pac?'

'Yeah. Let me in, would you?'

'Sure. Just a second.'

She heard water come on, thumping into a metal basin.

For a moment, it seemed strange that Bass should have a wash basin inside his garage. Then she remembered his boasting about it last year. He'd had it installed, along with a garbage disposal, so he could clean his fish without bringing them into the house. 'That's what *you* need,' she had kidded

Harney, who rarely returned from fishing trips with more than a sunburn.

As the door started to open, she lowered her pistol. Not wanting to give Bass a fright, she held it out of sight behind her back.

He saw her, smiled, and flicked off the garage light. 'You got me fair and square,' he said, using a tough-guy voice Pac recognized as his mediocre Bogart impression.

'I guess you're all right,' she said.

'I haven't been abducted or murdered. Not yet.'

She backed away as Bass stepped out of the garage and shut the door. 'Nice outfit,' he said. 'Harn buy that for you?'

'I bought it for Harney.'

'Shall we go into the house where we can throw some light on the subject?'

Even in the dark, she could see his playful leer.

'Let me get my purse,' she said. 'I'll put *this* away.' She swung the pistol around and showed it to him. 'I didn't know who I might be running into.'

'Just me.'

'Yep.' She turned away from him.

'Wow!' he said.

'Yeah, I know. I should've changed.'

'Not on my account.'

'Glad you like it.'

Bass close behind her, she stopped for her purse. Pressing a forearm across her chest to hold the front of her gown in place, she bent down and picked it up.

As she straightened, Bass said, 'Let's go in the back door. I'm still a bit nervous about the front.'

'No problem,' Pac said.

She slipped the .380 into her purse as she followed Bass to the rear of the house.

He pulled open the screen door of the porch, letting her enter before coming inside himself to open the kitchen door. 'I swept up the broken glass,' he said, and turned on the kitchen light.

The house was warm and a bit stuffy.

Bass led the way into the living room. He turned on a lamp.

Pac expected him to sit down. Instead, he faced her and pushed his hands into the pockets of his jeans. He chewed his lower lip. His eyes looked somber.

'Did you come about Faye?' he asked.

'I phoned her parents. She's not there yet. She hasn't been in touch with them.'

'So she's still among the missing?'

'For the time being.'

With a loud sigh, Bass took a hand from his pocket and rubbed the side of his face. 'Well, that's something, anyway. You dropping by at this hour . . . well, it scared me. You know? I was afraid . . . I don't know . . . that something might've turned up.'

'Something did turn up, but not about Faye.' From her purse, she took the photos Rusty had given her at the hospital. She held them out toward Bass. 'Do you recognize this man?' she asked.

Bass glanced at his hands. They were black with grease. He wiped them on the front of his shirt. Though neatly tucked in, his shirt was smudged and streaked. 'Working on the car,' he muttered, and reached for the photos. He studied them for several seconds, frowning. Then he asked, 'Am I supposed to know this guy?'

'He's shaved his head since those were taken.'

'Ah.' Bass studied the face. Finally he said, 'This is him, isn't it? Yeah. It's him, all right. The one who chased me tonight. And the one we saw at the Bend – the guy who killed what's-her-name. Parker?'

'Parkington. Alison Parkington.'

'Yeah, her. Do you have him?'

'Not yet. Not that I know of, anyway.'

Chapter Forty-seven

MERTON'S TALE

A quiet rapping on the rear door of the van awakened Merton. He opened his eyes and stared up at his reflection in the enormous mirror. His naked body, lit in red, looked bathed in blood.

The boy was gone.

What a kid. Steve? Yeah, that was his name.

He'd been an easy make. Reluctant all the way but giving in, giving in, until there was nothing more to give and he found himself doing what he'd always been taught that only perverts do. And loving it. And crying afterwards because of his shame.

Maybe the kid had come back.

Maybe he squealed.

The knocking came again.

Merton sat up, swung his legs off the bed and reached down for his jeans.

'Who's there?' he called.

'I'm looking for Mister In-Between.'

The voice sounded familiar, but it wasn't Steve's.

'Who is it?'

'Bill.'

'Are you alone?'

'Yeah.'

'I don't want to see that freaky bitch you hang out with, so if she's with you send her back to your truck.'

'She isn't here.'

Merton pulled on his jeans. On his way to the rear door, he fastened the waist button and slid the zipper up. He opened the door. Bill was standing a few paces behind the van. He wore a pale T-shirt, dark shorts, and no socks or shoes.

Leaning out the rear of his van, Merton scanned the moonlit clearing. He saw Bill's car, but no sign of Trink. 'I hope you dumped her for good.'

'Yeah, I did,' Bill said. 'We had a fight.'

'Good deal. Lose her for good, that's my advice.'

'Yeah. I've had enough of her. But I think she tried to follow me out here. Someone was tailing me a while ago. I'm pretty sure I lost whoever it was, but . . .' He glanced around.

'You'd better get in here fast,' Merton said.

'Sure.'

He crawled backward, giving Bill room to enter. Once inside, Bill pulled the door shut.

'She comes along,' Merton said, 'she'll wish she hadn't.'

'Yeah.'

'She likes body-piercing, *I'll* pierce her.'

Bill nodded, chuckling softly.

'So, what can I do for you?' Merton asked him.

'How about some hash?'

'How about a free sample?'

'Hey, great.'

'Make yourself comfortable,' Merton said, and crawled to a cupboard. He opened it, took out the pipe and a baggie of hash, then sat on the edge of his bed. Reaching into the plastic bag, he picked out a small chunk of hash. He placed it onto the wire mesh of his pipe. He lit it with a match, drawing on the pipe, sucking the rich smoke into his lungs.

'Did you hear about that dead woman they found?' Bill asked him. 'The one without a head?'

'Sure I heard,' Merton took another puff. 'What about her?'

'They found her really close to here.'

'So what?'

'Some guy was seen with her body.'

'Yeah?'

'I read about it in the paper. The thing is . . . the guy who killed her? He sounded a lot like you.'

'Did he?'

'Yeah. A lot.'

'Is that why you're back tonight? Think I might be the killer?'

'Sort of.'

Merton eased himself down from the bed and crawled toward Bill, who was kneeling just inside the rear doors.

'I'm not the one who killed her,' Merton said. On his knees, he opened his jeans. They went loose and slipped down a few inches. He sucked some hash smoke into his lungs, then gave the pipe to Bill. As the boy smoked, Merton took his left hand. 'Here,' he said, drawing the hand toward him. 'Touch.'

He felt Bill's cool fingers.

'This hasn't touched a woman since I was sixteen years

old,' he said, his voice husky. 'And it didn't touch one last night.'

'I'm not saying it did.'

'But you think I killed her, don't you?'

'I don't know.'

'If I didn't fuck her, I didn't kill her. The same guy did both. And I saw it happen.'

'You *saw* it?' Bill asked, his hand sliding, gently caressing.

'Saw it,' Merton said, 'but didn't *do* it.'

'When?'

'After you and that bitch went back to the truck last night. You know how stoned I was.'

'Out of your gourd,' Bill said, still slowly stroking him.

'So I went for a little walk in the night. I wanted to see what the moon looked like on the river.'

Trembling, Merton took the pipe back. He sucked from it and held the smoke deep in his lungs. He let it out slowly. 'A man was naked on the other side of the river. Shocked the hell out of me, seeing him over there. I thought maybe I was hallucinating, but I didn't really think so.' He slipped the pipe back into Bill's mouth. 'Anyway, I didn't want to get caught spying on him, so I stayed hidden in the trees. Couldn't take my eyes off the guy. You should've seen him in the moonlight, Billy. He had himself a real good build. His skin was all wet and gleaming . . . His *saw* gleamed, too. His hacksaw.'

Bill's hand stopped moving. 'He had a *hacksaw* with him?'

'You bet he did. I couldn't figure out why, at first. But someone else was there with him. Someone I hadn't noticed.

269

A woman. I had my eyes on him the whole time, so I didn't spot her till he walked across the sand and knelt down over her body. For a long time, he just seemed to be staring down at her. Then he put down the saw and climbed onto her and fucked her.'

Bill took out the pipe. 'She was dead?' he asked.

Merton shrugged. 'No idea. Might've just been out cold. Either way, she just laid there.' He chuckled softly. Reaching out, he unbuckled Bill's belt.

Bill gripped his hand. 'What happened after that?'

'After he got done fucking her, he cut off her head. Let go of my hand.'

Bill released it.

With both hands, Merton worked to unfasten Bill's waist button. 'He sawed her head right off, just like a guy sawing a log for the fireplace.' The button came undone. The zipper skidded down. 'I couldn't believe it. I had to be hallucinating. All that hash.' He pulled down Bill's shorts and underwear. 'So later that morning, when I was sure he'd gone, I swam across the river to find out for sure. Even when I touched her, I wasn't completely sure the whole thing was real.' He reached for Bill's genitals.

Bill grabbed his hand and stopped it. 'Don't.'

'What's *your* problem tonight?'

'*Sheriff!*' Bill shouted.

Merton lunged at Bill, tumbling the boy backward. He raised his fist, ready to hammer it down.

Then the van's rear door flew open.

A voice he knew from long ago shouted, 'Stop!'

He looked up.

A big, freckled hand, washed in crimson light, aimed an

enormous revolver at his face. Behind the hand and out of the light was the broad, grim face of Sheriff Rusty Hodges.

'We meet again,' Hodges said.

'Fuck you.'

'Pull up your jeans and climb out.'

Chapter Forty-eight

FISHY BUSINESS

Ready to leave, Pac started across the living room of Bass's house.

'Do you think I'll be safe here?' Bass asked, walking beside her.

'You'd be better off back at the motel. You were supposed to *stay* there, you know.'

'You know what?' Bass said. He made an embarrassed smile. 'Going off to hide in that motel made me feel like a chicken. You know, like I was running away. I didn't like that feeling, so I came home.' He laughed once.

Pac, stopping a stride away from the front door, reached out for the knob.

'Almost didn't make it, either,' Bass said. 'My brakes went out about halfway here.' He frowned. 'You don't suppose . . . ? Maybe Merton tampered with them?'

'Possible,' Pac said. Her hand dropped away from the door knob. Turning, she faced Bass. 'What's the matter with the brakes?' she asked.

'I didn't get a chance to find out. I was just in the process of taking a look when you showed up.'

'That's what you were doing in your garage?'

'Right.'

'You're braver than I am,' she said.

'How's that?'

'If *I* lost my brakes, I'd park my car on the street. Or I might risk pulling into the driveway. But I sure wouldn't drive into the garage. I'd be afraid of taking out the back wall.'

'Guess it wasn't a real smart move,' Bass said.

'No. It wasn't.' Pac slipped her right hand inside her purse. She took hold of her Sig Sauer but didn't pull it out. 'Let's take a look in your garage, Bass.'

'Hey.' He laughed. 'You're kidding, right?'

'Wrong.'

'Do you have any idea how *late* it is?'

'I know exactly how late it is.'

'I'm tired,' Bass said. 'I bet you are, too.'

'I'm tired, all right. But I'd still like to have a look in your garage before I go. I'd like to find out why you lied.'

He shrugged. 'I didn't lie. You're gonna feel like a real ass.'

'I'd *be* a real ass if I didn't check.'

'What do you think you'll find in there?'

'Let's have a look and see.'

'You're gonna feel like an ass.'

'Knock it off, all right? Just take me out to the garage and we'll get it over with. If it checks out, fine. I'll be on my way.'

'Let's go, then. I've got nothing to hide.'

Turning away, he started toward the kitchen.

273

'Let's go out this way,' Pac said, and opened the front door.

'You're getting awfully pushy, you know that?'

'Just doing my job.'

'I've had a tough day,' Bass complained. 'It was bad enough my canoe trip got ruined by that damned body and I had to spend half the day explaining. Some asshole has to kidnap Faye and try to kill me. But now, to top it all off, I'm being treated like a criminal by my best friend's wife.'

'You're starting to behave like one.'

'And what's your hand doing in your purse?'

She showed him by pulling out her pistol.

'Very nice,' Bass said. 'Now what're you gonna do, shoot me?'

She stepped away from the door and waved him toward it. 'Get out there and open the garage.'

'I ought to make you get a search warrant,' he said, going out the door.

'That's your right.' She followed him outside, keeping her pistol down by her leg.

'Maybe I'd better do that. I don't see why I should be so cooperative, you treating me like a piece of shit.'

'If you insist on a warrant, I'll place you under arrest and take you in. Just to make sure you don't try to dispose of whatever it is that you don't want me finding.'

'This is what happens – give a woman a little power, all of a sudden she turns into a fuckin' Nazi.'

'Do I have your permission to search your garage?'

'Sure. *Sieg Heil!*'

'Grow up, Bass.'

They walked to the garage's side door. Muttering words

that Pac couldn't quite make out, Bass unlocked the door and swung it open. He reached into the darkness. Moments later, the garage filled with light.

Pac entered it behind him.

Built for two cars, the garage housed Bass's red Pontiac and a fifteen-foot powerboat on a trailer. The air was still very warm from the long, hot day. Pac smelled grease, gasoline, and other odors she couldn't place. The mixture was unpleasant, but not overwhelming.

'Well?' Bass asked. 'What do you want to see?'

Pac didn't answer. Standing just inside the door, she scanned the garage. Sheets of cardboard covered the two windows. On the wall near the front was the control panel for the automatic door opener. Above the powerboat, the canoe lay across the ceiling beams. There was a refrigerator in the corner near the sink. Next to it stood a freezer chest. Then a workbench.

Tools hung on a pegboard behind the cleared workbench: a level, a ball pean hammer, a claw hammer, assorted sizes of screw drivers and wrenches, and three varieties of saws.

'I see you have a hacksaw,' Pac said.

'You've got wonderful eyesight.'

'What do you use it for?'

'I saw heads off with it.'

'Try answering me straight, Bass.'

'Try asking me a smart question. Of course I've got a hacksaw. As you can see, I have lots of tools. And I'd be willing to bet that *that* isn't the hacksaw somebody used on Alison Parkington.'

'It isn't. We *have* that saw.' Pac stepped past him. She turned her head, keeping an eye on him as she crossed the garage to the freezer chest. She pulled its handle. Locked. 'Would you mind opening this for me?'

'Think I've got a body hidden in there?'

'I don't know what to think. But you're acting weird and you lied about the brakes. And why the hell have you got the windows covered like that?'

'I just like a little privacy.'

'Come here and open the freezer.'

'Open it yourself,' he said. 'The key's on top of the refrigerator.'

The top of the refrigerator was above Pac's eye level. She switched the .380 to her left hand. Without taking her eyes off Bass, she reached up and patted the dusty metal surface. As she searched, a drop of sweat slid down from her armpit, trickling down her bare side all the way to her hip where it encountered her dress. At last, her fingers touched a key ring. She pulled it down. A single, small key dangled from the ring.

It fit into the freezer's lock.

'Are you sure you want to know what's in there, Pac?' His grin was smart. 'Are you sure you'll be able to *live* with it? Seeing it over and over again in your nightmares?'

'I'll manage,' she said and raised the freezer top.

Through curling white clouds of vapor, she saw cartons of ice cream, a stack of TV dinners, several small packs of white paper bearing the colored tape seals of a local butcher, possibly a dozen aluminum foil packs that she assumed contained fish, and a turkey.

Turning sideways so she could keep an eye on Bass, she bent over the freezer and reached down with her right arm. And felt the front of her gown fall away from her body a few inches like a boat sail catching a breeze.

Where Bass was standing – over to the left but a few paces in front of her – she doubted that he could see much.

Glancing away from him, she looked down into the freezer and shoved some of the packages around.

'Ghastly, huh?' Bass asked.

Pac shut the freezer. She returned the key to the top of the refrigerator.

'Why don't you check the fridge, too?'

'I was about to do just that.' The refrigerator had no lock. She looked inside. It held mostly beer and soft drinks. She shut its door.

'No body? Geez, I hate to disappoint you, Pac. Sorry I couldn't be more helpful.'

She walked alongside his car, peering into the windows.

'If I'd known you wanted a body so much, maybe I could've bought you one. Do you think we could send out for one? Like a pizza? Maybe there's an all-night mortuary that delivers.'

At the rear of Bass's big red Pontiac, Pac saw that its trunk lid was held down by three strips of wide, gray duct tape.

'Why'd you tape your trunk shut?' she asked.

'It hasn't worked right ever since—'

'You never taped it before.'

'It started popping open. Is there a law against taping your trunk shut?'

'Would you like to open it for me?'

'Sure. Why not?'

She stepped backward as Bass approached. Turning away from her, he bent down and started to peel the duct tape off the lid of the trunk. It made sounds like ripping cloth. He left each strip attached at the bottom, hanging over the rear bumper.

When he was done, the trunk remained shut.

He pounded the lid with his hand. It jumped under the impact, then started to rise.

He stepped out of the way.

Springs lifted the trunk lid.

Inside the trunk, the naked body of a woman was curled on its side. It ended at the shoulders. The head rested face up against her belly.

Pac heard herself gasp.

Before she could move, the back of Bass's fist struck her nose and she was walking backward, falling.

Chapter Forty-nine

THE MAN AT THE BEND

'Did you recognize the killer?' Rusty asked. He stood beside the open passenger door of his patrol car, crouching slightly to see Merton better. Merton, handcuffed, sat sideways on the back seat with his legs hanging toward the ground.

'I'm not sure my lawyer wants me to answer that,' he said.

'Your lawyer isn't here.'

'Well, why don't we wait until he is?'

'I'm in something of a hurry, Merton.'

'Tough shit.'

'I can get you for contributing, possession, dealing, breaking and entering, assault and battery on Ina Jones, the attempted murder of Bass Paxton . . . And it shouldn't be any trick at all to nail you for the murder of Alison Parkington.'

'I didn't kill that bitch.'

'That's not what Walter said.'

'Walter's full of shit.'

'Look, Mert, I had my ear to your window. I heard your whole spiel to the kid.' Rusty nodded toward Bill, who was sitting in the front seat of the patrol car. 'It sounded like the truth, to me. But if we can't hang it on the fellow with the moonlit, gleaming skin, we'll hang it on you. So try to cooperate.'

'I knew you'd be a bastard about this. I should've dumped those creeps who saw me. You wouldn't have shit.'

'Which reminds me . . . Where's Faye Everett?'

'Who's that?'

'The blonde who was with Bass this morning by the river.'

'*Yesterday* morning.'

'Whatever. Where is she?'

'Got no idea. I've been looking for her myself.'

'What about your gleaming killer? What did he look like?'

'I couldn't see very well.'

'It didn't sound that way when you were talking to Bill.'

'I couldn't see his *face*. It was *night* you know, and I was all the way on the other side of the river.'

'What *could* you see?'

'He had a nice body on him. I'd say he was young. Had a good build.'

'How young?'

'Maybe mid-twenties.'

'How tall?'

'Who knows? Maybe six feet. Maybe six-two, six-three. Probably a couple hundred pounds or more. He had good-looking muscles.'

'What color was his hair?'

'Dark. Brown or black, I guess.'

'Was his hair long or short?'

'Medium.'

'Facial hair?'

'I couldn't see well enough.'

'Did you hear him speak?'

'No.'

'Anything unusual about him?'

'Unusual? Sure. He fucked a babe and sawed her head off. I'd say *that's* unusual.' Merton laughed softly.

'What did he do with the head?'

'After he cut it off? He wrapped it up. In his shirt, I think. Then he knelt down in the sand. He started digging. I figured he was going to bury it, but he didn't. What he buried was the saw. And some clothes or something. Then he got dressed and took the head with him.'

'Where?'

'Up the trail. He must've had a car at the top. Pretty soon, I heard him drive off.'

'You're *sure* he took the head with him?'

'He had it as long as I saw him. Carried it by the hair. He sort of swung it back and forth beside him.'

Frowning, Rusty muttered, 'Strange.'

'You're telling me.'

He looked into Merton's eyes. 'It's strange because we have a witness who saw *you* with the head. He says you swam back across the river with it this morning.'

'Who's this, Paxton?'

'That's right.'

'If he said that, he lied. Now why do you suppose he'd lie about a thing like that? You think maybe *he's* the killer? Could be. Yeah, could be Paxton. He might be the guy I saw. Has that nice build . . .'

'Pull in your feet.' Rusty threw the door shut and ran to

his side of the car. He climbed in and turned the key in the ignition.

'Where are we going?' Bill asked from the passenger seat.

Ignoring him, Rusty lifted his radio mike. 'Car One to headquarters.' The car lurched forward, its headlights reaming the darkness.

'Go ahead, Car One.'

'Any available units in the vicinity of Malfi Drive?'

'The nearest is Tac Four answering a four fifteen at one six three eight Harding.'

'Won't do us any good. I'll handle it.'

Chapter Fifty

BLOODY BUT UNBOWED

Pac, sprawled on the cool concrete, watched Bass search her purse. He pulled out her handcuffs.

'Where's Faye?' she asked. Her nose was blocked with blood and she sounded as if she had a cold.

'Didn't you recognize her?' Bass asked.

'That wasn't Faye.'

'Why thank you. That's the nicest thing you've said all day. I appreciate it.'

He stuffed the handcuffs into a rear pocket of his jeans. Bending over Pac, he picked up both her wrists. She neither helped nor resisted as he pulled her to a sitting position, but when blood began trickling from her nose she tried to pull a hand free to wipe it. Bass held her wrists more tightly. She sniffed, but the blood continued to spill. She licked it off her upper lip and tilted back her head.

'I couldn't just murder Faye,' Bass said, sounding pleased with himself. 'Christ, any halfwit would figure I'm the guy with the best motive for that.'

'What motive?' Pac asked, and licked more blood.

'What do *you* think? She was stepping out on me,

dropping her pants for that bastard Parkington.' Releasing one of Pac's wrists, he scurried around behind her with the other and fastened the cuffs. 'The bitch should've known better,' he said. 'I forgave her for fucking around with that asshole in Burlingame last time, didn't I? Gave her a second chance. So what does she do? She starts fucking around with her fucking *summer school professor*!' He grabbed Pac's other arm and jerked it back behind her. 'She blew it. No third chances, Pac. She had to die. But she wasn't gonna take me with her. No way. No way at all.'

'So you hired Merton LeRoy to kill her?'

Bass laughed. Pac felt his warm burst of breath on the back of her neck. 'I never saw that queer till this morning,' he said. 'Guess that was *yesterday* morning, now, huh? He sure came in handy, though. My God, when I saw him lying there with the Parkington bitch, *I* almost believed he'd killed her.'

'*You* killed her?'

'Sure. I needed a body for my big plan.'

'What *big plan*?'

'Any body would've done, as long as it had blonde hair.' Pac felt a hand stroke the hair on the back of her head. 'Yours would've done fine. I would've had to cut your hair, of course. Faye's is so much shorter than yours. But you would've done fine. I gave you some hard consideration at first. But then I found out that Parkington's wife was a blonde. So much better, using her. That way, I wouldn't just be killing Faye, I'd be getting back at the good professor who fucked her. If he gave any sort of shit at all about his wife, that would hurt him.'

'It did,' Pac said. She licked her upper lip. There didn't

seem to be as much blood as before.

'That Alison was a beautiful woman,' Bass muttered. 'And wild. She jumped at my idea of a midnight rendezvous. So beautiful. She thought I was hot stuff, too. Hell, I am hot stuff. Don't you think so, Pac?'

'You're not my type,' she said.

She tensed as his hands came down on her bare shoulders. 'Sure I am. I'm *every* woman's type.'

'Sure.'

His hands began rubbing Pac's shoulders in a slow, deliberate way. 'That Alison was one eager beaver. She jumped at the chance to have a little fun with me in the middle of the night. I ended up enjoying it, myself. She was a really beautiful gal. Only not so beautiful by the time Faye got to see her. That was part of Faye's punishment – give her a look at a naked, headless corpse. It was also part of the big plan. After a sight like that, it was perfectly reasonable for Faye to make a blind dash for her folks' place – or for *any* place. Right? Just to get away. Ina bought it. You bought it. Everyone bought it.

'Before you know it, Faye's car is going to turn up in San Francisco. Just her car. Right now, it's nicely hidden at the marina. I drove it down this afternoon, all loaded with her luggage. I'll leave it there till things calm down a little, then I'll drive it to San Francisco.'

Bass slid his hands from Pac's shoulders to the back of her neck. He pulled slowly on the tied cords.

'When they find her car, they'll figure Faye made it to the Bay Area, after all. Maybe she was on the way to her parents' house and ran into some sort of trouble. They'll probably search high and low for her, but they'll never find her. Never never never.'

Pac felt the cords come loose. The front of her gown fell, leaving her naked to the waist.

'Rusty put out an APB on that car,' she said, her voice shaking. 'You try to drive it *anywhere*, you'll be picked up.'

'Oh, I'll make it. I changed the license plates.' He kissed the side of her neck. His breath tickling her skin, he said, 'I'll just put Faye's own plates back on after I'm there.'

'Real smart,' Pac muttered.

'I'm a very smart guy. *And* a hunk.'

'*And* a comedian,' Pac said.

He slipped his arms around her. His hands took hold of her breasts.

Fucking bastard.

Stay clam, she told herself. *Just take it easy.*

'What did you do to Faye?' she asked.

'Didn't you see her in the trunk?'

'That wasn't Faye.'

'Like I said, thanks. But you're wrong. That *is* Faye. Minus a few parts. Like her fingers. Like her tongue. Like her *nipples*.' He pinched Pac's nipples.

She flinched and gasped, '*Ow! Don't!*'

'Like a few other choice parts of her. They're down the garbage disposal. And like her head.'

'Her head?'

'She's *minus* her head. I didn't put it down the disposal, though. Wouldn't fit.' He laughed. 'Her poor little noggin got run over tonight by an eighteen-wheeler out on Highway Forty.'

'That was *Faye's* head?'

'Yep.'

'Why?'

'Because I put it in the road. Did it right after that queer smashed Ina on the head and chased me around.'

He jerked Pac's hair, pulling her down backward to the garage floor.

She lay on her arms. The sharp edges of her handcuffs bit into her wrists and lower back.

Bass, on his knees, leaned forward. Looming over Pac so his face appeared upside-down, he grinned at her. 'They all think it's *Alison's* head that got mashed tonight. Don't they?'

'I don't know.'

'Sure they do. Alison's the stiff with the missing head. Now they've found it. Nobody'll even think twice. You know what they'll do? They'll bury Alison's body together with *Faye's* head. Just wait and see.' He laughed and said, 'Woops! No, I guess you won't have a chance to wait and see, will you? You'll be dead, just like them.'

'There's no point, Bass. Killing me won't help.'

'Oh, I *have* to kill you.' Reaching down, he gently squeezed her breasts. 'I've talked too much. You know *everything*.'

'Let me take you in, Bass. I'll do everything I can to help you . . .'

'Very generous offer,' he said. 'But I've got other plans.' Leaning far over her, he slid his hands down her ribcage, her belly. At her hips, he shoved the gathered fabric of her dress. But the dress didn't move. 'Lift your ass,' he said.

'I can't.'

'Lift it.'

'Why don't you just wait and do this after I'm dead, okay? I'll be a lot more cooperative then.'

'A gutsy bitch to the end.'

'That's me.'

'Pick up your ass.'

'Fuck you.'

'Do you want me to hurt you, Pac? I'm capable of . . . hurting you *very* badly. I'd *love* to do it. I hurt Faye *a lot* before I killed her. She didn't like it very much, I'll tell you that. Neither will you. I don't care how gutsy you think you are, darling, I'll have you screaming for mercy. Want a taste?'

'No,' she muttered. She raised her knees slightly and lifted her back off her tightly clenched fists.

Bass, leaning way over her, gripped her dress with both hands. As he started shoving it down her hips, he lost his balance. He let go quickly with one hand and caught himself. Braced up with his left hand on the garage floor, he dragged the dress down with his right.

Pac shot a knee up. It struck his forehead. His bracing arm collapsed. Even as he started to drop, Pac twisted, throwing herself sideways.

His belt buckle scratched her shoulder as she rolled.

Then she was out from under him.

He lay face-down, barely moving.

Pac kicked off her shoes. She rolled onto her back. Ignoring the pain as the cuffs cut into her, she sat up. On her rump, she crossed her legs. Then she rocked forward and lunged to her feet. The gown slipped down to her ankles. She scowled at it.

No way to put it back on. Not with her hands cuffed behind her back.

So she stepped out of it.

Bass, now on his hands and knees, looked at Pac with

dull, half-shut eyes. Then he looked down at the floor. At Pac's pistol near his right hand.

He reached for it.

With a quick sweep of her foot, Pac knocked it skidding away.

Bass grabbed her ankle.

She jerked free, jumped away from him and rushed to the wall.

To the garage door opener.

She rammed her shoulder against its button, but nothing happened. Turning to face the panel, she crouched and shoved the button with her nose.

The equipment let out a thump and hum. Rumbling, the garage door began to rise.

Not fast enough.

Bass was standing, his legs wobbly. He stumbled backward, stopped himself, and shook his head as if trying to clear it.

Pac dropped to her knees and rolled. The concrete was cool and smooth against her skin. The first roll took her underneath the rising door. The second brought her to her knees. With its momentum, she gained her feet and started to run down the driveway.

Running was hard with her arms cuffed behind her back. Hard and slow and precarious.

More than anything, she needed her arms for balance.

In moments, she heard footfalls behind her. She didn't look back. The pounding shoes gained on her.

She almost made it to the end of the driveway before Bass clutched her right shoulder and jerked it. She spun around, falling.

The lawn was wet and she slid when she hit it.

Then Bass was on her.

She screamed.

That's when he punched her just below the ribs and she felt as if her insides were exploding through her skin. As she gagged for air, he picked her up.

'Hey!' someone yelled. 'What's going on?'

'Mind your own fucking business!' Bass shouted.

Pac felt herself flop over Bass's shoulder. He started running, his shoulder pounding into her belly like a club.

'What the hell you doing?' the voice called again.

This time, Bass didn't answer. He stopped abruptly. From the brightness of the lights, Pac knew they were inside his garage.

He suddenly bent down and threw her backward.

She expected a long fall and a terrible, jolting blow as she struck the concrete floor.

But the fall was brief.

She didn't hit the floor.

For a moment, she was glad. Then she felt Bass pushing her legs, and she suddenly knew what had broken her fall.

She opened her eyes in time to see Bass fling down the lid of his Pontiac's trunk.

When it pounded her upraised knee, she passed out.

Chapter Fifty-one

THE CHASE

From his speeding patrol car, Rusty saw the red Pontiac shoot backward out of Bass's garage. A bald man rushed into the driveway, shouting. The car struck him and threw him tumbling through the air.

'Fuck!' Bill blurted from the passenger seat.

In the back seat, Merton said nothing.

Rusty mashed the accelerator. As his car surged forward, he recognized Pac's car parked by the curb. His eyes shot back to the Pontiac in time to see its tail drop into a dip where the driveway met the road.

Its trunk lid sprang open.

Rusty saw an upraised knee inside.

He hit the brake pedal. His tires grabbed pavement. His headlights reflected on the polished red of the Pontiac's side and he saw Bass hunched behind the steering wheel.

'Watch out!' Bill yelled.

The headlights of Rusty's car shattered against the Pontiac's side. Rusty threw open his door and jumped out, drawing his revolver. Crouched behind the door, he aimed the .44 magnum at Bass's head. 'Climb out!'

Bass ducked below the window. His car darted forward, sparks bursting as it scraped the front of the patrol car.

Rusty glimpsed the dented door. Its metal looked like crumpled paper. He followed it briefly in his sights, then squeezed the trigger. The pistol blasted and bucked. Its bullet punched a hole through the door. He heard Bass yelp with pain and anger. But the car gained speed. Just in front of the garage, it swung onto the lawn. The open trunk shielded its rear window.

'Get out!' Rusty snapped at Bill.

The boy, holding his head, looked at Rusty with confusion. 'What?'

'Get out! Get out!' Rusty slammed his own door shut as Bill pushed open the passenger door.

'How about me?' Merton asked from the back seat.

'You stay.' He fastened his seat belt and stomped on the gas pedal.

Ahead of him, the Pontiac was angling across a neighbor's lawn, speeding toward the street. It tore through a hedge, raced across the sidewalk and leaped from the curb. When it hit the street, the trunk bounced almost shut and flew open again.

Rusty picked up his mike. 'Car One to headquarters.'

'Car One go ahead.'

'Hit and run at four three two Malfi. Send ambulance. A man is down. Suspect vehicle is a red on red Pontiac Grand Prix, Charles-William-David eight four three. I'm in pursuit.'

For a long time, the siren screamed in Pac's mind. She thought she was home in bed, and tried to reach out for Harney. Her arm wouldn't move out from under her. It felt asleep. Both arms were asleep and ached with a numb tingle when she tried to move them. She attempted to straighten her legs and pain shot through her left knee. Something blocked her feet. A sudden claustrophobic fear shocked her fully awake.

Above her, the trunk lid bobbed, bright with light from the spinning flashers of the patrol car that was obviously pursuing them.

But she could feel a cool touch against her right shoulder. A touch of skin that vibrated and bounced with the car's motion.

Finally, she turned her head and looked.

In the darkness, it took several moments to recognize the shape pressing against her shoulder.

Faye's knee.

Faye! Oh, God!

She turned her eyes away.

And remembered Bass taunting her. *That is Faye. Minus a few parts. Like her fingers. Like her tongue. Like . . .*

NO!

She turned her eyes away and stared at the lights flashing on the bottom of the trunk lid, at the dark treetops, at the sky. If stars were out, she couldn't see them. She looked hard, trying.

Trying not to think about the dead knee against her shoulder. Trying not to think about the other places where parts of Faye were touching her bare skin. She clenched her teeth. Trembling. Trying to hold her scream inside.

'If it makes a quick stop,' Merton said from the back seat, 'you'll make a lovely impression on the bitch in the trunk.'

Rusty didn't answer. He'd already thought about the consequences of a rear-end collision.

Probably, the person in the trunk was already dead.

He couldn't be sure, though. Maybe he should drop back even farther.

He eased off the accelerator and watched the gap widen.

The bare knee, he was certain, belonged to a woman.

Probably Faye. God, I hope it's Faye's knee. Not Pac's. But that was Pac's car in front of the house. So it might be Pac.

Don't let it be Pac. Please.

Suddenly, the Pontiac's brake lights flashed on.

'Watch out!' Merton yelled.

Rusty had already hit the brake pedal.

He bore down on the Pontiac's tail, watching the upraised knee, ready to swerve away if a crash seemed imminent.

Just as he was about to wrench the steering wheel right and take his chance with the road's shoulder, the Pontiac made a quick left turn. Rusty didn't try to follow. He shot past it, braked to a stop, shoved the shift lever to reverse, and started backward.

It was then that he saw the sign pointing up to the narrow rising road taken by the Pontiac.

The sign read, INDIAN POINT, 1 MILE.

The abrupt slowing had flung Pac against Faye's body, but the turn had pulled her back almost at once. She heard the sound of the siren fade. Opening her eyes, she stared at the bobbing lid of the trunk. The flashing red light was gone.

Then the car started to climb.

Something heavy rolled against her hip.

She lifted her head to see what it was.

Then she sat up screaming.

With both his headlights smashed, the only light Rusty had to steer by was the red of his flashers. The eerie hue turned the road and enclosing woods into a weird nightmare of crimson.

Finally, rounding a curve, he saw the twin red eyes of the Pontiac's tail-lights. And he saw the pale brightness that its headlights cast into the darkness ahead.

He sped up. The gap diminished.

As he drew closer, he saw a human shape inside the open trunk. His flasher caught it, left it dark, and caught it again, coloring the skin red as blood. 'My God,' he muttered.

'Know her?' Merton asked.

Rusty said nothing.

'Bet you like those jugs.'

'Shut up.'

'At least *she* has headlights.'

'Shut the fuck up.'

Merton laughed.

Rusty wiped the sweat off his upper lip.

Pac. My God. What am I going to do?

What if he kills her?

He's got no reason to kill her, Rusty told himself. Things had already gone too far. Hitting the guy in the driveway and kidnapping Pac, Bass had dug his hole too deep. No way out. If Rusty didn't get him, someone else would. Tomorrow, next week, next month. It was already the end for Bass. He'd already lost.

What if he isn't trying to get away?

What if he's already admitted defeat?

Bass was driving toward Indian Point.

Toward Loser's Leap.

Rusty went cold and tight inside.

'Oh Christ,' he muttered.

He picked up the mike. 'Car One to headquarters.'

'Go ahead, Car One.'

'We need assistance up here. Indian Point. Send backup and an ambulance.'

The horror left Pac as if startled off by the noise of her scream. Her mind seemed clear. She watched Rusty's car. It appeared to be about twenty or thirty feet away.

Doesn't he know what'll happen if he rear-ends us?

Sure he knows.

He knows, all right.

He'll just make damn sure he doesn't do it.

The road opened. In the flashing lights, the area looked familiar to Pac. At first, she couldn't place it. Then she recognized the curving line of trees along the back of the paved area.

The Indian Point parking lot.

He was speeding straight across the lot toward Loser's Leap.

Shit!

'Rusty!' she yelled. 'Drop back!'

But he didn't. He apparently couldn't hear her.

And she couldn't wave him off – not with her hands cuffed behind her back.

The patrol car sped closer, closer.

'*Get away!*' Pac shrieked.

As if he'd heard, Rusty suddenly swerved to the left, picked up speed and raced ahead.

Pac drew in her knees, thrust upward and rolled sideways. The edge of the trunk scraped her hip. Then she was falling. The pavement battered her bones and tore at her bare skin, mauling her as she skidded and rolled.

'What the fuck are you doing?' Merton shouted, his voice ragged with panic.

Rusty floored the gas pedal, drawing alongside the Pontiac.

'You're gonna *kill* us!'

'Bail out,' Rusty yelled.

The headlights of the Pontiac reached the walkway and the stone parapet at the far edge of the parking lot. The wall, less than a yard high, blocked and held the lower halves of the bright beams. Their upper halves continued far ahead, reaching into the night's emptiness.

Rusty pulled ahead of the Pontiac. He flicked his head sideways for a glance. The car was slowly dropping back. Too slowly for a stop. In moments, it would smash through the parapet and make a long, tumbling dive for the lake. Taking Pac with it.

No way.

No fucking way!

Rusty whipped his wheel to the right, cutting in front of Bass's car.

The Pontiac's headlights swept across his hood, glared on his windshield, held him. He clutched the steering wheel with all his strength.

The crash stunned him.

The impact tried to jerk him free, but he held on. He held on as the Pontiac knocked his car sideways, as the curb tripped his tires, as his patrol car flipped and the stone wall smashed his windshield, crunched his roof. He held on so tightly that his hands cramped as the car continued to roll, righted itself, and dropped.

God, this is it!

Taking a deep breath, he braced himself and watched through the break in the windshield. The moon was a brilliant, pale disk. Never before had he seen it looking so pure and bright.

His car tilted backward and its hood blocked out the moon.

Chapter Fifty-two

THE KILL

Pac was lying belly-down on the parking-lot pavement when she heard the collision. She raised her head. The wheels of Rusty's patrol car turned skyward like the paws of a dog rolling over. Then the whole car dropped out of sight.

She stared, uncomprehending at first.

Then she knew.

Oh God, no! No!

She lowered her head and pressed her cheek against the rough cool pavement.

A long time seemed to go by. Then she heard the huge, distant thump of the car punching through the surface of Silver Lake.

She looked up.

And saw Bass staggering backward, eyes on his big red Pontiac. Though its front was smashed in, Rusty had stopped it from plunging over the cliff.

Below the raised, crumpled hood, flames flapped in the breeze.

Bass kept backing away. He was hunched over at the waist. His right arm was crossed against his chest.

He lurched toward the rear of his car.

Pac watched him look into the trunk.

Then she lowered her head. Through the slits of her nearly shut eyelids, she watched him turn away from the trunk and look for her.

She didn't breathe.

Bass turned again to the trunk. Reaching into it, he pulled out the severed head.

Faye's . . .

No, not Faye's.

It was Faye's *body* in the trunk – what was left of it. But it was Alison Parkington's head.

Faye's head got mashed by the truck.

Alison's head swung by its short blonde hair, ruddy in the firelight, as Bass rushed with it to the parapet.

He swept the head forward, whipped it high over his own head and down again, around and around like a nutty kid winding up for a killer pitch.

Finally, he let go. Alison's head soared away into the darkness.

Pac waited.

She didn't hear it hit the water.

Bass started coming back.

Flames licked under the rear bumper of his Pontiac as if tasting carefully before rushing over it.

Bass bent into the trunk. The flames seemed to hold back until he had Faye's body out. As he staggered away with it, they curled into the trunk.

Ready!

Get set!

Bass stumbled and dropped the body. Then he crouched,

hauled it off the pavement, and hoisted it again until it flopped over his shoulder.

He trudged toward the parapet.

Pac stared at Faye's bare back, at her dangling, swaying arms.

At the empty space below her back and between her arms – where her head should've been.

That's Faye!

Faye?

He'll do as bad to me . . .

Go!

Pac hesitated.

What if he looks around?

At least his hands are full.

Yeah. And mine are cuffed behind my back.

Terrific.

GO!

Pac rolled onto her back, sat up and sprang to her feet. Though her left knee throbbed, she started running. The pavement sent shock waves up her leg. Each time her heel came down, she strained to keep her knee from giving out and dropping her to the asphalt.

The harsh shocks diminished when the parking lot ended and she ran on the solid dirt of the trail. But the downhill slope seemed to rip at the fibers in her knee, tearing gasps from her as the pain seared.

In the moonlight that mottled the trail with milky puddles, she saw a turn too late. Her shoulder slammed into a tree trunk. The blow twisted her around and she fell. The ground hit her hard.

'PAC!' Bass shouted from somewhere above.

Here he comes!

She struggled to her feet and ran.

She saw the next switchback in time, slowed herself, and made the turn. As she ran, she listened for Bass. She heard nothing except her own harsh breathing, her own quiet gasps of pain, her own blood pumping inside her ears.

He was on his way, though. She was sure of that and the certainty made her keep running.

Soon, she heard Bass behind her.

She ran faster. Hammers seemed to pound her kneecap. She could hear Bass huffing for breath. She ran faster. Then her knee gave out. Her leg collapsed and she plunged forward through the darkness. Making a half-turn, she hit the ground shoulder first. She slid. When she stopped, she held her breath for a moment and listened.

The panting came from above her.

Rolling onto her back, she looked up.

Bass stood a few feet away, pressing his right arm to his chest. A patch of moonlight showed his agonized, bloody face. The streaks of blood looked black.

'Stupid bitch,' he muttered. Bending down, he grabbed her under an arm and pulled. 'Get up. On your feet.'

As she rose to her feet, she staggered against him. He held her up and began walking her slowly down the trail toward the lake.

A few minutes later, she thought she recognized the place on the trail where she and Rusty had grabbed Trink and Bill.

She remembered tripping the girl. Now she wondered if maybe this was some sort of cosmic pay-back.

However much Trink had gotten banged up when she

fell on the trail, Pac had already gotten it ten times worse. And Rusty . . .

Oh, Rusty. Rusty.

I can't think about that.

Anyway, I'll probably end up the same way.

Soon, the ground leveled off. Pac saw a trail sign, but trees shaded it from the moonlight so she couldn't make out its letters or numbers.

Bass led her to the right, toward the picnic area, toward the shore of the lake.

Maybe that woman'll still be here.

Fat chance.

Maybe someone . . .

'What are you going to do?' she asked.

Bass didn't answer.

'Are you going to drown me?'

'Not exactly.' His voice was tight with pain. 'I'm going to sink you. You'll be dead first.'

'How?'

'You'll find out.'

She felt his body go tense with pain then relax as the agony subsided. 'Get a little banged up in the crash?' she asked.

'That fuck shot me.'

'Good.'

His fingers squeezed into the skin of Pac's upper arm until she winced.

'If you get treated for the gunshot,' she said, 'they'll have to report you.'

'So who's gonna get treated? It just nicked me. Hurts like shit, though.'

Ahead of them was the moonlit clearing. Bass led Pac into it, past a picnic table, past another.

She saw no one.

'Bass,' she said, 'don't do this.'

He flung her to the ground. She cried out as the cuffs bit into her. A few moments later, the pain subsided and she felt the wet grass against her back and buttocks. She sat up.

Just to her left, the ground dropped off.

That's where the woman had been sunbathing this morning.

But nobody seemed to be there now.

At the bottom of the embankment should be the lake shore. Only ten or twelve feet away, probably, but Pac couldn't see it.

I can't see it, but it's there.

If I can just get away from Bass for a second . . . throw myself in . . .

'Do I get a last wish?' she asked.

'Sure.'

'Take off these cuffs.'

'Oh, I will. Soon as you're dead.'

'Do it now, okay? I don't want to die with my hands cuffed behind my back. Please?'

'You think I'm a fucking idiot?'

'No.'

'The cuffs stay on.'

'Thanks a heap.'

'You're welcome.' He knelt on the grass beside Pac, shoved her down, then straddled her hips. Bending over, he took hold of her breasts. He rubbed them, squeezed them, pinched her nipples.

She jerked rigid.

Then she was crying.

Crying from the pain, crying from the shame of being naked under this man, cuffed and at his mercy, crying for the death of Rusty and for her own death, soon to come. Crying for poor Millie, made a widow tonight, her husband down in the line of duty. Crying for Harney, who would have to face the loss of his father *and* his wife – both gone the same night – along with whatever children she might've given him if things had gone differently.

The children *she* would never see, hold, kiss, watch grow.

'This is great,' Bass said. 'Mary Hodges, *the Pac*, crying like a baby. Never thought I'd see it.'

'You . . . you don't . . . have to do this.'

'Sure I do.' He suddenly slapped the side of her left breast.

'*Ah!*' she cried out.

'Awww, poor Pac.'

'Get *off* me!'

'Sure.'

'Get off me right *now*, Bass. Right *now!* Or I swear to God I'll kill you.'

'Oh, really? Going to come and get me from beyond the grave?'

'*If that's what it takes!*'

'Good luck,' he said, smiling down at her. Then he slapped her other breast . . .

And Pac swung both her legs up very fast, curling her back, spreading her legs wide and bringing them up and forward, past Bass's sides . . .

Forward very fast, ignoring the pains of her battered body.

Almost like one of the backward somersaults she used to do with such ease during the floor exercises . . .

Curling her back, bringing her legs over the top . . .

She pistoned both her legs, shooting her bare heels straight and hard into Bass's face.

She cried out with pain.

Bass let out a grunt.

The impact slammed him backward.

His weight no longer pinned her down.

She flipped herself clear of his sprawled, squirming body. Away from him, she leaped to her feet.

Bass shoved at the ground, trying to sit up.

Pac rushed in and kicked an arm out from under him.

He flopped on his back.

She stomped his face with one foot. Her heel crunched his nose. He grunted.

Standing by his side, she bent her knees then hopped off the ground.

Hopped as high as she could.

Which seemed pretty damn high, considering that she'd been out of training for a few years.

On her way up, she did a ninety-degree turn in midair.

At the highest point in the jump, she brought her feet up behind her. Her handcuffed hands were right there. She gripped her ankles.

Then she dropped.

Dropped straight down, fast.

She landed, knees first, on Bass's ribcage.

Pain shot through her injured knee.

But both of them crashed through Bass's ribs, punching an ear-ripping squeal out of him.

Spreading her legs, she eased herself down Bass, straddling him.

He squeaked and thrashed and squirmed.

'What've you got there?' Pac asked, gasping for air. 'A little respiratory failure?'

He squeaked some more.

'Miserable, pathetic bastard,' she said. 'I hate to tell you this, but you just got yourself killed by a girl with both hands tied behind her back.'

'And by her pissed-off father-in-law,' someone said. A few feet away, a pistol roared. A blast of fire, bright as lightning, lit the stainless steel frame of an enormous Smith & Wesson revolver and Rusty's dripping face a small distance behind the weapon.

Bass's head jumped sideways as if it had been struck in the temple by a sledgehammer. Pieces flew off.

'Holy shit,' Pac said.

But she couldn't hear her own voice through the ringing in her ears.

Chapter Fifty-three

AFTER

Pac started crying again.

'Hey, it's all right,' Rusty said, his voice soft and husky. He holstered his revolver. Then he crawled the rest of the way up the embankment and sat down beside Pac. She was still straddling Bass's body. 'Everything's fine,' he said.

'I thought you were dead.'

Rusty shook his head. 'A little wet, that's all. Hell of a ride. I guess Merton's still down there.'

'Hmm.'

'I damn near drowned, myself. Remind me not to drive off Loser's Leap again, will you?'

'Don't drive off Loser's Leap again, Rusty.'

He laughed softly. Then he said, 'You gonna sit on Bass all night?'

Sobbing, she nodded. Then she stammered out, 'My . . . hands are cuffed.'

'I'll take care of that.' He crawled behind her. 'You sure did a job on him, Packer. A hell of a job.' He unlocked the handcuffs and removed them from her wrists.

'Thanks.' She brought her stiff arms slowly in front of

her. Both wrists were deeply grooved, cut and bleeding. Her hands were numb.

She climbed off Bass's body and sat down on the cool, dewy grass. Rusty sat down beside her.

'You okay?' she asked.

'I've been better.'

He ruffled her hair. She smiled and wiped her eyes.

Though her ears still rang from the gunshot, she heard a distant siren.

'Cavalry to the rescue,' Rusty said. He took off his shirt and helped Pac put her arms through the sleeves. It was wet and cold and stuck to her skin.

Pac tried to fasten the buttons, but her numb fingers felt thick and useless. 'I can't get 'em,' she said.

'Allow me, ma'am.' Rusty buttoned the shirt for her, slowly and gently. 'There you go,' he said when he was finished. 'Can you walk?'

'With a little help.'

Rusty gave her the help.

Together, they made their slow way through the darkness. When the walking became too hard for Pac, Rusty carried her. They were halfway up the trail when two deputies appeared, running, flashlights streaking the night with white beams.